The
DEVIL'S TEETH

by

SABRINA FLYNN

THE DEVIL'S TEETH

A RAVENWOOD MYSTERY

SABRINA FLYNN

www.sabrinaflynn.com

THE DEVIL'S TEETH is a work of fiction. Names, characters, places, and incidents are either the product of the author's overactive imagination or are chimerical delusions of a tired mind. Any resemblance to actual persons, living or dead, events, or locales is entirely due to the reader's wild imagination (that's you).

Copyright © 2019 by Sabrina Flynn

All rights reserved.

This book or any portion thereof may not be reproduced or used in any manner whatsoever without the express written permission of the publisher except for the use of brief quotations in a book review.

Ink & Sea Publishing

www.sabrinaflynn.com

ISBN 978-1-955207-10-2

eBook ISBN 978-1-955207-11-9

Cover Art by MerryBookRound
www.merrybookround.com

ALSO BY SABRINA FLYNN

Ravenwood Mysteries

From the Ashes

A Bitter Draught

Record of Blood

Conspiracy of Silence

The Devil's Teeth

Uncharted Waters

Where Cowards Tread

Beyond the Pale

Legends of Fyrsta

Untold Tales

A Thread in the Tangle

King's Folly

The Broken God

Bedlam

Windwalker

www.sabrinaflynn.com

to my readers
you make the journey worth it

Envy is thin because it bites but never eats.
– A Spanish Proverb

THE DEADLY PEST

ISOBEL

Wednesday, June 13, 1900

ISOBEL AMSEL CURSED UNDER HER BREATH. SHE NEVER imagined a light would be the death of her. But then it wasn't precisely the light buzzing around her face that would do the killing. It would be the fall. A flash of light danced over her face, then landed a third time, stabbing her eyeballs. She pressed her cheek against stone, and squeezed her eyes shut.

Sweat curled down her spine. It wasn't fear; it was the damn sun. It baked the rock, giving her would-be murderer ammunition.

Whoever was trying to kill her was persistent. She'd give them that.

Stalled a hundred feet above ground, a crimp and a tiny crevice were all that were keeping her alive. And pure stubbornness.

A tremor started in her left big toe. The abused

appendage was jammed into a crack. Her muscles ached, her nerves screamed, and the tremor began to shake her whole leg. Isobel shifted her weight, placing all her hope in the left side of her body. With her right hand she explored greywacke, searching blindly for a handhold.

Climbing was not so much brute strength as balance, calling on the nerve of either the supremely confident or truly mad. It did not require sight, or so she told herself.

She pinched a bit of rock, and straightened her leg. Her toe went numb, but the maneuver rewarded her with a kindly protrusion of rock. She moved to a better position. As the blood rushed back into her toe, she took turns shaking out one arm, and then the other.

She cracked open an eye. The light was still zipping around her face like an annoying fly. As tempting as it was to linger on the relative safety of a solid inch of rock, she couldn't cling there forever.

Isobel took in a slow breath. She was too experienced to look down, or to ponder her precarious situation, or to think about the rocks waiting to catch her if she fell. Fear was the swish of a blade—the moment before death. And she had been dodging that old foe for twenty-one years.

Isobel exhaled. Felt herself relax. Felt fear wash over her. When she was free of its hold, she moved slowly up the rock face, and then surged, reaching for her life. For a breadth of a second there was only air. And her mortality.

A blink later, she gripped the top ledge, and pulled herself up onto a slab.

With her feet on solid ground, she ducked behind a jagged rock and searched the valley for her attacker. The Oat Hill Mine Road hugged the base of the Palisades, winding from Calistoga towards a mercury mine. Trees of oak and fir, pine and cypress gave way to meadow and the homestead of a lone Finnish man. A dust cloud rose from the distant road—a wagon—but no light.

Isobel shifted to the side, and a flash from the valley announced her adversary—at the edge of a meadow. She frowned. Was she overreacting? For a twenty-one year old, she had accumulated a number of dangerous enemies. But perhaps it wasn't an enemy out for vengeance. The light could be wielded by a mischievous child, or coming off the lens of an enthusiastic bird watcher.

Isobel chucked a pebble off the ledge, and watched it soar for a few blissful seconds until it dropped to the road and bounced down the steep slope. The only question she was presently concerned with was how in the hell she was going to climb back down with that pestering light.

Isobel chose a different route down the cliff, one where the light could not follow her. Climbing down wasn't easy, but then nothing worthwhile ever was. With her forearms feeling like bricks and her hands like noodles, Isobel hurried from the base of the Palisades into the cover of trees.

Standing under the canopy, she listened to leaves and a trickling stream, savoring the relative coolness. Summer in Napa Valley was slightly more tolerable in the shade. She squinted through the branches. It was high noon. Lotario would be expecting her at Bright Waters. But curiosity nagged. And that was never good.

Confident that her twin could stand in for her in whatever place she was supposed to be, Isobel struck off towards the meadow. If someone had purposefully been trying to make her fall they'd likely be long gone, but tracks would remain. And if it hadn't been *someone*, then it was *something*. A something that was pulling her farther away from Bright Waters Asylum.

The trees sighed from a welcoming breeze, and she crouched to dunk her head in the stream. Refreshed, she hopped from one bank to the other, relying on her mental map of the valley. Could it have been Riot playing games with her? No, she thought, he wouldn't distract her on a cliff.

Sunlight dappled golden grass, the trees broke, and Isobel walked into a meadow. A flash caught her eye, a reflection from the sun. She hurried to the lure, and stopped. An object swayed in the breeze, catching the sun's light. Back and forth with a branch's creak. Isobel searched the tree line, then slowly stepped forward. Of all the things she'd considered, this was not one of them—her would-be murderer was a magnifying glass.

2

CRACK IN THE LENS

Isobel turned the magnifying glass in her palm as she walked. The lens was cracked, and the fracture mesmerized her, catching sunlight and sending it careening to the four points of the world. Silver, polished to a mirror finish, circled the lens, and the oak handle had been skillfully molded for a hand. Well made, and therefore expensive. Why leave it in a forest? The lens could be replaced, or at the very least, the silver salvaged.

Music drifted in the lazy afternoon, and broke her musing. Isobel found herself on the edge of Bright Waters Asylum. She looked out onto a stretch of green surrounded by shade trees. Private cottages for its more affluent patients dotted the land around a main building. With its adobe walls and the large courtyard that smelled of flowers, the facility reminded Isobel of a mission.

A group of patients played croquet as a phonograph scratched out *O Sole Mio*. A lone woman lounged under an oak reading a book. Strands of gold gleamed in her dark hair, and a frilly white tea dress draped elegantly over her lithe body.

A rush of relief traveled to Isobel's toes. Lotario was still playing his role—that of herself. Belatedly, Isobel remembered her own role. She quickly slipped her arm into a makeshift sling and adopted Lotario's careless gait.

As she made her way to her twin, a number of female patients waved greetings. She flashed one of Lotario's charming smiles in return. One of the women blushed. Isobel could never account for her twin's way with women.

Lotario kept his nose buried in a book as she neared.

"Have you moved at all?" Isobel asked.

"Where the hell have you been?" he said through his teeth.

"You've always had a knack for voices, Ari. That sounded just like me."

He slapped the book closed, and glared. A wave of dizziness hit Isobel. Whenever Lotario assumed his 'Isobel' guise, she always experienced a moment of disorientation.

"I'm not acting," he said.

She arched a brow.

"You were supposed to be back *hours* ago."

"I lost track of time. Were there any telegrams for me?"

"Of course." Lotario looked her up and down. "You were climbing, weren't you?"

It was obvious. Her fingertips were scraped raw. "I'll put on gloves so you don't have to damage your delicate skin for my sake." The only way they could swap places was to assure that each had the same injuries, scrapes, bruises, and skin coloring. Most inconsistencies could be easily fixed with makeup, or concealed with clothing. But some things could not be concealed. And Lotario had always been one to throw himself into a role—even if it meant injuring himself.

Lotario was shaking his head. "There won't be any more swapping."

Isobel chose to ignore the declaration. "How is your shoulder?"

Lotario huffed, and looked away.

She sat on the divan by his side. "Ari, I had to get out of here. My muscles are atrophying."

He didn't reply.

"I needed practice," she persisted.

"You climbed the walls of your cell for months."

"Yes, well, I needed to test my prowess on something more challenging. I've become quite adept at climbing, by the way. I would have been perfectly safe, except..."

His eyes sharpened on her. "You nearly fell?"

"No." She took a breath. "Well, nearly." Isobel brandished her would-be murderer.

Lotario frowned at the cracked magnifying glass. "You killed Sherlock Holmes?"

Isobel snorted.

"Please tell me you didn't go into town."

"I found it."

"Where?"

"In the woods. It was hanging on twine tied to a branch. It caught my eye while I was... on the rock I was climbing."

Lotario frowned. "Odd."

"Odd isn't the word for it. Singular, more like."

"*Singular* is a soon-to-be-married woman with two children who's climbing a *cliff*. You should not be climbing the Palisades."

"I've always climbed them," she defended.

"You have a family now."

"I'm not married *yet*."

"And you won't be at this rate." Lotario snatched the glass from her hand. "There are initials on here."

"I *had* noticed."

"*TS*," he muttered.

"There was dried blood on the handle, and I found more blood on the ground."

"Maybe someone cut their hand."

"I don't think so." She plucked the glass from his hand, and peered at the crack in the lens as if it held the answers she sought.

"Bel, there are a dozen possible scenarios."

"And yet someone took the time to tie a bowline hitch around this magnifying glass and hang it from a tree. One could replace the lens, or simply use it as is. It's still functional."

"Perhaps it was intended as a signal?"

"Or a warning."

"For vermin?" Lotario mused.

Isobel smiled. "A glass scarecrow." She spun it in her hands.

"A ward or a lure? It could be the signal for an illicit liaison between lovers." Lotario snapped his fingers. "A liaison between detectives."

"You should write penny dreadfuls."

"I have."

Isobel blinked at her twin. "You have?"

"Hmm." He waved away her questions. "You'd hate them."

"I might not."

"You would."

"I didn't realize you wrote books."

Lotario gave her a patient look. "While you were being shipped off to Europe to subsequently ditch your chaperone—"

"I didn't ditch her."

"Fine. While you were running around God knows

where for two years and marrying a blackguard to protect our family, I was living my own life. Do you think I just twiddle my thumbs and wait for you while you're gone?"

Isobel was at a loss. She didn't know which was more disturbing: nearly falling from a cliff or discovering her twin had secrets. "Speaking of waiting..." She stood. "I need to—"

"No."

The sharpness in his tone brought her up short. "I didn't ask you," she said.

"You were about to. And the answer is no. Wherever, whatever—I'm not doing it." Lotario crossed his good arm over his chest.

"Ari, there's only one general store and one post office in town. They might know who this belongs to."

"You have a talking session in," he paused to check his watch, "fifteen minutes."

"It's your turn to sit in for me."

"Not today."

"But you enjoy them."

Lotario said nothing, only tilted his chin. She knew that look. Isobel saw it in her mirror's reflection every morning. There was no arguing with that chin tilt. So she tried reason. "Someone might be in trouble."

"You said the blood was dry." He sat up, though it pained him. "And, Bel, if you're caught outside the asylum, they'll send you to somewhere with bars."

Isobel looked towards the men and women laughing on the green. Flowing white dresses and white linen suits, music, tea parties, and relaxation—part of her would rather be in confinement with hardened criminals. At least she'd have something to occupy her time.

"Mingle. Be social. Meet your fellow inmates," he said.

Isobel scowled at the group.

"I don't scowl, Bel," Lotario said.

"I don't have anything in common with those people. My head isn't full of trifles, Ari."

"Oh, yes, of course." He climbed to his feet and looked her in the eye. "We lesser beings can't converse with the likes of you unless there's murder afoot and you're lying through your teeth."

"Whatever gets results."

Lotario smoothed his skirts. "I'm not covering for you again. Not until you make an effort."

"An effort for what?"

"*Empathy*, Bel. And some awareness that you are not the center of the universe."

"That's your spot." The quick reply left her lips like a slap. Lotario flinched, and moved his injured arm a fraction. There might as well have been an elephant sitting between them.

Lotario had taken a bullet for her. He might never regain the full use of his arm.

"Ari, I'm sorry."

Without a word, he turned and walked towards his private cottage.

3

TALKING SESSION

"Miss Amsel, how is your shoulder?" Doctor Julius Bright smiled at his patient-cum-prisoner. But instead of returning his infectious greeting, Isobel considered the question of the chicken and the egg. Which had come first?

"Do you think your temperament would be the same if your father had borne the surname 'Grimm'?" she asked.

Julius smiled, again. He practically wore the thing. On any other man it would have seemed ridiculous. But it was sincere, touching the alienist's bright eyes. "We all assume names," he replied cryptically. "Won't you sit?"

Isobel ignored his offer. She'd be damned if she was going to lie down for a talking session. "Are you implying you were not born with that surname?"

"Would it matter?"

She considered his question. "To some."

"To you?"

"Of course."

"Why?" Julius asked.

"I would suspect you of hiding something."

"And this would trouble you?"

"Only so far as to question your credentials."

"You seem disinclined to accept my help regardless."

"I never asked for it," she replied. "The court ordered me here."

Isobel took his consultation chair. Julius seemed unfazed, which pricked her nerve. Instead he settled himself on the settee. He was a tall man, over six feet, and his shoes dangled off the end of the consulting couch. He folded his hands over his waistcoat. She wouldn't call him corpulent, not precisely. Only solid.

"Which are more meaningful: the names we are given, or the names we choose for ourselves?" he mused to the ceiling.

"A child is unformed," she stated. "I think the Chinese tradition of giving a child a milk name until they reach maturity is a fine idea."

"But then we come back to your question: does the name shape the child? Even a milk name?"

Isobel toyed with a lone cufflink on the table beside the chair. She thought of Atticus Riot. Left with only an acronym after his mother hanged herself, he had named himself. Riot had chosen 'Atticus' because he fancied it sounded important, and he had plucked his surname straight from a penny dreadful. A street urchin aspiring to greater things.

"I think not. We take names that suit us," she said.

"Captain Morgan. Huckleberry Finn. Charlotte Bonnie. Am I forgetting any?"

Isobel tapped the cufflink on the table. "Violet Smith."

"Ah, yes, your slap-happy prostitute disguise."

Isobel nearly snorted with laughter. She hadn't expected it, but she schooled her reaction. She had no intention of revealing anything to Dr. Bright.

"Why Violet?" he asked.

She lifted a shoulder. "Arthur Conan Doyle chose that name for a number of his 'women in distress'. Faceless women, lacking character or resolve."

"But you were hardly helpless."

"A flower seller once told me that violets are thieves. A flirty flower that comes and goes as it pleases. It suited the disguise."

"Is that how you generally choose your names?"

"I don't put much thought into it."

"Ah."

Isobel narrowed her eyes at his profile. That "Ah" had sounded very knowing, but she refused his bait.

"How is the shoulder?" he asked again.

"It hurts."

"So sorry. A bad slip in a tub, wasn't it? The same arm as your twin."

The alienist did not look at her. She did not answer. But he kept talking, musing to himself. "No doubt it was the strain of the trial. Distracted lately?"

With boredom, she thought.

Julius rubbed the bridge of his nose. His next words were said with a sigh. "How much time do we have left?"

"You could end this now," she suggested.

"Do you enjoy dodging my questions?"

"I'm required to be here for an hour, twice a week. I am *not* required to answer your questions."

"You were quite talkative the other day." Julius turned his head to look at her. "What was it? You were dreaming excessively of your fiancé—Atticus Riot—and cucumbers. *Large* cucumbers."

Isobel suppressed a sigh. One of the drawbacks of

sending Lotario in her place was the things he tended to say. "I'm not in the mood today."

"For cucumbers or Atticus Riot?"

Isobel searched him for any sign of innuendo, but he had turned back to the ceiling. She might have thought him asleep accept for a single finger tapping the other, like a ticking clock, or maybe a tune.

"For talking," she said. In the weeks she'd been there, she had been scheduled for twelve sessions. She had only been present for five of those. Lotario had sat in for the rest. Sometimes she talked, and sometimes she did not. And just to confuse the good doctor, Lotario had done the same. Tried and true tactics that kept people guessing.

"Another brown study, is it?"

"I'm incarcerated. What do you expect?"

"How many more days?"

"One hundred and seven."

"Not near as bad as it could have been."

Doctor Bright's gentle reminder tightened her throat. Isobel's world had nearly ended when Parker Gray burst into the courtroom. Lotario had thrown himself in front of the bullet meant for her, and he'd nearly died for it. "No." The single word was clipped and hard.

"You don't do well with confinement?"

She did not answer.

"I don't either," he admitted.

"You assumed the name Bright to conceal that you were in prison?" It wasn't a serious question. Isobel had only aimed to get under his skin. She never expected an answer. Let alone the truth.

"Yes, as a matter of fact. As a child."

Isobel leaned forward. "What crime did you commit?"

"I wasn't my older brother."

Stone and bars shattered in her mind's eye, replaced by something more sinister. "A relative locked you up."

"My turn," he said quickly. "Are you looking forward to your nuptials?"

"I'm in an asylum."

"And Alex Kingston walked free."

She ground her teeth together.

"Does it worry you—marrying another man so soon after?" he asked.

"My relationship with Atticus Riot is none of your concern."

"You spoke of him during your last session."

"I was in a rare mood."

"As well as the session before. Not so rare, is it?"

She raised her brows in a kind of shrug.

"Do you often experience drastic mood swings?"

"Isn't that what alienists like to call 'female hysteria' and 'wandering wombs'?"

Julius chuckled. "'Female hysteria' is a vague, all-encompassing term for complexities that my colleagues don't want to bother themselves with. 'Male hysteria' is just as prevalent, if not more. I'm afraid the male of the species is prone to the worst kinds of mood swings."

She looked at him in surprise.

"I study human behavior. I would be useless if I were prejudiced in favor of my own sex."

"If only society viewed the world with such a scientific eye. When women fly into rages or break down in tears they're committed for hysteria. While men who lose their tempers and beat their wives are called firm."

At the word *beat*, Julius flinched. He went back to his original topic. "Are you concerned that you're leaping from one marriage to another?"

Isobel ignored the question, and countered with an observation. "Your mother favored you. It must have been your father who locked you in the shed."

Julius sat up, and planted his feet on the floor. "How did you know?"

She gave a dismissive wave. "Given root cellars store food, a shed seemed the most logical choice."

"How did you know it was my father?" he demanded.

"You're jovial, uncoordinated, not corpulent, but hardly athletic. Definitely not the strapping young man in the photograph you keep tucked away behind your desk. You *are* kind, and that is hardly a trait most fathers appreciate in a son. Mothers on the other hand…"

The look in his eyes made her hackles rise. "Does your twin's behavior trouble you?"

"It troubles me when others ask," she shot back.

"I'm not referring to his carnal desires."

Isobel matched the doctor's sudden chill. It radiated from them both. He had pricked her nerve in return, and he had known precisely where to place his barb. Was he threatening her twin?

Lotario lived on a knife's edge, and she would kill to keep her brother from falling off that edge.

Julius relaxed, his features softening "I'm an alienist; not a judge. I only want to understand. And I can't do that unless people talk to me."

"Why meddle in minds?"

"Why meddle in crimes that don't affect you?"

Isobel stared, and Julius stood abruptly. "Thank you for your time. It was most insightful." He left her sitting in his consulting chair.

A FLURRY OF TELEGRAMS

A magnifying glass tried to murder me. Qd4 -B

Crazed patient? Kxc2 -R

No. Twine. Qc3 Check -B

Death by reflection. Unique. kd1 -R

A reference to my appearance? Having second thoughts? Qxd3 Check -B

No. You? ke1 -R

JB is having them. Bc3 Checkmate. -B

Is it possible I'm getting worse at this game? -R

I could be getting better. -B

A LEGAL MATTER

RIOT

"Sign here."

Atticus Riot looked to the two young girls at his side. Sao Jin glared, and Sarah Byrne fidgeted. Jin's jaw was set, as usual. But Sarah... he couldn't quite pin her unease.

"You look like you're having second thoughts," he said to Sarah.

"Mr. Amsel will be my uncle," she whispered. "Now it won't be right to marry him."

Riot swallowed down a laugh, as did the woman across from him. Donaldina Cameron cleared her throat and folded her hands on the desk, but amusement danced in her eyes.

"I'm afraid not, Sarah. But I think Lotario is a confirmed bachelor."

"The newspapers said you were, too," Sarah pointed out.

"I *was*. Plans do change. However, I think Lotario will make a better uncle than husband."

Sarah's shoulders slumped. "I suppose."

"Your heart will mend, child," Donaldina said.

"With your permission?" Riot looked to each girl in turn. Both nodded.

Riot applied his pen to the documents.

"And here," the attorney said.

Riot crossed his T's. There were quite a few in his name.

The attorney looked to Riot as he pushed the papers towards Donaldina. "After your wedding, Mrs. Riot can add her own signature with the judge as witness."

Well accustomed to the process, Donaldina Cameron signed as witness without prompt, and the attorney added his own signature and an official stamp.

"Congratulations, Atticus. Sarah Byrne Riot and Sao Jin Riot are officially your daughters." There was a fair amount of relief in Donaldina Cameron's voice. She looked like she had narrowly escaped a noose. If Riot hadn't adopted Sao Jin, the girl would have ended up at the mission.

"It's that simple?" Sarah asked.

"Thankfully, and unfortunately," Donaldina said. "Legal documents aren't required to adopt a child. But the papers help if there's ever a dispute. Keep those documents safe, Atticus. If the adoption papers for my girls were ever destroyed, every tong in the city would have their pet attorneys drawing new ones in under a day. And their pet judges would hand the girls straight over to slavers."

Jin shifted.

"I know," Donaldina said, nodding to the girl. "It's horrifying. But that's what we've been dealing with for years now. Until laws are changed," she looked heavenward, "I can only try."

"It goes both ways," the attorney said. "These legal

papers ensure that children remain with families who will care for them."

"Small blessings," Donaldina said. "Girls, may I speak with your *father* for a moment?"

Jin scowled and stomped out of the office, while Sarah beamed, practically skipping out.

"Congratulations, sir," the attorney said, although his tone was contrary to his words. After he left, Donaldina sat back in her chair, looking pleased.

"You couldn't resist, could you?" Riot asked.

"I never thought I'd see the day you settled down. With a wife and *two* daughters, no less."

"I'm not married *yet*." Riot smiled. "I never thought I'd see the day either. We're not precisely what you'd call a traditional family."

"No," Donaldina agreed. "Sarah is lovely. But Jin..." She faltered.

"Is spirited?"

"That's one way to put it." Donaldina leaned forward. "Atticus, you're in for trouble."

"Have you ever known me not to be in for trouble?"

"That's the only reason I agreed to this. That, and I'm not sorry to wash my hands of the girl. She seems to have taken to Miss Amsel, and you, as well." There was a question in the statement.

"Jin reminds me of myself at that age."

Donaldina raised her brows. "Your humor is so dry, I'm not always sure when you're edging towards sarcasm."

"I'm serious."

Donaldina looked at him for a moment, searching for that elusive humor. In the end, she took his word. "Well, whoever took you under their wing, I'm grateful."

"Tim shanghaied me."

"I'm afraid you'll have to keep shanghaiing as an option for Sao Jin. I've seen it a hundred times. A child can be so badly damaged that she'll strike out at those trying to help her. Jin is currently on her best behavior, but that's only because she doesn't want to go to China. As soon as Mei leaves, Jin will get comfortable and begin acting out. Worse than she has already."

"Bel and I are hardly proper parents, so it's a good fit. We'll take each day as it comes."

"Miss Amsel is a remarkable woman."

"Don't you mean perfectly suited to be Jin's adoptive mother?" he asked.

Donaldina laughed. "Maybe so. I wish the Riot family many… adventurous years."

"And you, Dolly?"

Color rose to her cheeks. "There is a gentleman, but…" She looked around her office and sadness shadowed her eyes. "Who would save these girls?"

JIN AND SARAH WERE SITTING ON OPPOSITE SIDES OF THE large entrance hall when Riot entered. Sarah, dark-haired with a spattering of freckles to match, looked sullen, her usually bright eyes puffy and red. Riot stopped in the center of the room.

"Did something happen?" he asked.

Jin didn't look up. She held a small clay jar in one hand, and scratched at her forearm with the other.

"Jin said the only reason you adopted us was because you feel sorry for us," Sarah answered.

"Do you believe that?" Riot asked.

"No."

"Then don't let anyone tell you otherwise." He gave Sarah a quick wink, and she smiled. He inclined his head towards Jin, and Sarah took his hint, turning to her sketchbook.

He sat beside Jin on the bench. "Did you say goodbye to Mei?"

Jin nodded.

"Is that her ointment?"

Jin looked away.

"Jin," he said softly. "Are you sure you don't want to go with her?"

"I knew it. You want me to go," she bit out.

Riot sighed, and turned his hat in his hands. "I want what's best for you. So does Bel. You might like China, or you might hate it. But it's your choice. Once you make that choice—you best put your all into it." He let the words settle, and watched her scratch at the skin under her large sleeve. Bel had told him that Jin was covered in scars, and the skin on her forearms was raw with scratches, scabbed over, and scratched again. "Bel and I have made our choice —and we'll put our all into it. I promise you that."

Jin looked up, her eyes smoldering. "You only feel sorry for me. I am a pathetic dog."

Riot gently took the jar from her hands, and unscrewed the lid. The green substance smelled of herbs and earth. "As a pathetic dog once upon a time myself, I can attest to the fact that, with a little care," he dabbed his fingers in the jar, and smeared some of the ointment over a scratch on the back of her hand, "we can amount to something. And maybe even one day, have friends."

He closed the lid, and handed it back to her.

"You do not own me," she said defiantly.

"The papers are to keep you safe. That's all."

Her lips pressed into a taut line.

"I'm not replacing your father," he said gently.

The girl flinched as if he'd slapped her. Riot had cut right to the heart of the matter. She tried to speak, but couldn't. Her knuckles turned white around the jar.

With a growl, she stood. "I will stay."

He extended his hand. "Your all," he said.

Jin hesitated, looked him straight in the eye, and gripped his hand with strength. "My all." They shook, sealing the promise.

Riot held the door open for the girls as they left 920 Sacramento. The papers against his chest were a different kind of responsibility—one he had never felt before. And he wished Bel were there.

They started up the hill in silence.

"What if Captain Morgan does not marry you?" Jin asked after a time.

"Then I suppose you're both stuck with just me."

Sarah took his arm. "Hardly stuck, Mr.—" She tilted her head. "Should we call you *Pa* now?"

"Whatever you like, Sarah. Though I feel like I've aged decades in an hour."

"You *are* old," Jin stated.

"Jin! He's not *that* old."

"I am *not* calling you father."

"Call me A.J."

Jin wrinkled her nose. "I will call you Din Gau."

"I'm not fond of that name," he said.

"Why?" Jin craned her neck to look up at him, puzzled.

"What does it mean?" Sarah asked.

"Rabid Dog," Jin said proudly.

Sarah mouthed the words in shock. "I like Pa better."

"*Boo how doy* gave him that name," Jin said. "Hatchet men fear him, because he kills them all."

Riot swallowed. He tightened his grip on his stick, focusing on putting one foot in front of the next. Sarah squeezed his arm. "I don't like that name either."

"Why not?" Jin asked. "One day I'll kill *boo how doy*, too."

Riot didn't respond. He only watched the girl out of the corner of his eye, trying to figure out if she were baiting him, or serious. Sao Jin was hard to read. Even for him.

Sarah's eyes widened. "Did you *really* kill those men?"

"Vengeance is a bitter draught," Riot said. But he wasn't looking at Sarah. He said it to Jin. "But yes, Sarah. I have more blood on my hands than I'd like to think on. I take the safety of the innocent personally."

"No one is innocent," Jin bit out.

"Maybe so, but some can use more help than others."

"Sounds like a knight to me," Sarah said. "There's nothing wrong with that."

The bite of a memory dug into his back. The blow of a bullet hitting chain mail armor under his coat—a protective tactic hatchet men used to great success. It was the only reason he was still alive.

"Are you all right?" Sarah asked.

Riot blinked. Both girls were staring up at him. He had stopped walking. Riot gave himself a mental shake. "Have you two ever tried gelato?"

Sarah perked up at the word.

"What is gelato?" Jin asked.

Riot switched directions. "To the Italian quarter, then. We need fortification for tomorrow."

"What happens tomorrow?" Sarah asked.

"We're interviewing teachers."

Sarah groaned. And Riot smiled. From gambler to gunfighter to father. His life had taken another surprising turn.

6

THE GREEK TEACHER

SMALL TALK SEEMED UNSUITED TO RAVENWOOD MANOR'S parlor. The guests whispered words like "foggy" and "uncommonly cold" and their nervous laughter fell hollowly in the room.

A prim woman, who was gripping her hands tightly, cleared her throat. "Are all the rooms similarly decorated?" she asked.

Three children sat on a settee. They were as different in color as they were in size and temperament: a dark little boy, a glaring Chinese girl, and a freckled white girl from Tennessee. And then, of course, there was the cat, Watson, who sat in the center of the room, flicking his tail.

The freckled girl smiled pleasantly. "Not all of the rooms, Miss Hines." Sarah Byrne tapped a bell jar. It contained a shrunken head with a ruby in each eye socket. "This room is splendid for drawing."

Miss Hines paled, and quickly averted her eyes from the obscene decoration. Sarah didn't think the woman all that much older than herself. Certainly younger than Miss Isobel.

A second woman, Mrs. Famish, tore her eyes from an anatomy sketch. She was opposite of her name, and although severe, she was at least polite about it. "Do you draw, Miss Byrne?"

"It's my favorite thing to do."

"When you're not making doe eyes at Mr. Lotario," Tobias White said under his breath. Sarah discreetly jabbed an elbow in the boy's side.

A quiet gentleman across the way kept glancing at a stuffed raven by his arm. He smoothed his tie and licked his lips, and then quickly shifted the dead animal a fraction to the right. The base was now aligned with the corner of the table. Sarah liked the bird. Its eyes always seemed to follow her around the room. Although the gentleman wasn't unpleasant to look at, she wasn't so sure about him. For a teacher, he seemed awfully nervous, and he had not yet given his name. No manners at all, her Gramma would have said.

"This femur here—do you know what these marks are?" a second man standing by the mantel asked. Mr. Patten was not at all like the quiet man. His self-assured voice boomed in the room, and he looked down his nose at the trio on the settee. He had quite a long nose, and ears that made Sarah think of a mouse.

"Teeth," Sao Jin bit out. "*Human* teeth. After they ate him, the headhunters of Sumatra painted it as a trophy."

Watson yawned, displaying an impressive pair of canines.

"It belonged to that fellow." Tobias nodded towards the shrunken head. His feet swung over the floor, his heels hitting the settee in a bored rhythm. "The owner of this house had his head chopped off. It was done in the dining room over there." He pointed to a set of closed doors.

"Grimm, that's my brother, he don't talk, had to pull the panels off the walls to get the blood out."

Miss Hines raised a handkerchief to her lips.

"*Tobias*," Sarah whispered.

"That is quite enough," Mr. Patten said. "You know what they say about liars, young man."

"But it's true," Jin said. "There are restless spirits in this house."

Miss Hines wobbled on her seat.

Jin looked pleased. She turned her glare on the mousy man. Mr. Patten sniffed, and turned to Miss Hines. "Chinese are superstitious and uneducated," he assured.

"That's awfully impolite," Sarah said. "Jin is my sister."

"I am not," Jin growled.

Sarah looked away from the smaller girl. "There's a piece of paper that says so," she muttered.

"Yellow does not mix with white," Mr. Patten said.

Jin smirked. She leaned forward, and turned a teapot so the handle faced the man. Sarah rose, and offered Miss Hines a white-frosted teacake. The woman looked like she might be sick, but manners prevailed and she set the plate in her lap.

The door to the second parlor opened, and an impeccably dressed gentleman paused on the threshold. His raven hair gleamed, and a wing of white slashed across his temple.

His dark gaze swept over the room. When his eyes passed over Sarah, the corners briefly creased. Sarah had noticed that he rarely smiled. 'Deadpan' was the word her gramma would have said, and then promptly warned Sarah to keep away from men like him. But Sarah knew better. Atticus Riot smiled with his eyes. It wasn't easy to see—not with his spectacles and his trim beard, but it was a feeling she got when he looked at her. His eyes were warm, and that was good enough for her.

Riot looked to Tobias. "Will you show Miss Veld out?"

Tobias hopped to his feet. Riot gave the young woman whom he had just interviewed a polite bow, and turned to the remaining applicants in the room. The numbers had dwindled. Only two men and two women remained.

"As well as this gentleman here." He nodded to Mr. Patten "And the lady there." Miss Hines looked relieved. She hastily dropped her cake on its plate, offered farewell in a faint voice, and beat Tobias to the front door.

"Has the position been filled?" Mr. Patten asked.

Riot didn't answer.

The gentleman persisted. "I haven't yet interviewed."

"Good day." Riot gestured towards the exit.

Mr. Patten gathered himself up to shout, but took one look at the bespectacled man in the doorway and thought better of it. Sarah could practically see hot air cooling around his ears. Mr. Patten pushed past Tobias on his way out.

Riot looked to the remaining applicants: the young nervous man who hadn't offered a name and Mrs. Famish.

"Mrs. Famish."

The stout woman rose and marched into the second parlor. Riot winked at the children, and closed the doors. The subtle, prearranged signals they'd agreed on were proving helpful in weeding out applicants.

"Mrs. Famish, this is Mrs. Lily White."

Mrs. Famish didn't hesitate to shake Lily's hand. The women were of the same age, and carried themselves with equal confidence. "My references." Mrs. Famish handed her papers to Riot.

He took the letter, and waited for both women to be seated before sitting in a chair beside his housekeeper.

"How long have you lived in the city, Mrs. Famish?" Lily asked. Everything about Lily White was pleasant, from her eyes to her dimples and the gentle way she had of speaking.

"I live in the east bay. I'm a school teacher in Oakland. But the prospect of a smaller class size, as well as room and board in the city was too much to pass."

Lily smiled. "How long have you been a teacher?"

"I've held that position since my husband died, some two years now. Before I married, I was a governess."

Riot looked up from her references. "It says you speak French and Italian. Fluently?"

"I do. And I teach the fundamentals: writing, reading, arithmetic, and the social graces."

"How do you keep discipline?" Lily asked.

"It depends on the child," Mrs. Famish answered. "I find a good swat with a ruler works for most. Other children respond to a stern word, additional work, or forced idleness in a corner."

"We'd not allow the children to be struck. At all," Riot said. If striking a child produced results, then Jin would be an angel. And if Mrs. Famish attempted to strike Jin, even for a swat, Riot had little doubt the woman would find a knife in her gut.

Mrs. Famish gave a nod. "I'll certainly abide by your wishes, but some form of discipline will be needed. We can discuss your preferences at a later time."

"Are you capable of preparing the children for university?" Riot asked.

"If you like…" Mrs. Famish hesitated. "Will Miss Sarah be attending university?" She sounded puzzled. "How many students will I be teaching?"

"There will be at least five," Lily said. "My two sons and daughter, and Mr. Riot's daughters."

"Your *daughters*, Mr. Riot?" Mrs. Famish asked, putting emphasizes on the plural.

"Jin and Sarah."

She leveled the universal school teacher look on Riot. "The Chinese girl?"

"Yes."

Mrs. Famish straightened. "I thought Sarah was being silly when she called Jin her sister," she explained. "I don't mind teaching negro children, but by law orientals must be segregated in classrooms. It's illegal to teach white and oriental together. Might I suggest a Chinese school?"

"You'll be a private tutor, Mrs. Famish," Riot said.

"The Chinese girl will slow down the other children."

Lily raised her brows.

"Doubtful," Riot said crisply. "Thank you for your time, Mrs. Famish." He stood, and she followed suit, gathering her handbag.

Mrs. Famish paused at the door. "Legal consequences aside, I *would* be willing to instruct her along with the others."

"We'll do just fine," Lily said.

Mrs. Famish squared her shoulders. "I'll tell you both plain, because I prefer to be blunt instead of beating around bushes. With your reputations, the race of the children, and restrictive disciplinary rules, I doubt you'll find a qualified teacher."

"Our reputation?" Riot asked.

"I'm speaking of your future wife, Mr. Riot. There are few in California who didn't follow the trial in the newspapers. Miss Amsel… well…" She looked at him. "I don't need to go on, I'm sure."

"Thank you for your honesty," Riot said.

"And that's all it is. Plain honesty." She extended a hand, and shook both his and Lily's again. It showed a level of professionalism the others had lacked. And she was right. Their reputations were affecting the children. There was the rub.

"I'll contact you when we've made a decision." Riot opened the door for her. Three sets of eyes look up at him in a picture of innocence. All three looked bored. Too bored.

Riot searched the room with a sweep of his eyes. There were no new signals indicating their disapproval. Only a nervous young man trying to blend with the furniture.

"Would you show Mrs. Famish to the door?"

Tobias flung his arm toward the door with enthusiasm, and when the two were gone, Riot turned to the final applicant. The young man's brown hair was thinning at the top. He looked in danger of going bald before his thirtieth birthday. His eyes seemed too large for his gaunt face, and the thin little mustache clinging to his upper lip did little to soften his features.

"Mr...?" Riot fished for a name.

Without answering, the young man bolted for the adjoining parlor, only to stop at the threshold. Riot watched with growing concern as the man stepped past the threshold, stepped back out, and then back inside.

Sarah and Jin glanced at each other in alarm.

Riot looked for any telling bulges under the coat or irregularities in the sleeves. There were none that he could see. Riot closed the door and turned to the nervous young man, who had already taken a seat. He wore gloves, and his hands lay flat on his thighs. His gaze was fixed on the window.

Lily smiled, showing her dimples, but the gesture didn't seem to put him at ease.

"References, Mr...?" Riot tried again.

"Nicholas Stratigareas. Everyone calls me Nicholas." He had a soft voice, and he sat with a straight back, in perfect symmetry with the armrests, while his polished shoes were as straight and flat on the floor as could be.

Riot didn't take his seat. Something was wrong. "You're not here about the teaching position, are you?"

The man blinked in surprise. "How did you know?"

Riot shifted, placing himself between Lily and the stranger. "Why are you here?"

There was a plea in Nicholas's large eyes. "I need your help, Mr. Riot."

"I don't interview clients in my home. You'll have to make an appointment with my agency on Market Street."

"I can't go to your agency."

"And why is that?"

Nicholas shifted on the seat. "Because I'm being watched."

SILENCE FOLLOWED THE DECLARATION. RIOT WAITED FOR more, but the young man only kept glancing at the window. It looked out to the side garden, where San Francisco's Silver Mistress was caressing roses and jasmine, stirring lazily and taking her time to make way for the sun. Grimm was crouched in the garden, dead heading the rose bushes and clipping leaves. Miss Lily's son had a gift with plants and animals. A quiet way about him. But Grimm's manner didn't seem to put Nicholas at ease.

Lily leaned to the side, to look around Riot. "Who is watching you?" she asked.

Nicholas's Adam's apple bulged along his neck. "I don't know."

Riot took a seat beside Lily. Out of habit he tucked his coat back, but he hadn't brought a revolver to interview teachers. He inclined his head to Lily, and she took his cue.

"What do these people look like?" she asked. There was concern in her question.

"I... don't know," Nicholas said.

"How do you know you're being watched?" she asked gently.

Nicholas swallowed. "I can *feel* them watching me."

The intensity of this pronouncement raised Riot's hackles. "You're in my home, not my agency. I'm going to need more than a feeling, Mr. Nicholas."

Nicholas glanced out the window. "Faces," he blurted out. "I'm sure of it. I saw faces. I keep my rooms tidy. My shoes were moved... a half inch to the right."

The more Nicholas talked, the more unbalanced he appeared.

"Do you have any enemies?" Riot asked.

Nicholas shook his head.

"What about jilted women? A jealous husband?"

Nicholas flushed red. "No, Mr. Riot... I would never..." he stammered "...that is, I'm an honorable man." He glanced apologetically at Riot, but didn't meet his eyes.

The newspapers had made a racket over Riot's affair with Isobel. One would have had to be living in a hole not to have heard of it. As a gambler, Riot's reputation was already in the gutter, but that didn't matter much at all—a man could still run for President of the United States with a questionable past. Isobel was a different matter. Respectable society viewed her as a woman of the underworld (which amused her no end), while the rest saw her as a local legend.

Riot waited for Nicholas to expound; he did not. With the thin leather gloves and crisp sleeves, it was hard to read the man. His suit was store bought, but tailored to precise measurements. He wasn't a wealthy man, but clearly concerned about his appearance. Although the suit was worn around the edges, it was well tended. He was fastidious to the extreme. His long neck craned forward, and his shoulders were hunched. Riot had the impression that he spent most the day bent over a table. With the man's hands covered, Riot couldn't tell if he worked as an accountant or factory worker.

"What is it you do for a living, Mr. Nicholas?"

"I'm a druggist's apprentice."

"Has there been any trouble at your pharmacy?"

"None."

"Have you recently inherited money?"

Nicholas shook his head.

"Have you witnessed a crime?"

Again, a shake of his head. "No! Nothing at all has happened. The only thing that's changed is I'm being followed."

"When did it start?" Lily asked.

"A month ago."

Lily took a patient breath. "How do you know?"

"I saw a face in the window of my pharmacy. And then again, later that night, in my home."

"In your home?" Riot asked.

"Outside the garden window." He glanced towards the window again. Grimm had moved on from his roses.

Lily leaned to the side, catching Nicholas's attention. "What did this face look like?"

"Obscured. Blurred. It was dark."

"The skin color was dark?" Lily asked.

"No… I mean I don't know. The window is tinted."

"In your home?" she asked.

"No, at the store where I work."

"Where do you work?" Riot asked.

"Joy's Drugstore on California and Kearney."

Riot waited, but Nicholas wasn't one to give information away. "Have you seen the face again?"

Nicholas shuddered. "Here and there. In window reflections, in a crowd, on the streetcar."

"But you can't describe him?" Riot pressed.

"I know I'm being followed!" His shout made Lily jump.

Riot stood. "Mr. Nicholas, I suggest you leave *now*. Leave your address and I'll send a man around—"

"It must be *you*." The intensity in Nicholas's eyes was alarming. There was desperation in that gaze, and desperation was a close friend to madness.

"What do you wish of me?" Riot asked.

Nicholas smoothed his hair three times to compose himself. "I want you to make him stop watching me."

Riot was on the verge of bodily escorting the man out of his home. But he waited, and watched. Nicholas wasn't threatening—he was terrified. Unfortunately, desperate men were capable of nearly anything.

"I'll do what I can," Riot said softly. "But not *here*." He took a step forward, trying to catch his eyes, but Nicholas shied away from his gaze. "You may telephone my agency. You may approach me on the street. You may wire me. But *never* come here again. Do you understand, Mr. Nicholas?"

The man licked his lips. "I do, Mr. Riot." Nicholas stood like a spring. "I do apologize. It's only that I need your help."

"Do you have an address?"

Nicholas shook his head. "I shouldn't have troubled you. I'm terribly sorry." Before Riot could escort him out, the man headed for the door, and Riot watched as he hurried down the street, head swiveling every which way.

"Poor soul."

Riot glanced at Lily, who had followed them onto the front porch. "I'm afraid this sort of thing will only get worse."

"This sort of thing?" she asked.

"Petty cases, delusional clients, missing dogs—the price of fame," he said dryly.

"Did Mr. Ravenwood tolerate such things?"

The edge of Riot's lip raised as he leaned against a column. "I never could tell. He'd scoff at murder cases, but drop everything for an odd detail as trivial as a missing button."

"Do you think Mr. Nicholas is in danger?"

"I think Mr. Nicholas believes he's being followed with all his heart. But that doesn't mean it's true."

Lily nodded in agreement. "The largest lies are the ones we tell ourselves. Will you look into it further?"

"I don't know," he said truthfully. "Ravenwood Agency doesn't have the manpower to handle another case. I'm stretched as it is. What did you make of it?"

"I think that young man needs help."

Riot stroked his beard in thought. "We could use a healthy dose of help in finding a teacher."

Lily sighed, and glanced at her notes. "Those willing aren't fit, and those fit aren't willing. Mrs. Famish is our best candidate so far." There wasn't a hint of excitement in her words. Riot shared her lack of enthusiasm.

"Sins of the father," he murmured, as he opened the

door for her. "I hadn't considered the possibility that my reputation would affect the children."

Lily smiled at him. "People are responsible for others in all sorts of ways. Especially the ones who turn their noses up in the air. They're not worth your time, Mr. Riot."

Laughter burst from inside the house. Riot paused at the parlor door to listen. There were four voices in the room instead of three. He looked to Lily in question, hoping she had heard the same. "Was there another applicant?"

Lily shook her head.

7

AN IMPROPER APPLICANT

ATTICUS RIOT PULLED THE PARLOR DOORS OPEN. Conversation cut off, and five sets of eyes looked to him. Miss Annie Dupree set Watson down and stood, her eyes sparkling like sapphires. She was tall and shapely, with a careless tendril of auburn hair begging to be touched.

"Mr. Riot. Mrs. White. I was just telling the children about a boy who once brought a snake to school."

Tobias slapped his knee. "He tried to scare Miss Dupree with it." But the mere thought sent him into another giggling fit.

Jin didn't giggle. Instead, she explained, "Miss Dupree ate it for lunch."

"I've had some good snake," Sarah said.

Miss Dupree smiled, and extended her hand. Riot took it lightly. "Have you settled on a tutor?" she asked.

"Not yet."

"That's fortunate."

"And why is that?"

"I'm here to interview for the position."

Riot cocked his head, and the rest of the room went silent. Annie Dupree was renting Ravenwood's old consultation room—the French doors were discreet enough for the comings and goings of her nocturnal clients. The children did not know this, of course, or if they did they feigned ignorance.

Lily tolerated Miss Dupree. But only due to Tim. He was as unprejudiced as a man came—to color and profession.

Lily opened her mouth, looked to the children, and then gestured her into the second parlor. "Won't you come in."

Annie swept past with a swish of skirts, and Riot studied her back. Not for her hourglass shape or lush hair, but in a thoughtful, calculating sort of way. Charm and beauty were not lost on Riot. He noticed them, but only to tuck details away—to learn their 'tells'. Annie had a smile that would drop most men's brains between their legs, but Riot had grown up with such women. They were his mothers and sisters, and he had seen the pain in them that men left behind.

Riot waited for Watson to enter, and then closed the doors. He gestured for the women to be seated.

"You both appear speechless," Annie said. Watson hopped on her lap again. Her fingers idly stroked his fur.

He waited for a coy comment. A 'as most men are with me' but Annie held her tongue. Her eyes, however, communicated far more.

"Do you have teaching experience, Miss Dupree?" Lily asked.

"I do. No references, as I'm sure you understand." Annie averted her gaze. "I wasn't always a woman of the underworld. I was a governess in Boston—until the man of the house took a liking to me. I'm sure you both can fill in the rest."

"I'm sure I can, but I'd like to hear it all the same," Riot said.

Annie looked at him in surprise, her lips parting slightly.

"I wish I could say I refused his advances, but I was young. When he got me with child, he called me unfit and kicked me to the gutter without reference. I could no longer find respectable work. I heard a woman could make herself over in the West, so I relocated and began teaching. Only I couldn't live on a teacher's wage here."

It was a story Riot had heard countless times. Brothels were filled with teachers, widows, launderers, maids, nurses, shop girls, and everything else under the sun. Women were paid a fourth of what men made for the same work—except for prostitution. For the majority of women, it came down to starving or whoring.

"I'm sure you'll understand I have reservations," Lily said.

Annie looked down at the cat in her lap, unable to meet their eyes. Her voice was soft when she spoke. "I know you barely tolerate me as it is. And I know if it weren't for Mr. Tim, I wouldn't be allowed to board here."

Lily shook her head. "I don't have anything against you, Miss Dupree. I take issue with you running a brothel out of your rooms. You pulled yourself out of the gutter long ago, and there's no reason for you to remain there."

Annie arched a delicate brow. "Have I no reason?"

"Most folk get by without diamonds and fine food." Lily looked pointedly at the diamond nestled between the woman's breasts.

Annie smiled. "With all due respect, you don't know my

business. But you're right. I could move on, and for the most part I have, but I do enjoy the company of certain men." She glanced at Riot under her lashes.

Careful not to look at Riot, Lily calmly folded her hands on her lap, and waited.

As a ploy to get into Alex Kingston's inner circle, Riot had hired Miss Dupree to accompany him to a number of social engagements. He had enjoyed her company, but that was all. Dinner and opera, then parting ways in the entry. His housekeeper didn't know that, however.

"Mrs. White brings up an excellent point. You could retire to the country and live comfortably for the rest of your life. Why teach children in this house?"

Annie smoothed her skirts, collecting her thoughts. "I could live comfortably *outside* San Francisco, but not *inside* the city. And I'm not the type of woman to be kept. Once you're married, Mr. Riot, I imagine you'll give your boarders notice to vacate. Ravenwood Manor is the first home I've had in a long while, and teaching the children would ensure me a room in this house."

"And what of your 'select gentlemen'?" Lily asked.

Annie smiled. "What I do in my room remains my business."

"Absolutely not," Lily said.

"Do you speak for Mr. Riot?"

"I speak for *my* children."

"You won't find a more qualified teacher," Annie countered. "Especially for Jin. I've dealt with young women like her. Do you imagine a young, reputable teacher will know what to do when Jin begins speaking of brothel life? Because she *will*. It's been her life for the past two years."

Riot kept his face blank. But his heart beat quicker. How did Annie Dupree know so much about the children? But the answer was obvious. After returning from Calistoga, Riot had thrown himself into his work. The children had had little to occupy themselves with these past weeks.

And although it worried him, Annie was right—Jin's life was a world away from that of Tobias, Maddie, and Sarah's.

"Qualifications?" Lily asked.

"I speak French, Italian, and Latin. And as you know, Mr. Riot, I possess a passable knowledge on most subjects— finances, sciences, any topic that I might find myself discussing with one of my gentlemen. I can teach the girls manners and grace. And Tobias, too. The children are bright—they need a quick mind like my own. There isn't an emotion or situation that I haven't handled calmly and delicately in grown men, let alone children."

Riot let her words settle into silence. There was a lot she was not saying into that silence, and he'd be a fool not to suspect that Annie Dupree was involved with Siu Lui, his half-sister, who sat like a spider in a web of criminal undertakings.

But Riot wasn't prepared to show his cards. "Given recent events, you'll understand my hesitation."

"That was unfortunate." Then to his surprise, she showed him a card of her own—the card she wanted him to see. "You already have ears at the door, Mr. Riot." She gestured towards the closed door. Riot knew there would be three sets of ears pressed to the wood. "I'm only a pair of eyes. And I may prove useful one day."

RIOT GENTLY CLOSED THE DOOR BEHIND A SWISH OF EXITING skirts. Annie Dupree had left him with much to ponder. The moment one door closed, another pair slid open. Jin stuck her face through the gap. "We want her."

"I didn't say that," Sarah said. "It's not proper."

"What's not proper?" Tobias said.

Riot held up a hand. "We'll discuss it at another time."

"I want to see Captain Morgan," Jin demanded.

"In good time." There was an edge to his voice. One that made Jin duck back inside.

"Finish your chores. All of you," Lily said, shutting the doors.

Three pairs of feet hurried away.

Lily took sympathy on the man. The trial had been torture for him. She had seen it in his eyes, in the set of his shoulders, every single day. And while the torture might be over, Isobel was still in an asylum, more than five hours away. He had only spent a week at Bright Waters before responsibilities had pulled him back to San Francisco. Atticus Riot hadn't stopped since, and now he looked as severe as the day Lily had first met him.

"I'll make a pot of tea."

"I'm needed at the agency," he said.

"Mr. Riot."

He drew up short at the tone of her voice.

"We need to talk."

Riot followed her into the kitchen. While Lily put the kettle on, she heard him gathering the cups. The man never sat idle while others worked. He was a rare kind of man, which made what she had to say difficult.

They didn't discuss the elephant in the room straight away. Not until they were both settled at the table with a cup warming their hands. Riot raised his dark eyes to hers. "What do you think of Miss Dupree's offer?"

"I think she's qualified. And she's right. Jin will be an

issue. Even if we found someone willing to teach the children, Jin would make it a point to shock them the moment she became bored. I don't think we have much choice, Mr. Riot."

He considered the truth in her words.

"What did she mean by 'only a pair of eyes'?" Lily ventured.

Riot blew on his tea. "I suspect Miss Dupree is working for an old acquaintance of mine."

Lily waited as Riot sipped his tea, but he didn't elaborate. "Friend or foe?" she finally asked.

"Both."

"Sounds like family."

Riot grimaced. "The only one I have."

"We can't choose our blood, which is a shame because they're set to hurt us more than any stranger. Is Miss Dupree a danger to my children?"

Riot considered her question. "I can't be sure. In my youth, I would have been, but not anymore."

"If I don't know the whole story, I can't be sure either."

"The less you know the better."

"I've never found that true."

Riot's lip quirked. "You're probably right." And so he told her. Everything. Three cups of tea and a cold pot later, Riot fell silent.

The story seemed to exhaust him, and Lily itched to send the man straight to bed, but it wasn't her place. Instead she asked, "And this White Blossom, you suspect Miss Dupree is spying for her?"

"That, or Miss Dupree knows a part of the story, and she's using it to her advantage."

"Why would she bluff about something like that?"

"She'll know I'll want to keep her close so I can keep an eye on her."

"And do you?"

"*Keep your friends close, and your enemies closer,*" he quoted.

"Where is that from?"

"The Art of War by Sun Tzu."

Lily shook her head. "There's no art to war. It's more like what comes out of the back end of a horse."

"Miss Lily, you shock me."

The edges of her eyes crinkled with laughter. "Well, I wouldn't keep her too close. You're a married man, or soon to be. I can't imagine Miss Isobel taking kindly to a woman like that in the house."

"Bel isn't the jealous type."

"I've heard a number of men say that very thing. But it doesn't matter what her temperament is—or yours—people will talk. You and Miss Dupree were seen in public." She left the rest unsaid, but apparently suggestion bled through.

"That's as far as our relationship extended."

"If I wasn't even positive, what will others say?"

"They'll talk either way." He stood, and reached for his hat. "Thank you for the tea, and your listening ear."

"Don't thank me yet. There's something else we need to discuss."

"Oh?"

"I wouldn't bring it up now, but since you've returned, no time seems like the right time. And this can't wait much longer."

He sat back down. "What is it?"

"The state of your finances."

Riot narrowed his eyes. "I beg your pardon?"

"Your estate."

"Ravenwood's."

"*Yours*," she corrected. "Mr. Tim hired me to manage this house, and in order to do that I needed access to Ravenwood's accounts. Mr. Riot, I didn't take on boarders because I was lonely—we need their income to keep the house in good repair."

"But Ravenwood was wealthy."

"In land. And, yes, he had a sizable nest egg, but Mr. Tim and this house go through money like Tobias in a candy shop. I'm assuming you'll be giving the boarders notice soon? What with the children moving in and Miss Isobel."

"Aren't there enough rooms?"

"Jin and Sarah are sharing the spare bedroom, but I spend more time breaking up their arguments than cleaning up after them."

"They've been arguing?" he asked.

Lily fixed him with a look. And he realized just how scarce he'd been since he returned from Calistoga.

"We *could* fix up the attic, but that's a lot of bodies under one roof."

"I'll leave it to you to sort." He made to stand again.

"*Mr.* Riot."

Riot paused, and she heard a faint sigh.

"You have an estate. I need to know what you want to do with it. Without boarders you'll have no income, and begging your pardon for saying it, but your agency is more of a drain than a boon on Ravenwood's estate."

"It is?"

In answer, she stood and opened a cupboard, selecting a slim journal from the shelf. Lily laid the account book on the table, and opened it, placing a finger on the final figure.

Riot stared at the numbers. He adjusted his spectacles, and looked again. The numbers hadn't changed.

"As you can see, the income from the boarders pays for this house, groceries, utilities, and my salary while leaving a bit extra, but Mr. Tim has been using Ravenwood's... *your* money as a personal bank. Half the time he doesn't charge folk—not the ones who can't afford it. But he pays his agents generously all the same."

"I'll have a word with Tim, and see if I can sort out the agency. In the meantime..." Riot unconsciously reached for the deck of playing cards in his pocket. "How much do we need?"

Lily shook her head. "It's not that simple. A house this size needs *steady* income. There needs to be more planning than a trip to the nearest gambling hall. You have children to think about now."

"Miss Lily, the only things I know are gambling and detective work." Along with women and gunfighting, he added silently. He ran a finger along his deck, squaring the edges. "Do you have any suggestions?"

"You have a few options." She ticked off her fingers. "You could sort out the agency and try to turn a profit. But I'm not sure that's possible. Not with this kind of overhead." She gestured at the ceiling.

Finger two. "Ravenwood has property in England. You could sell it, but that's a temporary solution." She moved on to the third finger. "Or you can sell this house, and buy something smaller."

Riot considered her words. At one time he had been set to rid himself of this house. An arrogant building of turrets and grim windows that held too many painful memories. But now the thought turned his stomach. And property in England? Riot had to admit, he hadn't glanced at his inheritance after Ravenwood's murder. He had simply left.

"Any others?" he asked hopefully.

"It's a gamble."

"I'm a gambling man."

Lily took a deep breath. "Have you thought about investing what's left of Ravenwood's money?"

From his lack of expression, he had not.

Riot cleared his throat. "I've never paid much mind to business."

"I thought as much."

"I don't suppose you have?"

"Mr. Tim didn't hand Ravenwood's estate to a simpleton. I was raised in Nantucket. While the menfolk were off whaling, the women ran things. I've run businesses before, and I have a few ideas," she said.

Riot tucked his cards away. "You can keep fifty percent of whatever you make."

"I don't take charity, Mr. Riot."

"It's not charity. You're doing all the work."

"It's *your* money. Offering fifty percent is a terrible way to do business."

"That's why I'm making you a partner." He thrust out his hand.

Lily stared at him as if he had gone mad.

"I don't have a head for money, Miss Lily. It's this, or the gambling tables for me."

"What about Miss Isobel? She's sharp."

The edge of Riot's lip quirked. "When it suits her. I know her well enough to say this won't."

"Shouldn't you hear my proposals first?"

"If it would make you more comfortable, but I'm already late, Miss Lily."

"Then I'll make some inquiries, and we can discuss it later. If you like my ideas then we'll shake on it."

Riot stood, and slipped on his hat. He tipped the brim,

and walked out with that easy stride of his. The clink of imagined spurs whispered in her mind.

A gambler *and* a gunfighter, she silently added. Judging from the courtroom shoot out, she suspected he was better at the latter. The implications of what he had just offered stunned her, the reality worried her, and the eccentricity of Riot bordered on madness.

8

A FLURRY OF TELEGRAMS

Fancy marrying a pauper with two daughters? -R

A gold mine didn't suit me one bit. -B

That's a relief. -R

Did your hat obsession finally land you in the poorhouse? -B

I may have to sell my collection. -R

We'll join the circus. -B

Being a clown will suit me just fine. -R

Not a ringmaster? -B

I knew I forgot something. -R

I don't expect a ring from a pauper. -B

Our luck may turn. LW is working on it. -R

Smart man. Any luck finding a tutor?-B

9

ACUTE PARANOIA

ISOBEL

ISOBEL SHUT THE BOOK. "I CAN'T STAND THIS."

"Reading, or life in general?" Lotario asked.

"This book." She brandished *The Memoirs of Sherlock Holmes*.

"Are you *still* angry at Conan Doyle for killing your favorite detective? It's been *six* years."

"The 'Final Problem' didn't do Holmes justice," Isobel said.

"I thought it noble."

"It's riddled with holes. Moriarty is *never* mentioned before 'The Final Problem'. Then a 'Napoleon of crime' appears out of thin air—a mastermind whom Holmes suspected for years, but there are *no* details."

"The Strand has limited space," Lotario said dryly. "Besides, Watson was married and distracted, which I'm hoping will happen to you when you enter into that blissful state. *Again*. In the meantime, write another scathing letter to the author. That always cheers you up."

"My letters keep being returned."

"Here's an idea: why don't you stop reading 'The Final Problem'?"

"Why don't you stop buggering men?"

"I don't do the buggering," he said cheekily. "Does this have anything to do with your last case?"

Isobel stuttered to a stop. "No."

"Hmm."

"What's that supposed to mean?"

Lotario sighed, and closed his book. "You and Atticus faced your own Moriarty."

"But Bak Siu Lui is *still* alive, Ari. And I'm not so trusting of her word as Riot is. Three years of self-imposed exile doesn't mean she can't manipulate things in San Francisco from afar."

What Isobel wouldn't give to face that woman on the edge of Reichenbach Falls, or better yet on a nice cliff along the coast. She'd certainly sleep easier at night.

"Do you really think someone was trying to kill you with a *magnifying glass*? I doubt the silver frame would throw light that far."

"Someone was in that meadow shining *something* at me. Even if murder wasn't the intent, it may have been a warning—a reminder that the business with Bak Siu Lui isn't finished."

Lotario rolled his eyes, and returned to his book. After a time, he mused aloud, "If Holmes had survived the duel with Moriarty, do you think he would have developed paranoia?"

"I'm *not* paranoid."

"You're in an asylum, dear sister. Your opinion on the psyche is suspect." Lotario glanced at his twin out of the corner of his eye. "Let the magnifying glass go," he urged softly. "No one is trying to murder you—a rifle would have been easier. Personally, I'd use poison."

Isobel ignored the threat. "You're not even curious?"

"My curiosity is on holiday. Can I *please* read in peace?"

Isobel stared silently at her twin, until he put his back to her. In the end, she pressed her lips together, and looked out across the mineral pool. Patients floated like crispy seals in the water, while others lounged on divans. At least two of the women had been admiring Lotario for the past half an hour. One of them had a pale line encircling her finger.

What was it like, having a still mind? One that would allow her to drift the day away in leisure?

A shadow blocked her sun, and a grunt followed. Isobel glanced up to find a large man standing over her. The left side of his face and body looked like it had melted.

Isobel beamed up at the man. "Samuel."

Never able to meet her eyes, he ducked his head. A bit of drool had slipped from the corner of his mouth, and was stuck to his stubble. He thrust a Western Union slip under her nose. "Telly."

"Thank you," she said with feeling. "You're the only other man I look forward to seeing here." She ripped the missive open, and read the telegram.

Our best candidate is the resident in RW's old consultation room. -R

Isobel choked in surprise.

"Is something a matter?" Lotario asked.

"Would you hire a prostitute as a schoolteacher?"

Lotario arched a brow without looking up. "You're asking the wrong whore," he murmured under his breath.

Isobel glanced at Samuel, but he stood like a stone by her side, waiting. He gave no indication that he understood their conversation. She fished out paper and pencil from her satchel, and penned a reply.

Tread carefully. -B

"I never imagined I'd want a telephone at hand," she muttered. The closest telephone was in town, miles from Bright Waters. Unfortunately, her six month sentence prevented her from making the trek. She folded the slip of paper and handed it to Samuel. Without raising his eyes, he gently took it from her.

"Como está?" she asked. But her question in Spanish elicited no more reply than if she had asked in English. Samuel Lopez had the mind of a child and the build of a bull, but he seemed a gentle sort. Always bringing his dog, Bebé, along, or stopping to pet Mr. Darcy, the rabbit. Julius Bright hired him for odd jobs, but lately Isobel had commandeered his exclusive services. The flurry of telegrams she and Riot exchanged daily would feed Samuel for a year.

"One moment." She fished for a coin, and dropped it into his palm. "No Bebé today?"

Samuel gave his head a violent shake, curled his hand around the coin, and loped off at a quick pace. Her responding telegram would be delivered within the hour.

Isobel opened her mouth, a question on the tip of her tongue.

"*No,*" Lotario bit out.

Isobel sighed. He knew what she had been about to ask. To swap identities. Just one more time. She needed to talk with Riot. There were too many reporters loitering around telegraph stations. It was forcing them to exchange cryptic messages, and letters weren't any safer. They could be intercepted, too.

Maybe I *am* paranoid.

With that thought, she told herself to relax, and closed her eyes. Sunlight caressed her skin, and water lapped against the edges of the pool. Conversations drifted on a breeze along with the scents of earth and leaves. Lotario yawned. A page flipped. A nurse's heels clicked on terra-cotta tiles. A bumblebee buzzed by her ear. A flap of wings. *Click, click, click.* A burst of laughter.

Isobel opened her eyes. "I'll go mad at this rate!" She needed to stir the waters.

Carelessly, she stripped off her summer dress. Eyes widened in shock, and Lotario's admirers called for a nurse, but the cry was cut short as Isobel dove under the water. If there was one benefit to an asylum, it was that she was expected to be insane. Social niceties be damned.

"Miss Amsel!" A nurse came trotting from a wing. "Your clothes!"

Cooled and refreshed, she pulled herself out of the pool. A thin chemise clung to her body, and a puddle formed around her feet. The nurse attacked her with a towel.

"You know the rules, Miss Amsel."

"I forget them."

The nurse eyed her sharply, and pushed the loose dress into her arms.

"That's why we infirm need your reassuring presence, Miss Floyd. To guide us from our misery and folly," Lotario drawled.

"I'm simply doing my job, is all."

"You go above and beyond, while brightening my every day," Lotario crooned.

"Oh, Mr. Amsel. You're too kind." Miss Floyd blushed.

"I do try. Can I get you anything more? Another lemonade? A pillow? You do look pale today…" She continued to fuss over her favorite patient, forgetting all about the convicted criminal. In short order, Lotario sent the nurse away with a smile on her face.

Isobel plopped down on the divan beside her twin. "A bit overdone, don't you think?"

"Miss Floyd reads poetry and romance novels featuring long-haired poets in her spare time."

"Your Miss Floyd also likes to drag combs through the gnarled hair of her patients."

Lotario lifted his good shoulder. "Everyone finds a way to cope. If you found one, I wouldn't need to help you so often."

"Help me?"

"I've been distracting everyone here to keep you out of trouble."

She snorted. "Is that what you call it? I thought you were trying to make me sick."

"I doubt being near to death with pneumonia would keep you inside the asylum."

He knew her too well. Isobel would crawl off the grounds to die. "At least in a prison, I wouldn't be as tempted. I'm not sure what's worse: knowing I can escape at any time or being trapped behind walls."

"Now you're just whining."

The memory of her time confined to a jail cell during the trial drove her out of bed each night. Isobel hugged the towel to her breast.

Lotario's gaze slid sideways. "When is Atticus due for a visit?"

"I don't know."

"It's been a while."

"He has a life. Work. Cases. The children."

"*You.*"

"What drivel are you reading?" she asked, nodding to his book.

"I'm on holiday."

"A holiday away from your stress as a dancer and a whore?"

"And opera," he added, ignoring her stab. "Forced recuperation has been good for my voice. Although I've had trouble finding a spot to practice my scales without drawing notice."

"There's a cave a few miles—"

"No!" He swallowed. "No caves," he said in a weaker voice.

Isobel said nothing, which was far worse than prodding him about it.

"Oh, say it," he growled.

"Dr. Bright is worried about you."

"He should worry about *you* instead," Lotario said.

"He'll worry when I strangle the next nurse who speaks soothingly to me. I need stimulation."

Lotario opened his mouth.

"*Mental,*" she growled.

"Have you made any attempt to converse with your fellow patients?" he asked instead.

Isobel arched a brow. "I've talked with Samuel, Dr. Bright, Miss Meredith, Mr. Darcy, and you today."

"A rabbit doesn't count." Lotario stretched, his sleek muscles rippling. He winced at the last, and quickly shifted. Isobel bit her tongue. "What about those two?" he asked.

"You mean the two women who have been admiring you for the past hour?"

He glanced at his nails. "Oh, have they?"

"Yes. And no, I haven't spoken with either of them. She'll only tell me what I already know."

"Which one?"

Isobel made a gesture with her fingers. A code they had developed early on. Touching her right thumb to pinky. Six o'clock. "She recently lost her husband, in death."

"Liars go to hell."

"I'm not making it up."

Lotario huffed.

"If you used your brain, you'd come to the same conclusion." There was a challenge in that. Lotario turned a casual eye on the woman, then made an appreciative sound. "Delightful, but you're wrong."

"I don't think so."

"You're guessing," Lotario challenged.

"It's obvious."

"So you say."

Isobel took a breath. "The loose folds on her arms indicate rapid weight loss—a side effect of childbirth or grief. There's a pale line around her *digitus medicinalis*, but the rest of her is tan. She's been here a month, but the ring's impression is still there. She removes the ring when she goes into the mineral baths out of fear that it will slip off. Sentimentality of that sort can only be for a husband she still loves. She would hardly be wearing a ring of the man who abandoned her. It's possible she lost a child, too."

"And yet she's been admiring me."

"As one admires a classical sculpture."

Lotario fluttered his lashes, and shifted his leg ever so slightly to display a well-shaped calf. But flattery had not won him over. "It's easy to speculate," he said.

"It's not speculation."

Lotario waved a hand. "Yes, yes, it's deduction, but how do you confirm your far-flung theories?"

"I don't need to."

He rolled his eyes. "Arrogant witch."

"Go ask her," she challenged.

"And bring on a fit of hysterics?"

"A dollar says I'm right."

Lotario pursed his lips. "I don't flash an ankle for a dollar, dear sister."

Isobel scowled at her twin. Lotario was not a pauper, but he had expensive tastes and large holes in his pockets. "You won't go talk with her because you know I'm right," she said.

Lotario ignored the observation, and changed the subject. "What about the quiet one over there?"

"Easy. Circles under her eyes. Recently shorn hair. Cracked lips. And she's brought out to sit in the sun every day at noon. She's recovering from pneumonia."

"Wrong," Lotario said with relish.

Isobel arched a brow.

"Her beloved pet died, so she butchered her own hair. You two share something in common."

"Have you spoken with her?"

Lotario waved a hand. "It's obvious."

Isobel studied the woman with renewed interest. "It wasn't a dog. It was a cat."

"Did you just steal my deduction?"

"That woman *hates* dogs. She has an aversion to Samuel's dog."

"This is precisely what you're lacking, Bel. You might be able to name every poison under the sun, but when it comes to human nature, you're as blind as they come."

"If her dog died, why would she hate dogs?"

"Because seeing Samuel's dog brings up painful memories," Lotario pointed out.

"Possible," she conceded. "But wrong."

"Only a moment ago, you claimed it was pneumonia."

"I'm certain of it."

"How?"

Isobel scrunched her brows together in consideration. Too far away. Determined, she set her book down, walked over and stopped beside the woman's divan. The woman looked up in alarm. There was a wrap around her short hair, red nose from crying, loose clothing that all the patients wore, pale... Yes, all the signs were there. Then what was wrong? "Your pet cat recently died," Isobel stated with authority.

The woman inhaled sharply. "Do I know you? Miss...?"

"Amsel. Isobel Amsel."

"Tibbles *didn't* die, I had to give her to a new home."

Isobel blinked. "She's not dead?"

"No!" she sniffled, and sneezed. "I developed severe allergies. It nearly killed me."

With head held high, Isobel marched back to Lotario and sat. "I was right. It was a cat." She thrust out her hand, waiting for payment.

"Her cat didn't *die*," he said out of the corner of his mouth. "That was horrid, Bel."

"What was?"

"The woman is crying now."

Isobel frowned. "She has allergies."

"On second thought, *please* don't interact with the other patients." Lotario sighed, closed his book, and walked over to the woman. Instead of a frown, Lotario was welcomed with a shy smile. The two fell instantly to talking.

With nothing to do, Isobel sat back and plucked the

magnifying glass from her satchel. As she turned the handle over, she watched a pair of nurses stroll along the veranda. Their blue dresses and starched aprons made them stand out from the patients. And in town...

Energized, she stuffed the glass back into her satchel, and hurried towards the main building. Bright Waters was not a secure asylum. It relied on its remote location to keep patients in place. She could walk about freely, and as long as she (or Lotario) checked in every morning and night, no one appeared concerned with her whereabouts.

Escaping wasn't the issue, it was recognition. During the trial, her likeness had been plastered all over the newspapers from California to New York. Depending on the person, she was either a local legend or an infamous harlot. What Isobel needed now was something even more recognizable. Something to distract the eye.

A man of her own age drifted down the hallway, shuffling his feet with a scratch, his eyes vacant, his movements aimless. The right side of his face was horribly scarred, and he had lost his right arm. A soldier who had fought, and probably wished he had died, in some far-flung war. She thought of her older brother, Merrik, fighting in the Philippines. Would he return? And if he did, would he come back whole?

Two nurses walked down the hallway, each with a stack of blankets. Isobel shook her head when they asked if she needed anything. "That one-armed fellow might need some help. He looked lost."

"That'd be Mr. Stewart." They both nodded in understanding and picked up their pace.

Isobel waited at the end by the stairwell. Most nurses were busy with duties elsewhere—taking care of patients outside in the gardens or in the baths. Julius Bright believed nature was the ultimate healer. Perhaps he was right, but it was certainly no cure for curiosity.

Isobel slipped into a nurse's room, and gently shut the door. She went straight for the wardrobe.

"Well, hello," she whispered to a blue dress. Recognition was a funny thing. It caught ones attention, but as soon as the mind categorized a thing, the niggling question of 'who' was dismissed. She reached for a dress, and the door behind her opened. She nearly dropped the garment.

Isobel spun around, an excuse on the tip of her tongue. "Lotario," she hissed.

"What are you doing?" He held up a hand. "No, never mind. I don't want to know."

"Good, I wasn't going to tell you."

"You're going into town, aren't you?"

"Only for a short while."

"Only?" He took a step closer. "Are you mad? If you get caught you'll lose what freedom you have."

Isobel shook the dress at him. "No one will look twice at me."

"Don't risk your happiness for a *magnifying glass*."

"Tied to a tree. With a crack," she said. "Go read. Finish your book. I'm not asking for your help, so stop meddling."

Lotario snatched the dress from her hand. "I'm trying to keep you out of trouble."

"Did Riot put you up to this?"

"Of course not. The man is not an idiot," Lotario said.

"Agreed. So why are you stopping me?"

"I happen to like Atticus, and I don't want to see his heart broken when my twin ends up in a grave."

"Since when has a mercantile been dangerous?"

"*Everything* is dangerous with you. Since you've been

back, I've been seduced by a mad coroner, abducted, nearly drowned, *and* shot."

"I'm not asking for your help." She took back the dress, and briefly considered shoving her twin into the wardrobe, but Lotario always made such an awful racket.

"Well, you should."

"You told me you wouldn't swap places with me anymore."

Lotario arched an imperious brow. Finally, he gestured to himself.

Light dawned, and Isobel cursed under her breath. She was an utter idiot at times. "Will you take the magnifying glass into town and inquire after the owner?"

"Ask nicely."

Isobel batted her lashes. "Please, oh wonderful brother of mine."

"That's better."

"Can you telephone Riot, too?"

"You don't have to ask nicely for that." Lotario smiled like a cat. "Besides, mother and father are visiting today." Before she could retract her request, he snatched the magnifying glass from her hand and darted from the room.

10

A SIMPLE TASK

LOTARIO

Sunlight touched the dirt road, playing over leaves and a trail of wagon ruts. Lotario Amsel frowned at the long road. From silks to fine cuisine and four-horse carriages to this. And, by God, the parties he was missing. He could be in Paris, with ancient cobblestones under his feet, or on the Riviera. Tan bodies, carefree love, and Venetian balls. Instead, he was here.

Lotario curled his lip as he side-stepped a steaming pile of manure. The things he did for his twin. He was exhausted, his shoulder hurt, and the trees were swaying. But he didn't dare let on. Otherwise Isobel would beat herself up for making him walk to town. And then she would fuss. If there was one thing worse than a restless Isobel, it was a fussing Isobel.

Light-headed, Lotario stopped to rest on a rock. The shade cooled him, and he adjusted the sling on his shoulder. As a general rule, he tried not to ponder the future. It led down dark places and Lotario preferred the light. But weeks here—a place of recuperation—had forced him to slow down. To contemplate his life. And that was something Lotario had always tried not to do. His usual life involved fluttering from one party to the next, moving between johns and lovers, and swapping personas whenever he grew bored with who he was. But now he was stuck with himself. Lotario Amsel, black sheep, outcast, and now, cripple.

Lotario squeezed the magnifying glass until his knuckles turned white. It sent pain arcing up his wounded shoulder. Angry with himself, he pushed off the rock, and continued his walk towards Calistoga.

A rattle of wheels sent him hurrying to the side of the road. He stopped under a tree, and turned. The driver was covered in grime from his Stetson to his overalls. Not an ideal ride, but it would do.

Lotario hailed the driver. "Can you give me a lift into town?"

The man pulled on the reins, and eyed Lotario's sling and suit. He plucked a pipe from his lips. "Amsel's boy, are you?"

"One of them. Lotario Amsel," he introduced.

"Finneas O'Conner." The driver thrust down his hand, showing off a bright pink palm. A mercury miner.

Lotario took the hand with his good one, and his arm was nearly yanked from its socket. He was deposited on the seat with a thud. Lotario turned to look in the bed. A bandaged Chinese man sat beside a bloodstained blanket with a telling bulge underneath.

"We're due at the undertakers," Finneas explained, snapping the reins. The wagon rolled forward. "So where do you fall in the Amsel line? I can't recall all your names."

"I'm one of the twins."

Finneas laughed, and slapped his knee. "One o' the 'wee

devils'.""

Lotario hadn't heard that nickname in years. He studied the driver, and recognition touched memory. The mines had worn Finneas down, stolen his teeth and youth, but Lotario remembered the man. "You're Finn!"

Finneas flashed a gummy smile.

"You used to work at the vineyards," Lotario said.

"'Tis a shame 'bout that. Your ol' da was a good man. Paid us our worth."

"It *is* a shame." Aside from a few of Isobel's childhood expeditions, Lotario had fond memories of the vineyard. They had wandered for miles, and slept under the stars— with or without parental permission.

"Couldn't believe when he sold it. Then I heard 'bout some trouble with a rich fella and higher ups takin' what wasn't theirs." Finneas glanced at Lotario's bandaged shoulder, and frowned. "Those rumors, about your sister and you, they true?"

"Which ones?"

Finneas chuckled. "I can't read, so I have to divine the truth from what I hear. Never sure with that."

"I *can* read, but I'm always skeptical of what's in the newspapers. But if you're referring to the business with Alex Kingston and the court case that followed, then yes."

"And you took a bullet for her?"

"I did."

Finneas slapped him on the back, jarring his shoulder. Lotario swallowed down a wave of dizziness. "There's a lad. Good thing it wasn't my own dear sister. I'd have took a step back." Finneas wheezed for a few seconds. "I'll be damned. You wee devils turned into something good after all. Always figured you two for bank robbers."

"Bel was sentenced to an asylum."

The man barked. "Crazy, the both of ya. Is your ol' da going to buy another vineyard?"

Lotario lifted a shoulder. "I don't know. With the aphid infestation, I'm not sure there'll be any vines left. It's the vines that make the wine. But all the same, it'd be nice to keep some land here."

"Nasty pests," Finneas agreed. "Maybe it's good he got out when he did. I always said you two might be devils, but you're lucky ones."

Finneas hacked and gagged, and spat out a wad of thick phlegm. Lotario remembered a young, red-headed man full of energy. But then that was nearly a decade ago.

"How are the mercury mines?" he asked.

"Hellish." Finneas wiped his sleeve across his mouth. Lotario was on the verge of asking why he'd left the vineyard, but he didn't want to prick a nerve. If his father had sent Finneas away for some transgression, Lotario didn't want to be at the receiving end of the man's forgotten anger.

"Was there an explosion?" Lotario asked, nodding towards the corpse and injured passenger.

Finneas shifted. "Yep."

Lotario glanced over his shoulder, but the injured miner kept his eyes down. Accidents were common in mines, but so was malicious intent. It was none of his business. Still, Lotario was never one to pass up an opportunity to wheedle information from someone. He turned back around to Finneas and tried not to listen to the man's hacking—a common ailment among quicksilver miners.

They talked of the good old days at the vineyard, which turned to California's aristocracy. "A pompous, greedy bunch, the lot of them." And by the time Finneas dropped Lotario off in front of the general store, Lotario knew the man's favorite food (oysters), drink (whiskey), the lazy workers, and the whore Finneas wanted to marry (Sabine). Lotario had found that most men liked to hear themselves talk, and it took very little to nudge them in the right direction.

As the dust cleared, Lotario stepped onto the boardwalk, and gazed wistfully across the street to the hotel *Magnolia*. He longed for a good soak and a long sleep. But duty called.

A bell above the door clanged as he entered *Smith and Sons General Store*. Specialty cheeses and wines mingled in with breads and chocolates, among the more practical items. It wasn't a San Francisco boutique, but it was certainly civilized. Calistoga catered to a wide clientele, from vacationers to miners to the infirm.

The storekeeper's smile was at odds with his drooping mustache. The greeting only puffed out his cheeks until his eyes disappeared. "Afternoon, sir."

"Afternoon," Lotario said, dabbing at his brow with a handkerchief. "I'd forgotten how brutal summer can be here."

"You must be from the city."

"One does become dependent on our lovely fog."

For a minute, a pair of lacy gloves distracted Lotario.

"Shopping for the missus?" the storekeeper asked.

"Hmm." Lotario cleared his throat, and pulled himself away from the reams of cloth. "I need to replace a magnifying lens. It's cracked."

"I don't keep them in stock, but I can order one."

"That'll do."

The storekeeper reached under the counter for his ledger. "Make?"

"I'm not sure, but I have it here." Lotario placed the glass on the counter. The storekeeper hesitated a fraction, then picked it up and turned it over in his hands.

"A fine piece." His voice was rough. "I may have a lens in the storeroom. Excuse me." He hurried through the back door, taking the magnifying glass with him.

Lotario frowned. That had been far easier than expected. Never one to question luck, Lotario took advantage of the storekeeper's unexpected exit. He spun the ledger around, and ran his finger down a list of names and goods sold. There. A magnifying glass, ordered and arrived a week before, for a Mrs. Sheel. That fit the second initial on the handle. No address, but never mind that—there hadn't been a postmaster yet that Lotario couldn't trick into giving him an address.

Lotario spun the ledger back around, and waited. The minutes ticked on, and he turned to the merchandise. He collected a bag of hard candy, a pair of silk stockings, and those lovely lace gloves. He turned his nose up at the selection of dresses, and became enamored with a tiny book of poems.

The bell chimed, and Lotario snapped out of his book, wondering where the time had gone. A determined man with broad shoulders strolled inside. He had a star on his chest, and a scowl in his eyes. At that same moment, two more men walked in from the storeroom. Lotario swallowed.

"Stay where you are," the determined man ordered.

Lotario raised his hand. "I intended to pay for the candy."

Two quick steps and the Deputy Sheriff grabbed Lotario's arms, twisted them around, and slammed him onto the counter. "Miss Morgan, or should I say, Miss Amsel, you're in a heap of trouble," the sheriff growled in his ear.

White hot pain raced up Lotario's bad arm, right into his skull. Robbed of the breath to answer, his only reply was a strangled cry.

11

THE PARENTS

ISOBEL

"*MOTHER*, I'LL SAY IT ONE MORE TIME: I WILL NOT HAVE another wedding." Isobel put all her stubborn will behind the words.

Catarina Saavedra Amsel scowled at her only living daughter. Catarina had a presence that sent most men in retreat. But Isobel was immune. The emotion crackling between the two could power the city for a day.

"You *will* have a wedding, Isobel. I will not have a daughter living in sin."

"That ship sailed long ago. The entire country knows about my adulterous ways." Isobel delivered the statement with relish, provoking her mother to trace a cross over her breast.

"You must make this right. It reflects on the entire family." Catarina glanced to her husband and butler. She doubtlessly imagined the two of them already covered in filth.

"A man's reputation doesn't matter one jot. My brothers

can whore their days away, and still run for congress," Isobel said.

"That judge should have put you in a work camp!" Catarina snapped.

"My dear, please," Marcus said, then looked to his daughter. "She did not mean that, Isobel."

"The *hell* she didn't."

Catarina's eyes flashed, and Marcus Amsel quickly put his hand up. "Stop antagonizing each other," he said firmly.

"I am not," they said as one. Both women clicked their mouths shut.

Isobel rolled her eyes, growling under her breath.

"Are you done yelling at each other?" Marcus asked.

"No," said his wife. "We need to discuss arrangements— her dress, flowers, guests…" She counted down on her fingers.

"I'm in jail!"

"Pfft. You're on holiday." Catarina gestured towards the lush gardens. "What did you do with Lotario?"

"I didn't do anything with him. And don't change the subject, Mother."

Catarina blinked at her. "Would you like to discuss your wedding?"

Isobel took a breath. She managed to count to five before her mother's piercing gaze dashed any chance of calm. "I've already had a society wedding. In a church. I don't want to do that again. Riot and I aren't part of society. We would only have a handful of guests, most of whom would be ex-convicts."

"You have family. What will they think?" Catarina asked.

"Probably that I'm an adulterous liar, or simply mad." And then, despite her better judgment, she tossed one more thing into the pot. "Were you planning on inviting Curtis's widow and orphaned daughter to my wedding?"

The words hit Catarina like an answering slap. Her mother took a step back. The air cooled, and Catarina's face went hard with grief.

"You should have told us about Kingston," Marcus said softly, shying away from the son who had tried to murder his own sister.

Catarina swallowed, keeping a tight grip on her cane.

"I can't change things," Isobel whispered.

Her father wrapped a long arm around her shoulders, and placed a kiss on the top of her head. "My Isobel. Always courageous."

Words caught in her throat. She was on the verge of telling them that she wasn't—far from it. She was a coward who had killed her brother.

Catarina gathered herself up. "I thought your attempt to handle Kingston foolish."

"Well, she's always taken after you, *Schatz*." There was a twinkle in Marcus's eyes.

Catarina put her hands on her hips. "Marcus, surely you agree with me about the wedding?"

"*Wie bitte?*" Marcus asked in German. He always forgot his Portuguese when it suited him. Her mother huffed, and looked to Hop, arching a brow in question.

Hop wisely held up both hands. "No sabe, Miss."

"Mr. Hop, you spend far too much time with my husband."

"He is a wise man," Hop agreed.

Catarina turned her back on the traitorous butler. "Where *is* Lotario?" she asked again.

"He went into town."

"No doubt to gamble," Catarina said.

"Mother, I'm *marrying* a gambler."

Catarina waved the observation away like an annoying pest. "Señor Riot is a good man."

"Yes, he is," Isobel agreed.

Marcus Amsel clutched his chest, and began to wheeze. Hop reached for his arm, but Isobel grabbed her father first, and shoved him into the closest wicker chair.

"Marcus?" Catarina asked, clutching his shoulder.

"I'll get a doctor," Isobel said, tensing to run.

"No, no," her father wheezed. "I've always said the day you two agreed would be the death of me." He was laughing so hard that breath was coming hard.

Isobel smiled as her mother playfully slapped the side of his head.

"Señor Riot *is* a good man," Catarina repeated.

"An honorable one," Hop added with approval.

Isobel looked to the man. "I'm glad you think so."

"My own daughter cares more about the butler's opinion than mine," Catarina huffed.

"Hop is a butler? I thought he was your advisor," Isobel said.

"Does Mrs. Amsel ever listen to advice?" Hop asked.

Marcus wheezed again. "You are trying to get me in trouble, Hop."

"I am sorry to say, sir, you were in trouble long before I came to your household."

Catarina turned her back on the men. "Isobel," she said softly. "I only want to see you do something right."

Always a backhanded compliment.

"Mother, St. Mary's won't marry us."

"Do you mean Señor Riot isn't Catholic? We'll fix that." Catarina pursed her lips. "Unless he's Protestant?"

"It doesn't matter."

"Of course it does."

"Except if it's the man *you* love?" Isobel pointed out.

Catarina clicked her mouth shut.

Marcus took his wife's hand, and kissed the back of it. "I married a rebel, and have never had a peaceful day since." It earned him a glare, but Catarina curled her fingers around his hand.

"Riot and I haven't discussed wedding plans." Isobel took a breath and dove in head first. "But we have decided to adopt Jin and Sarah."

Both of her parents stared at her, speechless. Hop's eyes widened a fraction in alarm.

"And if you say *one* word about Jin being Chinese, I will disown you here and now, Mother." Isobel meant every word. But rather than anger, something far worse happened: tears sprang to Catarina's eyes.

Marcus climbed to his feet, and guided his wife into the chair, kneeling despite his arthritic knees. "There, there, *mein Schatz*," he soothed.

Isobel stared, horrified, as her mother wept silently into a handkerchief. She glanced at Hop, who tilted his head slightly towards the weeping woman. Isobel had only ever seen her mother cry once—shortly after her older sister, Liliana, had died in childbirth, along with her newborn daughter.

Isobel tried to make amends. "I said, *if...*"

"Shush, Isobel," Marcus said.

Isobel sighed, and turned to pace, but a bony hand snaked out and held her fast. It was her mother's. Catarina looked up at her with red-rimmed eyes. "How could you think me so cruel?"

"You generally have something critical to say," she replied truthfully.

"Hop is part of our family. Do I say such things about him?"

"Perhaps not in English," Hop said.

Catarina dabbed at her eyes. "Yes, well, the same could be said of your convoluted tongue. Who knows what you say about me, Mr. Hop." But there was gentle humor in her voice—an old back and forth between them.

"I always say it to your face, Mrs. Amsel. It is more amusing that way," Hop replied.

"You have an odd sense of humor," Marcus muttered.

Catarina took a steadying breath. "I am overjoyed, Isobel."

"You are?"

The hand around her own tightened. "Yes."

"Why?" Isobel asked with no small amount of suspicion.

"Because Sao Jin will give you every bit as much aggravation as you give me."

Marcus and Hop guffawed. When their laughter died, Isobel looked her mother square in the eye.

"And I'll love her as you loved me," she said.

"*Love*," Catarina corrected. And smiled. Her mother had a captivating smile. The kind that transformed her. Rare as a diamond, but every bit as beautiful.

Both uncomfortable with sentiment, they returned to familiar ground. "But Isobel, these children, *my* grandchildren, are not some stray cats that you pick up and leave at home."

"I know, Mother."

Catarina scrutinized her, and finally satisfied with whatever she saw, she nodded. Marcus clapped his hands, and planted another kiss on his daughter's temple. "I think them both delightful girls. We will have them visit for a week or two."

"I don't think that's a good idea, Father."

"Why not?" he asked.

"I'm not sure Jin's ready for… that." *Mother* was the word she'd wanted to say. "Jin is a difficult child."

Catarina waved the statement away. "You act like I did not have children of my own. I doubt there is any child more difficult than you."

Isobel would have pointed at Sao Jin, had the girl been present. "I'll speak with Riot when he visits."

"It is done, then," her father announced.

Isobel bit back an oath—her mother would find the closest bar of soap if she used the Lord's name in vain.

"When is Herr Riot visiting again?"

"I don't know. Since the trial, he's been bombarded with cases." She swallowed down the disappointment those words brought. But it did nothing to lessen the keen ache in her breast. A flash of annoyance washed it away. She was not some lovestruck woman.

Both her parents were nodding in sympathy. "Your father once went away on business for two weeks. It was dreadful."

"I can't sleep without *mein Schatz*."

Isobel tried not to think overly much on the implied meaning. Eleven children was proof of their affection. She cut the thought out of her mind. But it was hard to ignore the look in her father's eyes when he gazed at her mother. Catarina was his world, and he was hers.

Catarina was ten years younger than her husband. But childbirth had taken its toll—especially the twins. Isobel and Lotario had done their mother in, and she'd been using a cane ever since. Although her parents were fit for their ages, time was closing in, and Isobel found herself hoping they would both die in some accident—together. If her mother died first, Marcus would be an empty shell. But if her father were the first to go, Isobel would be left to deal with her mother.

The thought might seem callous to some, but Isobel thought it practical. The memory of Riot in the witness stand, gunpowder in the air, and a bullet hole through his coat made her sick every time it flashed in her mind. And blood. The smell of Lotario's. Now she had two men she hoped to beat to the grave. A cold, selfish thought, but it was the truth.

Love was overwhelming; all consuming. And it could hurt like hell.

"Isobel?"

She looked back to her parents. Her mother's eyes held an ever-present suspicion, and her father's held concern. "Are you well?" Marcus asked.

"Of course I am," she replied quickly. She avoided her parent's gazes, and looked to the leaves, the green, so idyllic, so… restful. This place was wearing her down. Alone, idle with her thoughts, with nothing to distract her or stimulate her mind. If she weren't mad already, she'd be sure to go mad by the end of her sentence.

"Dr. Bright seems an amiable gentleman," her father noted, fishing for more information.

Isobel said nothing.

Marcus shifted uncomfortably. "I think he is worried about you."

"I hope you are taking advantage of his care," Catarina said.

Isobel narrowed her eyes. They really were too much at times. "What has he told you?"

Catarina and Marcus glanced at each other. But they were rescued by a curly-haired woman waving a white handkerchief. Miss Meredith stood with her pet rabbit, Mr. Darcy, at the far end of the green, motioning frantically. "Miss Amsel!" Mr. Darcy twitched on his leash.

Without excusing herself, Isobel darted across the green, scattering patients like hens.

"It's your brother. Inside with Doctor Bright," Miss Meredith said without prompt. And there it was: love. One of the men in her life was in danger. Isobel rushed into the main wing of the asylum.

JULIUS BRIGHT WAS BENT OVER LOTARIO, WHO SAT HUNCHED in a chair. A nurse hovered nearby. A man with a star on his chest and a Stetson on his head stood close to them, along with his deputy. Both had revolvers on their hips. The sheriff wore an unpleasant scowl.

Isobel's heart skipped. "What happened?"

All eyes went to her as she hurried across the lobby. The second man placed a hand on his revolver in alarm, while the man with the badge turned at her approach. She recognized him as the sheriff who had led a posse after Virgil Cunningham. "This is official business…" he hesitated when he saw her, and glanced back at Lotario. Her twin was pale and slumped in the chair. There was a bruise on his cheek.

Isobel ignored the sheriff. "Are you alright, Ari?"

"I was tackled, accused of being you, and groped. And I've apparently abducted a child. Or you did. I'm not sure what the sheriff thinks anymore. Only that I did it all with just one arm," he added dryly.

Julius placed a comforting hand on his patient's good shoulder. "I'm afraid his shoulder was wrenched," he said to Isobel.

Deputy Sheriff James Nash had a chiseled jaw that meant business. When she rounded on him, he steeled himself, and looked down at the diminutive woman in a tea dress. "Sheriff Nash," Isobel said between teeth. "Why did you accost my brother?"

"You're not in a position to demand answers, *Miss Amsel*." He stressed the name. When she had first met him, she had been posing as Mrs. Morgan. Nash looked to Julius. "Why isn't this prisoner in a cell?"

"She's under my care, Sheriff."

"Well, get her out of here, or I'll have my deputy lock her in a room."

"Shouldn't you be looking for the missing child?" she shot back.

Nash narrowed his eyes. "What do you know about the boy?"

"That he's missing," she said cheekily. "When did he disappear? Are there witnesses? Why do you suspect my twin?"

"It's none of your business," Nash argued.

"It *is* my business. A child is in danger." Nash started to argue, but she bullied right over him. "When you believed I was posing as Lotario, you tackled me, and groped me. Me, a *woman*." She spread her arms. "Would you like to see if I'm really a man? Maybe we're twin *brothers*."

Heat turned Nash's cheeks pink. "That's not what happened," he said quickly.

"What did?" she demanded.

Julius folded his hands behind his back, and leant slightly forward, waiting in anticipation for the sheriff's reply.

But Nash had a stubborn set to his jaw. "I don't have to answer to you, Miss Amsel."

"But you do have to answer to *me*." Catarina Amsel's

voice cut across the room like a knife. The sheriff and his deputy quickly removed their Stetsons as her cane clicked across the terra-cotta.

Catarina took in her children with a steely gaze, then aimed it at the sheriff.

"Mrs. Amsel," Nash shuffled his hat in his hands, and looked over her head to Marcus and Hop. Relief filled his eyes.

"Jim," Marcus enthused when he neared, patting the man's shoulder. "You've grown into such a fine young man."

"Yes, sir, thank you, sir."

"You're acquainted?" Julius asked.

Marcus beamed. "Of course, he watered down the streets of Calistoga for years."

"Well now he's accused Lotario of abducting a boy," Isobel said.

"That is not what I..." Nash shifted under the sudden scrutiny of Catarina.

"But you wish to search his cottage," Isobel said.

"Who told you that?" Nash demanded.

Catarina bristled at the man, but before her mother could take over, Isobel steered the conversation in the direction she desired. "*Who* is missing? Details, Sheriff. I may be able to help."

Off-balanced and outnumbered Sheriff Nash sighed. "Do you know the Sheels?" He looked to the Amsels.

Her mother's eyes darkened, and her father's face fell. But the name wasn't familiar to Isobel. Not surprising since she had been traveling the continent since she was fifteen.

"Which boy?" Julius asked.

"Both of them. Titus *and* John."

"The magnifying glass belonged to Titus Sheel," Isobel stated.

Nash frowned down at her. "How'd you know?"

"The initials on the handle. T.S. You think my brother abducted them because of a magnifying glass?" she asked incredulously.

Nash inclined his head towards her twin. "Mr. Amsel *claims* he found it, but he can't remember where. 'Out in the woods' isn't much to go on."

"Lotario used to get lost in his own backyard," Catarina stated. "And presently he can hardly walk without exhausting himself."

"That's why I intend to search his cottage. It's suspicious. That, and he was asking the storekeeper about *replacing the lens*, not asking after the owner."

"Circumstantial evidence. Hop, fetch our attorney," Catarina ordered.

Isobel closed her eyes, and took a breath. Lie after lie had gotten her here. And she was done with it. Resolved, she said, "Don't waste your time, Mother. And that goes for you, too, Sheriff Nash. Lotario can't tell you where he found the magnifying glass, because I was the one who found it. I asked him to go into town and ask after the owner."

Lotario clucked his tongue. "She's lying. Really, Bel, you don't have to throw yourself on a sword for my sake."

"No, I'm not lying," she corrected.

"You're really quite bad at it," Lotario tried again.

She ignored her twin. "I found the glass hanging from a branch, tied in a bowline hitch with twine. The lens was cracked, the surrounding grass crushed, and there was blood on the handle."

"Where?" Nash asked.

"Out by the Palisades."

"That's a long way from the asylum."

Isobel didn't answer.

"You were sentenced to Bright Waters, Miss Amsel," Nash said.

"Under my care, Deputy Sheriff," Julius reminded him again.

"Were you with her, Doctor?"

Isobel held her breath.

"No, but I've prescribed daily walks as part of her reha-bilitation." Not a hint of dishonesty. Julius Bright was a smooth and practiced liar. Isobel swallowed down her surprise, and her gratitude. But why would the alienist lie for her?

"Why would you do that?" Nash asked.

"Nature heals the mind and body, Sheriff. Not stone walls and cages. I think you'll agree that Miss Amsel is not a criminal."

"I certainly do," Catarina said. "My daughter was wronged—*our family* was wronged. And what did the author-ities do?" She prodded Nash with her cane. The man winced. "Surely you aren't one of those crooked police offi-cers, James?"

"No, ma'am." Nash glanced down, and nudged the floor with his boot. His shoulders lost some of their breadth. He looked at Isobel, resigned. "You best show me where you found that glass, Miss Amsel."

12

A LEASHED HOUND

Isobel rode on the Oat Hill Mine Road, surrounded by Sheriff Nash, his deputy Mr. Sharpe, and Julius Bright. From the way the good doctor rode, Isobel surmised he was not comfortable in the saddle, but he had insisted on accompanying his patient nonetheless.

Isobel studied the sheriff's broad back. "It would help if I knew more about the boys."

"As of right now, your brother and you are my prime suspects," Nash replied.

Isobel bit back a rude comment. As if she needed the reminder. The irons around her wrists were impossible to ignore. When Nash had insisted on putting her in cuffs, Catarina Amsel had flown into a rage, but instead of keeling over dead she'd taken out her anger on Nash's toes. With her cane. It had been an accident, of course.

"Why do you think the boys were abducted?" Isobel asked.

"I didn't think so, until your brother showed up with Titus's magnifying glass."

"When were they reported missing?"

"Yesterday."

"And you waited an entire day?"

"An evening," Nash corrected.

Isobel waited for more. But Nash was reticent. "When were the boys due back home?"

"The boys were camping," he said. "They left Tuesday, and were due back Thursday. I just figured Mrs. Sheel was overreacting, and the boys were taking their time."

"I used to disappear for a week at a time," Isobel admitted. "The police stopped taking my parents seriously."

"Are the boys usually tardy?" Julius asked.

Nash adjusted his hat. "Not especially, but they do tend to roam."

"And how is their home life?" Julius asked.

"Nothing seems out of the ordinary."

"Ordinary can conceal a great deal of horror," the alienist noted.

"Aren't you chipper," Nash said.

"What about the father?" Isobel asked.

"He left home Monday on business in the city."

"You should verify his whereabouts."

Nash looked at her in puzzlement. "Mr. Sheel left on Monday. You claim you found the magnifying glass on Wednesday. Are you suggesting he traveled all the way back here to do his children harm?"

Isobel took a breath.

"Leave no stone unturned, Sheriff," Julius said cheerfully.

"I don't intend to, which is why I'm having a prisoner show me where she found a missing boy's property."

"There was blood on the ground, too," Isobel said.

"And you didn't think to report it?" he shot back.

Isobel bristled. "It wasn't a significant amount. If I had

appeared at your jailhouse on Wednesday with a magnifying glass—what would you have done?"

"Confiscated it, and then arrested you for attempted escape."

"At least you're honest."

"Wish I could say the same for you."

She narrowed her eyes. Had she done something to slight him?

"This is a long way to walk, Miss Amsel," Nash said, glancing between the doctor and her.

"I'm very restless." Isobel urged her horse into a trot, forcing the others to follow.

The miles melted under the afternoon sun. A single track hugged the valley, with a crag rising like a wall to one side, and a steep slope on the other that plummeted to the valley. Isobel nudged her horse off the road before a sharp climb. The horse knocked rocks loose as it stepped carefully down the slope into a forest.

Sound was dampened under the watchful presence of trees whose branches offered much needed shade. Julius wiped his brow with a handkerchief. His panama hat was covered in dust, and collecting leaves.

Eventually the trees parted, revealing a sun-drenched meadow of poppies and wild lilac. "There." Isobel pointed to a branch that reached into the meadow. "That's where the magnifying glass was hanging."

Nash nudged his horse forward, but Isobel quickly leaned over and grabbed a rein, bringing his horse to a halt. "We need to walk," she said.

"You said you found the glass across the meadow."

"I did. But I'd like to look for tracks."

"You were here on Wednesday."

"And I should have widened my range, but I had a

talking session to attend." Isobel let go of his rein, and dismounted.

Nash followed suit. "Sharpe, search over there." And then he grabbed her arm. "You best not run." With that warning, he let her go, and the group fanned out, eyes on the ground.

"Do you know him?" Julius asked as he took her reins.

Isobel shook her head. "Not really. I met Nash briefly when I was posing as Mrs. Morgan during the Virgil Cunningham incident."

"But had you met before that?"

"Not that I recall. But I'm sure I have a list of enemies somewhere as long as my name. Why did you lie for me?" she whispered.

"I didn't lie."

Isobel nudged the brim of her hat up to see him better. He wore his ever-present smile. "I don't recall you prescribing long walks, Doctor."

He chuckled. "No, but then you naturally rebel, Miss Amsel. It's quite fascinating."

Isobel stopped, and cocked her head. "You feared I'd do the opposite of what you suggested?"

"Wouldn't you?"

It was her turn to smile. "I've changed some."

"Your mother certainly hasn't."

Isobel ignored the baited comment. She wasn't about to get into a psychological debate when two boys were missing. She hoped that was the case—that the boys just had a streak of independence to rival her own, but her instincts said otherwise. Isobel pushed grim thoughts out of her mind. She'd not jump to conclusions. It was too soon.

Something caught her eye.

"Over here, Sheriff." Isobel crouched in the flowers. A

gathering of poppies had been crushed. The sun baked the earth in summer, but flowers were delicate and easily disturbed.

Sheriff and deputy converged.

"Careful," she warned. Isobel gestured at the patch. "See this petal? And here, on the ground? Dried blood. Here and there." She studied the pattern, and looked over her shoulder to the tree line. "I think someone, or something, was shot here."

"How can you tell?" Julius asked.

"The spray pattern," she murmured, looking towards a grouping of trees. "The bullet would have come from that direction."

"It could have been a hunter aiming for a deer," the deputy said. He was a wiry man, who was quick to reach for the gun on his hip.

Isobel nodded. "A possibility. There's deer track, and droppings over there." She headed back towards the tree line to where she estimated the shot had originated. It took her a few minutes of searching to find two spent cartridges. She handed them to Nash. "See here—the leaves are torn, and spread out."

"And?" Julius asked.

Isobel rubbed the back of her neck, gazing down at the spot. "There was a struggle."

"You don't sound so sure, Miss Amsel," Nash said.

"I'm not positive. Someone may have simply tripped and fallen here."

Nash frowned at the copper casings. "John Sheel, the younger of the boys, got a ninety Winchester short for his birthday on Monday. Titus got the magnifying glass. A gift from his mother."

"Twins?" Isobel asked.

Nash shook his head. "A year apart. Titus is twelve, John is eleven, but you'd think John was older. He's a big boy. This looks like a twenty-two gauge casing."

"Not much more than snake shot," the deputy pointed out.

"Which explains the drops of blood. It's certainly possible they were hunting a deer," Isobel said. "Or someone else was."

"Do you remember hearing any gunshots?" Nash asked.

Isobel thought back to the day of her climb. "I did. Five shots. But I hear gunfire every day out here. There's a whole lot of hunters and rowdy miners."

Nash nodded.

A mark on a fallen log caught her eye. She brushed the scuff with her fingertips. In her mind, she imagined two boys, one with a rifle and one with a magnifying glass. She planted herself where the cartridges had been found, raised her arms, and mimed aiming at an imagined deer in the meadow. She squeezed the trigger.

John might have hollered with excitement. A brand new rifle and a first kill. She ran to the fallen log, hopped up beside the scuff mark, and crouched. Searching the ground below.

"There!"

Isobel hopped down. A perfect shoe print, where one of the Sheel boys had jumped down and darted after his prey. The impact had been enough to mark the ground.

"A boy's shoe," she said.

No one argued. Their gazes were on the distant branch. What had happened in the space between where the rifle was shot and the tree across the meadow?

Fanning out, the four made slow progress, until they finally converged under a branch. Nash looked thoughtfully at the limb. The Palisades towered over the meadow to one side. Isobel shielded her eyes, spotting the crag she had been blinded on. Gunshots had been fired, but that wasn't uncommon here. She heard their bark on every walk.

So when had the magnifying glass been tied to the branch? On Tuesday, or was it Wednesday, the day she climbed the Palisades? Had the beam been directed at her by someone, or had the sun's position caught the frame's reflection and simply thrown it at her?

Isobel stepped forward to examine a gouge in a nearby tree. She reached for her tickler, but it wasn't there. The weapon had been confiscated for the duration of her sentence. "I need a knife."

Nash drew his bowie, but instead of handing it over, he nudged her aside with a shoulder. She swallowed down anger as Nash applied the tip to the gouge. A flat bit of lead fell into his palm. "The second bullet missed," he said.

Isobel moved deeper into the woods, pointing out a bent twig, a torn leaf, and finally another boot print on the bank of a stream. But this wasn't a child's print. It was made by a large, heavy boot—worn down to the nails on the left front toe. Indicative of a scuffing gait.

Isobel frowned, trying to reconstruct events. There were too many possibilities. Too many unknowns for her to be sure of anything.

Nash removed his hat and ran his fingers through his sandy hair. "I'll round up a search party."

Isobel held out her cuffs. "First, unlock these."

"I don't think so."

"I can search for more tracks while you get help."

"I'm not leaving a convicted felon out here," Nash growled.

"I'm with Doctor Bright."

"He's no lawmen. You'll come back with us."

"Are any of *you* trackers?" she asked.

"We'll bring a search party. And dogs."

"You'll trample over what's left of these tracks. Those boys could be in trouble."

"Don't tell me how to do my job."

"Watering down the streets?" She instantly regretted the slip.

Nash grabbed her arm, and pulled her towards the horses.

"Sheriff Nash," Julius called. "Please put your pride aside for a moment. Miss Amsel has experience with this sort of thing. There's no harm in letting her remain here with me while you get help. She's right, you know. The Sheel boys might be in trouble. Can we really risk a delay?"

Nash stopped. Isobel resisted the urge to run her knee into his groin. Nash took a breath. "Sharpe. Ride back and round up some willing men."

The deputy nodded, and darted back to his horse.

Nash tightened his grip on her arm. "You're not getting rid of me that easy."

"BORED YET, DOCTOR?" ISOBEL ASKED AS THEY SLOSHED UP a stream. Despite the sheriff's insistence on keeping an eye on her, Nash had moved downstream. He was likely hoping she'd run so he could gun her down.

"Only concerned."

"What do you make of the glass being hung from the branch?"

"Context is always important," the alienist said.

"Without any, I can come up with a dozen possibilities. What do *you* make of it?"

"It's troubling, especially the blood on it. But I tend to think the worst."

"Have you always?"

She glanced at him. "Hardly the time to dig around my brain."

Julius chuckled, and nearly slipped on a rock. He reached out to catch himself, and froze. "Miss Amsel?"

She was by his side in an instant. He pointed to a spot on the bank.

"Good work, Doctor." A twig had been pushed into the mud, and a tuft of grass hung limp. She climbed the bank, and spotted a print. "Sheriff!" Her sharp call echoed in the forest. Without waiting for either man, she followed a sparse trail: a snapped twig, a leaf pressed into the ground, and finally a faint smell that tickled the back of her throat.

Julius stopped beside her, wheezing. Isobel looked at him in alarm. She did not relish the thought of dragging such a large man back to the asylum for burial.

"A breathing condition," he explained. "Did you find something?"

"Can't you smell it?

Julius shook his head.

"Wood smoke," she explained.

Crumbling leaves and snapped branches signaled the sheriff's arrival. With a clink of chain, Isobel put her finger to her lips. She plunged after the faint aroma. Boulders, fallen from the crags overhead, had come to rest against a charred tree. Vines and ferns clung to its sides, nearly covering a hollowed out core. Isobel stuck her head in the dark opening. She smelled sweat and fear, and heard the click of a lever. She ducked back out.

"We won't hurt you!" she called. And then in a softer voice. "There's a boy with a rifle inside," she said to Nash.

"John? Titus? It's Sheriff Nash. Put that rifle down, and come on out, boy."

Sniffling came from inside the tree, then rustling movement, and finally a boy edged into the sunlight. He was covered in grime, and what Isobel suspected was blood—his face swollen with bruises. His knuckles were raw, and the rifle in his hands shook.

"Why don't we put down that rifle," Julius said, smiling at the boy. "There we are." He plucked it from the boy and started to hand it to Isobel, but Nash grabbed the rifle first.

"Where's your brother, John?" Nash asked.

But that was the wrong question. The boy crumpled to the leaves. "He's gone."

"Where?" Isobel asked.

The boy gasped for air. "The man... the man got him."

"What did the man look like?" Nash pressed.

John flinched at the question.

Julius gave Isobel and Nash a firm look. He carefully placed his hands on the boy's shoulders. "Let's get you some water." Julius led him back to the stream. Nash followed. Momentarily forgotten, Isobel ducked inside the hollow. A ring of stones with glowing embers offered some light. The boy's pack lay on the ground, along with a bedroll and a cooking pot—everything needed for a camping trip. Isobel crouched to pick up a feather. Quail. She searched the edges of the fire pit, and found tiny bones buried in the warm ashes.

She gathered up John's things, and ducked out to join the others by the stream.

"There we are. Good as new." Julius had just finished wiping the grime from the boy's face. John's eye was bruised and swollen, his nose puffy. He had black hair, striking blue eyes, and a spattering of freckles.

"Do your ribs hurt?" Julius asked.

"Yes, sir."

"May I?"

"No, sir. They hurt."

"I'd like to see if any of your ribs are broken."

John shook his head.

"Lift up your shirt, and let the doctor look at you," Nash ordered.

Reluctantly, John did so. For an eleven year-old he was tall and well-muscled. An outdoorsman in the making. Julius gently probed his ribs. A purplish bruise decorated his right side.

"They appear to be intact," Julius said.

Nash hooked his thumbs beside his belt buckle. "I need to ask you some questions."

Questions weren't necessary. John offered up a narrative in a rush of words. "The man came. He chased us both, but Titus is slower, and I didn't know... I didn't know he couldn't keep up. I thought he was right behind me."

"What did the man do?" Nash asked.

"I told you. He chased us. I don't know where Titus is!"

"You did what you had to do," Julius soothed. "Did the man grab Titus?"

John shook his head. "I don't know. Titus was screaming..." The boy choked to a stop.

Nash put a hand on his revolver, searching the woods. Isobel kept her eyes on the boy.

"Why didn't you get help?" she asked.

Julius looked sharply up at her.

John swallowed. Warmth spread across his face. "I should have went back with my rifle, but I froze. I couldn't move. I just *couldn't* do it. And I couldn't go back home. My father will say I'm a coward."

This was too much. Although John made a mighty effort to hold them back, tears came. And a single, choking gasp. Julius handed over a handkerchief, and patted the boy's shoulder as they waited for the storm to pass.

"One more thing," Nash said. "Did you get a good look at the man?"

John nodded, wiping his nose on a sleeve. "A tall Chileno with big shoulders—one was higher than the other. And one side of his face looked funny... droopy like."

Julius gave a start of surprise, and Isobel arched a brow. It was Nash who voiced their realization. "Samuel Lopez." Isobel's messenger.

13

THE LIMPING MAN

"Samuel isn't violent," Julius insisted.

Nash grunted. "He was chasing those boys, Doctor. Sounds violent to me. Should I dismiss John's story?"

Julius grabbed the saddle horn to center himself as he slid from one side to the next. "I'm not suggesting that. But the man who chased those boys might not be Samuel. Surely there are other men who fit the description?"

"A droopy-faced Chileno fellow?" Nash asked.

"There's an entire mine of workers only miles from here," Julius pointed out.

"Maybe so, but Samuel Lopez is a damn good place to start. Sounds to me like you're trying to protect him."

"I… no," Julius said. "Just be gentle. He's easily startled."

"As gentle as he was with those boys?" Nash spurred his horse into a run.

Isobel was following quietly. If she said a word, the sheriff would realize she had come despite being told to stay behind. They had left John in the care of the Bright Waters nursing staff, and sent a nurse to fetch his mother. What would it be like? Realizing your child had been missing for days? Isobel thought of Sarah—to those long days when she and Riot hadn't known the girl's fate. She hoped to never feel that way again.

Samuel Lopez lived in a little shack along the road to Calistoga. It was miles from where John had been discovered. And even farther from where the Sheels lived. It seemed odd that Samuel would have been walking in the shadow of the Palisades, but then what did Isobel know of the man?

She eyed the hobbled-together shack. Scavenged from rotting lumber, tarps, and an old rowboat. Sheriff Nash and Deputy Sharpe dismounted, guns drawn. Nash nodded to his deputy, and both men charged the flimsy door. A swift kick knocked it off its hinges.

Primal shrieks shattered the peace of the valley. Alarmed, Julius tried to dismount quickly, but nearly fell from his saddle. Isobel hopped down to assist the alienist.

A minute later, Sheriff Nash dragged out a terrified man. Tears streaked through the blood on Samuel's face.

"Where's the boy?" Nash growled, giving Samuel's collar a shake.

"Sheriff, please, there's no need for this!" Julius begged.

But Isobel barely heard the words. Every muscle in her body went rigid. Her nostrils flared at the scent that permeated the little homestead: sickly sweet rot. There was only one thing that caused that smell. Death. She plunged into the shack. A small fire in the pot-bellied stove lit the single room, illuminating a basket covered by a blood-stained blanket. Steeling herself, she twitched the blanket aside.

"Sheriff!" Isobel called.

Voices cut off, and Nash stepped back inside. "It's his dog, Bebé. She's dead." A wail from outside emphasized her words. "There's no boy in here."

There was nowhere to hide. The single room was surprisingly neat. A bed of old grain sacks was dressed with a tattered quilt that had seen better years. But Samuel Lopez had smoothed the creases and tucked the corners like any good child.

"Doesn't mean he didn't do something to that boy," Nash murmured. He went back outside, and resumed his questioning. She could hear their words through the flimsy walls.

"Did you see a pair of boys, Samuel? You chased them didn't you?"

The questions were answered with a long, frightened wail.

"Sheriff Nash, *please*," Julius said. "He has the mind of a child. Let me question him."

"Leave those cuffs on. Sharpe, check the outhouse and that shed over there."

Isobel crouched to examine the dead dog. It was stiff as a board, curled into a ball. A bandage was wrapped around its side, tied with a square knot. A red stain on the linen. A fresh bowl of water and food had been placed near the dog's bed.

Nash marched back into the shack.

Ignoring Nash's haphazard search, Isobel parted the dog's matted fur, and poked her finger into cold flesh. "This dog was shot," she said without turning.

"I don't give a damn about the dog." Nash upended the bed of sacks, dumping the quilt on the planks. He held up a pair of boots. "But I reckon this will match that footprint. Look." She did. Old boots with bad soles, worn down to the nails on the left side. The foot that Samuel Lopez tended to drag when he walked.

"No, no, *no!*" The word grew in strength until Samuel

was screaming them. He came crashing into the shed, hands in cuffs. Samuel fell to his knees beside Bebé, knocking Isobel out of the way. His hands gently stroked the fur, and he picked up the water bowl, holding it in front of the dead animal. Samuel Lopez either didn't realize his dog was dead, or he refused to believe it.

Sheriff Nash grabbed his arm, wrenching him back to his feet. Shocked, Samuel lost his grip on the bowl, and the clay shattered. Samuel made a mournful sound from deep in his throat, and tried to bend down to clean up the mess, but Nash wrenched him up again.

"You're under arrest, Samuel Lopez. I'm taking you in for questioning." He shook the boots in front of the man.

Samuel shook his head violently, repeating *No* like a mantra, as he struggled against Nash's hold.

"Feed Bebé." The words came out in a stutter and slur, and Isobel had to concentrate to make sense of them.

"Sheriff, could you release Samuel for a moment?" Isobel asked. She wanted to test a theory.

Nash ignored her, and shook Samuel again. But intimidation only made Samuel incoherent. Urine leaked down his trousers.

Annoyance flared. "Your dog is *dead*," Nash growled in Samuel's face.

The aggression flipped a trigger in Samuel. He flew into a howling rage. Sharpe and Nash had to wrestle him to the ground, and drag him back out of the shack. She followed them out to find Julius dusting off his trousers.

"Samuel," Isobel said, moving into his line of sight. Samuel stopped struggling, and looked at her. "I'll feed Bebé. All right?" She placed a hand on his shoulder, and he squeezed his eyes shut, tears streaming from his one good eye.

The sheriff and deputy cinched Samuel to a short lead, and wrapped the end around a saddle horn. "Bring those boots," Nash instructed Sharpe.

Julius grabbed Nash's bridle. "I have a secure room for him at Bright Waters. You can question him there."

Nash shook his head as he mounted. "He'll rot in my jail until he tells me where that boy is."

"He'd never hurt those children," Julius said with conviction.

Isobel wasn't so sure. Samuel had easily overpowered Julius, and knocked her flat. He might have the mind of a child, but he had the body of a man.

Nash clucked his horse forward. Samuel was dragged along the dirt road until he got his feet under him, then staggered behind the sheriff's horse.

Isobel turned from the sight, focusing her mind. She walked to a crude lean-to that sheltered a wood pile. Trinkets hung from the top support: a glass bottle, a rusty cow bell, corks, and crudely carved figures—all tied with twine in a neat bow.

Julius cradled a little carved man in the palm of his hand. "Sammy was half-starved when I first opened Bright Waters. He was one of my first patients." The words were quiet. "I taught him how to tie these bows." Julius closed his fingers over the figure. "It took a long while, but he finally got it. He was so proud of himself."

"Can he tie other knots?"

"What?"

She nodded to the baubles. "Did he learn more?"

Julius shook his head.

"Does he have family?" she asked.

He shook his head. "None that care. But he's full of caring. Sammy wouldn't harm a child," he said again.

"Not even by accident?" She nodded towards his hand. Gravel was imbedded into the doctor's palm from when Samuel had knocked him to the ground to get at Bebé.

His shoulders slumped.

"Can you get him to talk?" she asked.

"I may be able to, but Sheriff Nash…"

Isobel raised her cuffed wrists. "Is a bully."

"No," Julius corrected. "He's a man who's in over his head, and doesn't want to find another dead child on his watch."

"*Another?*" she asked.

"Last year. A girl fell down an abandoned well. He blames himself."

Isobel frowned at the empty road. "If he's worried about losing another child on his watch then he should accept my help."

"So sure of yourself?"

"After observing Sheriff Nash my confidence is rising by the minute." Isobel turned, and strode back to the shack. Closing her nose to the stench, she wrapped the dead dog in its blanket and gathered it up in her arms.

When she emerged into the light, Julius's face softened. "We'll bury her under Sammy's favorite tree."

"After we dig out the bullet. And after I make a telephone call."

14

LONGING

RIOT

A ROOM FULL OF EYES FOCUSED ON THE GENTLEMAN IN THE fedora. Riot paused in the doorway of Ravenwood Agency, and nodded to the assembled detectives.

"You're late, A.J.," Tim huffed. The wizened old man scowled at him. While everyone else sat at desks or on spare chairs, Tim stood, rocking back and forth on his heels. Even standing, he was about the same height of most of the men who were seated.

"So I am," Riot said, unhurried. He placed his hat on its hook and shrugged out of his overcoat. It was summer in San Francisco, but the Silver Mistress didn't abide by seasons. She did as she pleased. Fog swirled outside the windows, obscuring the buildings across Market.

"The rest of us dropped what we were doing for this here thing," Monty drawled. His dirty boots were on his desk, and his chair creaked as he leaned back. While Matthew Smith, neat and orderly, frowned at the gruff detective.

"We're getting paid," Mack McCormick rumbled. He was the newest addition to Ravenwood Agency. Isobel had recommended him after he was fired for helping her. He was proving to be a fine detective, although he tended to flirt with every woman he came across.

"I got cases," Monty grumbled.

"You've been sitting in a dive drinking," Tim said.

Monty shrugged. "It's surveillance."

"I apologize for being late," Riot said. He walked into his office, heard Monty curse, and when Riot didn't find what he needed, he came back out. "No telegrams?"

Tim leveled a stare at him that he hadn't employed since Riot was somewhere between hay and grass.

"Afraid not, sir," Matthew said.

Riot nodded as he cracked the window, letting cool air into the office. He put his back to the wall and waited, half watching the street below.

"As I was saying," Tim said. "We need more agents. So if any of you know a fellow or two, now would be the time to have him interview."

"Or her," Riot added.

"Gah." Monty spat. "We don't need any more women. Look at all the trouble that woman of A.J.'s caused. And now she ain't even here to pull her weight."

Mack chuckled. "Not much weight to be pulled on that one." The big Scottish man glanced at Riot, and cleared his throat. "I meant to say..." He stuttered to a stop under Riot's gaze.

"Jesus Christ," Monty swore. "Stop walking on ice around him. That woman of his is a lunatic."

Mack turned red. "Charlie isn't a lunatic." But he didn't sound convinced.

Riot's lip hitched upwards. "I'll let Bel know you both asked about her."

The telephone rang, and Matthew quickly answered it. "Ravenwood Agency."

Tim made a face, and shooed the others into the conference room. When everyone but Matthew was settled, he picked up where he'd left off. "I agree with A.J. about more womenfolk. We handle some delicate cases. It might be easier for a lady to talk to another lady."

Monty crossed his arms. "Where the hell we gonna put them? Bring in women and we need separate rooms for smoking."

"I've asked you not to smoke in here," Riot said.

Monty blew a cloud of smoke his way.

"Well, anyhow, keep your eyes out for new blood," Tim said. "I have my eye on Grimm."

"Who?" Monty asked.

"Miss Lily's son."

"The mute negro?" Monty asked.

Tim nodded.

"Better than some fainting woman."

"What do you have against women?" Mack asked. "I know a few reporting women who'd knock you flat."

Tim slapped his hand on the desk. "That's what we're looking for. See if any of your ladies want to interview for a position."

Mack considered it, and then nodded. "I suppose they could do both."

But Riot shook his head. "Discretion is key to an agency's integrity."

Monty snorted. "Except your woman can do as she pleases. She made a nice nest egg off your cases."

"They were her own cases, and it was after the fact."

"Well, she dragged our name through the mud properly," Monty said.

"Must have been some mighty fine mud," Tim crooned. "We've had more cases than we can handle since that trial."

"That was 'cause A.J. here had a shootout in a courthouse."

Tim ignored the fractious detective. "Just find detectives. We'll sort out the rest later. How's your case?"

"You mean *cases*," Monty grumbled.

"Which is why I'm trying to recruit more manpower."

"I don't 'ave anything against *man*power. It's the womanpower I won't tolerate."

Mack chuckled. "I once met this circus gal who—"

Matthew appeared in the doorway, and the Scottish man leaned in to tell Monty the rest. Matthew handed Tim a notepad, glancing at the snickering detectives. "A new client. They'd like to meet with Mr. Riot tomorrow afternoon."

"Was it a nervous fellow?" Riot asked.

Matthew shook his head. "A woman. Says she's in danger."

"Gawd almighty. What's that make? The fifth this week?" Tim thrust his cold pipe stem into his mouth. Only one out of those five had turned into a legitimate case. Isobel's newspaper articles had captured the imaginations of women in the city, and the subsequent events in the trial had moved more than one woman to attempt to live out her fantasy, which unfortunately involved Atticus Riot.

"The knight in shining armor," Monty sneered. "Always riding to the rescue of breathless females."

"Why don't you take this one," Riot said to the Scotsman.

"Mack already has two cases," Tim replied. "Monty has three. Matthew can only handle one case at a time, and I have a puzzle of one I was hoping to ask your help with. I thought you wrapped up your last case?"

Riot's heart flipped. The only thing he wanted to do was board the next train to Napa Valley. "I did." The case involved a missing husband whom Riot had tracked to the house of a second wife.

Tim eyed him, but didn't ask any more questions.

The telephone rang again.

Matthew hurried to answer the obnoxious device.

"That reminds me." Tim flicked his notepad. "We need someone to answer that damn thing. A presence in the office—"

"I need to speak with you about that," Riot interrupted. "Sir."

Riot looked to Matthew. "Telephone for you. It's uhm… Miss Amsel."

Riot shot out the conference room, ignoring Monty's bark of laughter. "Whipped!"

Riot picked up the base and earpiece in his office. "Bel?" He stretched out a leg to close the door with his foot.

"Riot." Her voice crackled over the line, and he smiled. There was silence for a number of heartbeats. He couldn't find his voice. And neither could she.

Isobel cleared her throat.

But he beat her to it. "Is everything all right?"

"I'm fine."

She always said that when she wasn't.

"Doctor Bright is here. He walked me to town."

"Thoughtful of him."

"I…" she stalled. But there were listening ears on the lines.

"I know," he said. He missed her, too.

A soft laugh came over the line. "You always know what

I'm thinking. Here I thought 'tells' were limited to the physical."

"I can see you perfectly," he said.

"I probably don't look precisely how you imagine." He could hear the blush in her words.

"You know me too well. I've finished my current case," he said.

"Did it go well?"

"No one died."

"You sound disappointed."

"I'm sure his *wives* were."

"Sounds eventful." She paused. "I've lost my telegram carrier."

"Oh?"

She switched to Italian. "Two boys went missing. It has to do with a magnifying glass I found. I don't have much time to explain. I found one boy safe, but the other is still missing. My messenger is in jail."

"Samuel?"

"You know him?"

"I spoke briefly with him when I visited for the week."

"Did he actually speak to you?"

"No, not really. I conversed with his dog. Gestures seemed to work with him though."

"I wonder if his hearing was damaged by whatever injured his face," she mused. And then she seemed to come back to herself. "If only the sheriff were as patient as you."

"Most lawmen aren't hired for their patience," Riot said. "I'm surprised the sheriff allowed you to search for the boys at all."

"I have a way with men."

Knowing Isobel as he did, there was far more to it. "You

certainly do. Will the sheriff let you search for the other one?"

"I don't know. He's questioning Samuel now. And not gently."

"Proof?"

"I found Samuel's boot print by a stream where the boys went missing. John, the younger one, described him as coming after them, and... Samuel's dog was shot with the same caliber bullet that was in John's rifle."

"That sounds like a motive," Riot said.

"Motive, opportunity, *and* evidence."

"But no boy."

"Right."

"I'll be there tomorrow."

"Don't you have cases?"

Riot hesitated.

"You don't need to drop everything on my account. I'm not sure the sheriff will allow me to investigate further."

"I was planning on surprising you."

"Well, it's not much of a surprise now."

"Should I wait another week?" he asked.

"You sound like you have something pressing to see to."

"I don't recall saying a word."

"Exactly."

He settled back into his chair, and told her about the interview with Nicholas Stratigareas.

"You should look into it," she said without hesitation.

"Do you believe Nicholas is in danger?"

"Sounds like it to me. Why do you think he's lying?"

"You made Ravenwood Agency famous, Bel."

"It was famous long before I came along."

"Then at the very least you breathed life back into it.

We've had a number of clients come in with fabricated stories."

The line crackled when she snorted. "Don't you dare pin all this on me—you did your fair share, Mr. Frequently-energetically-and-thoroughly."

"I didn't hear any complaints from you at the time." When her laughter died, Riot sobered. "Why do you believe Nicholas is in danger?"

"The shoes, Riot. His shoes were moved half an inch to the right," she said matter-of-factly.

"I'd rather visit you."

"I'll be bullying the sheriff into cooperation."

"And if that fails?"

"I think you know."

He winced. He knew. She'd break the law to find that boy. So he gave her the only advice he could. "Instead of bullying, try feeding the sheriff's ego."

"You know I'm dreadful at that sort of thing."

"I know. That's why you need the reminder."

"I feel like every second matters." There was a tremor in her voice.

"Every second *does* matter," he said simply. "I don't envy you." He hesitated. "These cases rarely end well."

Isobel swallowed. "Perhaps there's time yet."

"You have a way of bending it to your will. I'll be there as soon as I'm able."

"I know." The line went dead, and everything that was left unsaid twisted his heart. Riot wasn't sure if the telephone was a blessing or a curse. The distance between them had been amplified, and he ached to hold her—to run his fingers through her hair, to kiss the quirk on her lips, and feel her body sigh. Only three months remained of her sentence. The outcome of the trial could have been far worse.

"How's Miss Bel?" Tim asked.

Riot blinked at the old man. He hadn't heard him enter. He quickly straightened and started sorting through his case notes. It gave him a chance to find his voice again. "Despite the local sheriff's misgivings, she's trying to help him search for a missing boy."

Tim scratched his beard. "He'd be a fool not to take her help."

"I agree. Did you need something?"

Tim thrust his pipe at the mess of papers. "You said you wanted to talk about hiring someone to help in the office."

"Yes, of course." Riot gestured to the chair opposite. There was no easy way to broach the subject. "We need to talk about the state of our finances."

Tim nearly choked. "The *what?*"

"Ravenwood's estate."

"You mean yours."

"Yes."

Tim beamed. "Miss Lily takes fine care of that."

"That's why I was late. She spoke with me earlier."

"Oh." The little man seemed to shrink.

"We're near to broke, Tim. You've been using Ravenwood's estate like a personal bank."

Tim scratched at his bushy white beard, and mumbled something under his breath.

"Pardon me?" Riot asked.

"I need to pay the boys."

"In a month or two you won't have money to pay them. There's hardly any money left."

"It's not entirely my fault, boy. You think all those attorneys for Miss Bel's trial worked for free? We were swamped with legal fees."

"I'm not placing the blame entirely on your shoulders. But I will need to see your account books for the agency."

"You don't have time for all that, A.J. Leave it to me."

Riot folded his hands on the desk, and regarded his old friend. "You don't keep records," he surmised.

Tim spluttered. "Why keep damn records? Life is too short."

"Does the agency keep an account with a bank?"

"Hell no!" Tim slapped the desk. "How many bank robbers have we gunned down? And how many got away with hard-earned wages?"

"None that we chased."

"Exactly. I'm not putting my money into a safe so some slick-fingered fellow can pinch our gold. I pay in cash. And I don't trust no bank."

Tim was a gold-miner to his bones. And holding to that era's tradition, gold was spent. Even if that meant pulling out perfectly healthy teeth to replace them with gold ones. Riot glanced at the golden gleam between his friend's lips.

It was his own fault. Riot had left for three years—had run away and dumped everything on Tim's shoulders. The man had many talents, but money was not one of them. Although when it came down to it, gamblers weren't much better than miners with money. Riot was the lesser of two evils by a very thin margin.

Riot smoothed his beard, and stared at the scratched desk for inspiration. "We could hire an accountant." But that would cost money they didn't have.

"I don't trust them," Tim shot back. "How many murders have we traced back to a seedy accountant? I'll just ask Miss Lily to do it."

"Miss Lily has quite enough on her plate already," Riot said. "Do we have set prices?"

Tim thrust his pipe at the younger man. "You're set on turning us into the Pinkertons," he accused.

"No, I'm not. But considering their office is across the street, I think you've been wanting to thumb your nose at them. How much is the rent for this office space?"

Tim ducked his head, and mumbled a price that made Riot twitch. Market Street was prime real estate. "First thing we need to do is find a cheaper office. And I want receipts, Tim. From here on out. Write them out on whatever you have. I don't care. But every time money passes through those fingers of yours, write it down. Get Tobias to help you with figures if you need to."

Tim turned red, and sprang to his feet. "I can goddamn well put two and two together, boy."

"It's anything over two and two I'm worried about."

Tim slapped his hat on the desk. "Why you arrogant little runt."

Riot sat back. "An insult isn't a denial."

Tim gave him a rude gesture that amounted to two before stomping out. Riot put his elbows on the desk, and held his head in his hands. His fingers worried at the deep scar slashing across his temple. His life had been far simpler before Zephaniah Ravenwood had come along.

15

PLAYING WITH FIRE

ISOBEL

Isobel hung the receiver on its hook, and stared at the paneled wall. Her heart was somewhere on the floor. Aware of watchful gazes, she shook herself and dusted off her skirts.

The telephone operator, who had been pretending to read a book, looked up with a smile. "Is that all, Miss?" Her eyes flickered to the handcuffs around Isobel's wrists.

"Do you have a hairpin?"

The operator fished in a drawer and produced the required object, then cast a puzzled look at Isobel's short hair. With a smile, Isobel pinned back an annoying tendril. She had not accounted for growing her hair out. It was tedious.

She turned on her heel and walked out into sweltering air.

Julius leaned in close. "Just so you know, I do speak Italian."

"I know." She gave him a sidelong glance. "Tell me about the girl who went missing last year."

"Gabriella Banker. She was eight years old," he said. "After weeks of searching, Sheriff Nash eventually found her at the bottom of a dried up well on an abandoned homestead. The fall hadn't killed her. But..." His voice broke. "It appeared to be a combination of injuries sustained from her fall, and thirst."

"Was a post mortem performed?"

"It was an accident." He looked puzzled. "Do you always suspect foul play, Miss Amsel?"

"Given the long and brutal history of humankind, is there any reason why I shouldn't?"

"A misanthropist."

Isobel did not deny it.

"A dislike of rotted wood would be more appropriate in this circumstance. The cover broke, and Gabby slipped through. Nash took it as a personal failure, but it was miles from where she was supposed to be."

"Where was the homestead?"

"Along the Oat Hill Road."

"What was a little girl doing all the way out there?"

"I could ask what a woman was doing climbing the Palisades."

Isobel arched a brow. "Fair enough," she conceded. "But you didn't answer my question."

"I don't know the answer. Everyone assumed she got lost."

As they approached the jailhouse, a wail broke through the brick, followed by a shout, "Where's the boy?"

"Dear God," Julius said.

Isobel ground her teeth together, and quickened her

pace. "Small wonder Nash blamed himself if he used these same methods," she hissed.

Isobel shoved the door open.

Guttural, choking sounds answered.

Deputy Sharpe made to intercept her, but she ducked under his arm and slipped past his reach. He drew his revolver, but she ignored him. Nash stood in a cell with Samuel. He had the man by the collar. Blood ran down Samuel's nose and his teeth were stained red.

"Sheriff Nash!" Isobel barked.

Nash paused, glanced at her, and swore under his breath. He lowered his fist, and released Samuel. The man scrambled to the farthest corner, and curled into a whimpering ball.

Nash stepped out of the cell, and slammed the door. He crossed his arms over his chest.

"I would like to speak with Samuel. Alone," Isobel said.

"Get back to your asylum," Nash warned.

Isobel held up her shackled wrists. "You forgot to remove these."

"I will. When you get back where you belong—the crazy house."

"*No great mind has ever existed without a touch of madness*," Isobel quoted Aristotle.

"Sharpe. Get her out of here."

Isobel put her back to the bars. "Sheriff Nash, I realize you have a chip on your shoulder the size of the Palisades, but don't let your ego get in the way of finding Titus."

"I don't need your help."

"Clearly your fists aren't garnering results."

Nash curled that fist.

"Are you going to strike me? A woman in handcuffs?"

"You ain't no lady."

"I'm glad we agree on something."

Nash clenched his jaw. "Leave. Now."

Isobel took a step towards Nash, and looked him in the eye. "I can help," she said softly.

"I don't want your help," Nash said, taking out a key.

"Knowing what happened to little Gabby, would you have accepted my help last year?"

His eye twitched. And he grabbed the chain connecting her wrists, twisted, and wrenched the second cell door open. Sheriff Nash shoved her inside, and slammed the door on her heels.

"Sheriff!" Julius protested.

"Don't try me, Bright. You can pick her up in the morning. I think a night in a real cell will remind her what she is —a convicted criminal."

Julius Bright drew himself up to his full height. Whatever he had been about to do or say, Isobel would never know. He briefly closed his eyes and took a breath. When he opened them, he was the image of civility. Had she imagined that flash of rage?

"I understand," Julius said. "But I'm responsible for Miss Amsel's care and rehabilitation. If she comes to any harm under your roof, I'll hold you responsible."

"Rehabilitation?" Nash glanced at her. "The only place she'll ever be headed is somewhere other than heaven. When you come tomorrow, bring John Sheel. I want him to identify that man." Nash grabbed his hat, tossed the key on a desk, and called over his shoulder, "Sharpe, watch them. I'll be looking for the boy."

When the door slammed, Julius deflated. With a sigh, he started for Samuel's cell.

"Keep away from there," Sharpe called, with gun in hand.

"I'm a doctor. Surely you'll allow me to tend his wounds."

Sharpe sucked on a tooth as he fingered the trigger. "I'm locking you in there with him. It's on your shoulders."

"Fine."

Sharpe unlocked the cell, and closed the door when Julius stepped inside. Isobel watched as the doctor crouched beside the whimpering man. With soft words and patience, Samuel uncurled, long enough to let Julius wipe away the blood. "I don't suppose you have ice?" Julius called to the deputy.

"Sure. Soon as he tells us what he's done with that boy."

Julius looked to Samuel, but as soon as Sharpe had raised his voice, Samuel had curled back into his ball.

"Sammy," Julius said softly. "What happened?"

Only a whimper.

"Whatever happened, I know it was an accident. You can tell me," Julius urged. He smoothed back the man's hair. Like a parent would with a child, but the only word Samuel slurred was the name of his dead dog.

Eventually, Julius asked to be let out of the cell. "Your sheriff has sent his only witness into shock."

"He's doing his job."

"May I speak with Miss Amsel?"

Sharpe shrugged, and went back to his desk. He positioned the chair so he could watch both cells.

Isobel moved to the bars, and curled her fingers around the rough iron.

"I didn't tell you about Gabriella's death so you could wield it like a weapon," Julius whispered.

"A good slap can do wonders under the right circumstances."

"Your verbal blow landed you in jail. You dig and you dig, Miss Amsel. One day someone will strike back."

Isobel cocked her head. "One day?" She laughed. "More like daily. Isn't reaction what you strive for, Doctor? Do you recall our last talking session?"

"You have a way of needling under a person's skin."

"Your skin?"

"You do it intentionally," Julius said.

"And you don't?" she asked.

"Only when necessary."

"*Precisely*, Doctor. I'll not tiptoe around Nash's fragile ego when there's a child's life at stake."

"Well, congratulations. You stampeded yourself right into jail."

"It seemed the only way I'd get to speak with Samuel. I'm hoping Nash will be less inclined to beat him to a pulp when I'm present."

Julius blinked. "You did this on purpose?"

"Of course I did." She glanced at Samuel. "I figure he'll calm down eventually. What's the best way to communicate with him?"

It took a moment for Julius to recover from his surprise. "Be patient and gentle. The more you press him the more agitated and incoherent he'll get. But even at best, he can only manage a few words."

Isobel nodded. Small wonder the man had responded so well to Riot.

"Perhaps you can make peace with Sheriff Nash while you're in here," Julius said.

"I've never heard such cheerful sarcasm."

"More like delusional optimism. Are you sure you haven't wronged him in some way?"

"If I did it was in another life. There doesn't *need* to be a reason. I'm well used to men like him. Most men despise me because I'm not demure."

"That's just the thing. James Nash doesn't usually behave like this. But then, you do have a way with men." Julius gripped the bars. "Will you be all right in there? Shall I get your parents? They can summon an attorney."

"It's only for a night," she replied, brushing off his concern.

"Unless you keep needling the sheriff."

"Then you have my permission to call the cavalry."

"Have you done this before, Miss Amsel?"

"Been arrested? Plenty of times."

Julius shook his head. "Searched for a missing child."

"I have. And I assure you it's not a game to me."

"I wasn't implying—"

"You were thinking it."

Julius caught himself. "What can I do?"

"Bring John Sheel in the morning."

"You didn't tell the sheriff about the bullet in Bebé."

Isobel looked to Sharpe, who was sitting at his desk, spinning the chamber of his revolver. "Nash is too thick-headed to put a puzzle together."

"Anger isn't stupidity."

"But it blinds. And that's something Titus Sheel can't afford."

16

SISTERS

RIOT

Hat in hand, Atticus Riot climbed the steps to his room. The house was quiet, and it was late. He turned up the gas, but the light did little to chase away the emptiness. Riot hung his hat on its hook, removed coat, collar and tie, and unbuckled his holster. He wrapped the leather around his revolver and set it on the nightstand. It was an instant signal to his body to relax, but it didn't work tonight.

As he unbuttoned his cuffs and rolled them up, he gazed at the empty bed. Perfectly made. Untouched. A flash of tangled sheets, limbs, and the rake of nails down his back made him take a sharp breath. He ran his fingers over the bedspread, and bent, putting his nose to her pillow. Fresh linens, washed and sun-dried. Not a hint of Isobel remained.

For a man who had spent his life sleeping alone, it was hard to sleep without her now. He'd travel to Napa Valley tomorrow. Responsibilities be damned. There were other detectives. Other agencies.

Sudden shouting shattered his conviction. High-pitched insults in English and Cantonese flew through the walls. Riot cocked an ear, wincing at the words. Should he intervene? The shouting cut off, and a crash pounded the floorboards. The decision was made for him.

Riot shot towards the spare bedroom. Without knocking, he shoved the door open in time to see Jin bring her fist down on Sarah's face. He rushed forward, glass crunching under his feet, and pulled the girls apart. A flurry of kicks, fists, and growls convinced him he had taken hold of a wildcat.

"Jin!" The sharp order was intended to slap sense into her, but it only sparked terror. A foot connected with his shin, and he narrowly deflected an elbow aimed at his crotch. Riot wrenched the girl's arms behind her back, bodily picked her up, and sat her on the bed.

A string of Cantonese curses left her lips, followed by a growl, "I hate Sarah!"

"I hate you more!" Sarah yelled back.

Jin tensed, ready to spring.

"*Stay,*" he ordered. Both girls froze. With a sweep of his eyes he took in Jin's swollen eye, Sarah's bloody nose, and the shredded bits of paper that littered the floor around an overturned dressing table. Its mirror was broken. The girls weren't wearing shoes. He picked Sarah off the floor, and deposited her on the bed opposite.

Riot gently palpated her nose. She winced, but no bones crackled. He grabbed a hand towel from the floor. "Hold your head back, and pinch your nose with this." He turned to the glaring girl. "How's your eye?"

"I'm not a weakling," Jin spat.

"You still bruise." With one hand, he held Jin's head still

as he examined that glare. Sarah had a strong right hook. "Do either of you have glass in your feet?"

The girls checked their feet, and shook their heads. He tossed slippers at them. "I want both of you to go down to the kitchen and put some ice on your injuries."

The girls did not argue. Jin stomped out the door, but Sarah hesitated, tears shimmering in her eyes. "I'm sorry…"

Riot held up a hand. "Downstairs. Now."

When they had both exited, Riot turned to the mess and took a slow, calming breath. The floor was littered with Sarah's art supplies, shredded paper, and glass. He picked up her sketch book and laid it on one of the beds. A page had been torn out. That page was currently scattered on the floor. He gathered the torn strips and laid them out one by one, piecing together a puzzle. A face took shape, and Riot sighed. He knew what had sparked the fight.

SARAH SAT AT THE KITCHEN COUNTER. ALONE. BUT NOT entirely. The commotion had roused Miss Lily. She wore a dressing robe over her nightgown, and a cap on her head. "Jin bolted out the back door."

Riot nodded, unsurprised.

Lily glanced at Sarah, and clucked her tongue. "If I'd known there'd be a prizefight tonight, I would have ordered a slab of meat."

"It was the spontaneous sort," Riot said easily.

"Fights usually are. I have plenty of chores that need doing tomorrow if you're looking for a cure for their idleness."

"I'll send them your way."

After Lily sauntered out of her kitchen, Riot pulled out a chair. He studied the girl across the table. She had a cheese-cloth full of ice pressed to her nose. Wisps of hair stuck out in all directions, and her lips were pressed together. The longer he regarded Sarah in silence, the more tears threatened.

"Would you like to tell me what happened?" he finally asked.

Sarah mumbled something. With ice pressed to her nose, it took him a moment to decipher. "Jin ran away."

"I can see that, but her absence doesn't change my question."

"I don't especially want to answer."

Riot gathered the strips of torn paper from his pocket and laid them out, smoothing the creases. Sarah's lips trembled.

"You threw the first punch," he said quietly.

"Jin tore that page from my sketchbook!" Sarah said. Her words were so forceful that a fresh well of blood gushed from her nose. She hastily pinched her nose closed again.

Riot slid the last torn piece of the puzzle in place, and the sketch came to life. A pencil drawing of Sao Jin. Only she was transformed. The creases of rage and distrust were smoothed, and in their place was a small, sleeping child. Sarah had teased the truth out of a muse. Stark, detailed, and painfully honest. In sleep, that ever so vulnerable state, Jin's features were relaxed, her lashes brushed skin, and she looked little more than a babe. Save for the scars. Vivid and harsh, they slashed across the cherub-like face. The picture's honesty twisted Riot's heart.

"All I did was sketch her, and she turned into a wildcat."

"You mean she ripped this sketch out of your book and tore it up?"

Sarah set her teeth. "Seemed crazy to me."

"So you punched her."

Sarah slumped, defeated. "I don't know what came over me," she muttered.

Riot leaned forward and reached for her hand. "Do you know why she ripped this up?"

Sarah lifted a shoulder. "'Cause it was no good?"

"Because you have a gift. You have a way of seeing through the masks people wear."

Her brows drew together. "I just draw things as I see them. I don't mean anything by it."

"I know you don't, Sarah. But for some it's hard to take a good, long look in a mirror. And your drawings reveal far more than any reflection. That's a difficult thing to swallow."

Sarah studied the torn paper. "I thought she looked..." She hesitated. "Delicate while she was sleeping. Nothing like her usual, ill-tempered self."

"She's vulnerable here." He tapped the paper. "And for someone like Jin that's dangerous." *As well as for himself.* Riot had never rested easy. To sleep in the same room with another was to trust that person. He could count on one hand the number of people he had shared a room with, and only one of those had shared his bed while he slept. He could well imagine his own discomfort at finding a drawing of himself like this.

Sarah looked thoughtful. "I won't draw her again."

"Ask first next time." Riot squeezed her hand. "In the meantime, make sure you help Miss Lily with chores tomorrow."

"But we were set to visit Isobel at Bright Waters."

Riot climbed to his feet. "*We were.* But you have some penance to do tomorrow, and a room to clean tonight."

"But Jin started—" One look at Riot, and she fell silent. "Yes, sir." Without a backward glance, Sarah pushed away from the table, snatched up a broom, and stomped upstairs.

Riot frowned at the empty doorway. He felt a villain. As he walked out the back door to check for Jin, he marveled at how quickly his bachelor life had been turned upside down. And when he poked his head into Tobias's fort, any chance of a quiet night was shattered. Jin wasn't there, and the stash of clothes she kept was gone.

It appeared he wouldn't be on the train to Napa Valley either.

17

THE BLIND SHERIFF

ISOBEL

CRICKETS SANG TO THE SILENCE, AND AN OCCASIONAL BURST of drunken revelry punctuated the night like a cymbal. Isobel had not moved. She sat on a hard cot and was strangely still, save for an occasional drag on her cigarette. Her mind hummed with thought.

Deputy Sharpe slumped in his chair. Asleep. And Samuel Lopez had quieted some time ago. Isobel snuffed her cigarette on the stone floor, and stood, working out kinks in her muscles. Night had fallen without word from Sheriff Nash. She hoped the searchers had found the boy. It would make her life easier. But she held out little hope. The details were troubling.

Isobel slid to the floor, and rested against the bars of Samuel's cage. He was curled in the corner, hands held protectively over his head. She called his name softly.

Samuel peeked at her through his fingers.

"I'm not hungry." She covered a tin plate with a handkerchief, and slid it sideways through the bars. Sharpe hadn't offered Samuel any food or water.

Samuel didn't move. But after a while the temptation was too much. He edged towards her bars, and reached for the bowl. Samuel ate quickly. He was a grown man with meat on his bones, who never forgot the pangs of starvation.

"Bebé?" he asked, as he licked his fingers clean.

"She's under her favorite tree."

His face lit up. Isobel didn't have the heart to tell him Bebé was under the ground. "Who shot her?" Isobel mimed pulling a trigger, and he flinched. "Do you understand?"

Samuel nodded.

"Was it the boy?"

Samuel's features screwed into a knot. He gripped the bars, and growled from deep in his chest.

"Did you chase the boys who shot her?"

Another nod, and she held her breath. "What did you do?"

"Bebé," he said.

"Show me." Isobel picked up her cigarette stub, reached for the spoon in the bowl and a cup of water. "The cup is you. This is Titus." She pointed to the spoon. "Here is Bebé." A crust of bread. "And this is John, the tall boy." The cigarette stub.

Samuel stared at the items, and she feared the concept was too abstract. But then he began arranging the items like a child with toy soldiers. The bread stood alone on a stone with the cup some distance away. He butted the stub and spoon together. Then he made a gun with his fingers and tapped the stub, aiming it at the bread.

"Titus and John were fighting? And then John shot Bebé."

Samuel nodded. He walked the cup toward the boys,

and chased them for a few steps, before turning it back around towards the bread. Then slowly, he walked the spoon over.

"Titus came back?"

Samuel grunted. He placed the bread inside the cup, and scooted it away. Then reached for the spoon and tapped it after the two.

Isobel sat back on her haunches.

"Home," he said.

"Titus followed you home. Why?"

Samuel took out a tattered, blood-stained handkerchief, and reached through the bars. He held out his hand, and waited. When she didn't move, he grunted, fingers twitching.

Isobel placed her hand in his. He gently pulled her arm through, and tied the handkerchief around her palm with a neat bow knot.

"Bebé." Samuel sat back, waiting. And Isobel looked at the filthy thing lovingly wrapped around her hand. A bandage.

"Titus came back to help you with Bebé."

Samuel smiled, a bloody twitch of a lip that twisted his face. But it was a smile nonetheless. And it touched his one good eye.

"Where did Titus go after he bandaged Bebé?"

Samuel walked the spoon away, and shrugged.

Isobel studied the man, searching for deception. Was he playing the fool to hide his guilt? Or had Titus simply walked down the road and left?

"Samuel, did you tie a magnifying glass to a tree?"

He stared at her.

"A magnifying glass." She made a circle with her fingers. "To make small things look larger."

Samuel gave a twitch of a misshapen shoulder, and crawled back to his corner.

———

SHERIFF NASH WALKED INTO THE JAILHOUSE WITH STETSON in hand. The slump of his shoulders told Isobel all. He had not found Titus.

Deputy Sharpe sat up with a start, reaching for his gun. The trigger-happy deputy stopped short of a full draw. The two men nodded at each other. "Go home, Sharpe. I'll take over."

The deputy didn't argue. He donned coat and hat and walked out.

"You didn't find Titus," Isobel said from her cot.

"Careful, Miss Amsel. I'm liable to charge you, and send you to a secure asylum to finish out your sentence."

She took a drag on her cigarette, and blew out a line of smoke. "Don't take your frustration out on me. There's whores in town for that."

Sheriff Nash marched over, reached through the bars, and snatched the cigarette away from her. He crushed it under his boot. "You don't know when to stop, do you?"

Isobel climbed to her feet, and faced him through the bars. "I *don't* stop. That's my curse." She paused. "And my gift. Are you prepared to hear what I've discovered?"

He sneered. "I'd rather hang."

"You won't be the one to suffer, Sheriff. Titus will. Don't allow your prejudice to get in the way of practicality."

"Prejudice?" he asked in a low voice. He took a threatening step forward. A gun on his hip, unshaven and weary, anger boiling under the surface. Isobel was aware of her vulnerable position. A predator lurked outside her cage.

"That's what you call it?" he asked.

"Anger? Rage? Is it because I'm a woman?"

His lip twisted. "You don't even know, do you?"

"Enlighten me."

"I'll keep my pain private. It's mine. And I'm not about to 'enlighten' you as to the cause of it."

Isobel cocked her head as Nash walked to his desk. He brought out a bottle of whiskey.

"Did I wrong you in another life, Sheriff?" she asked.

He took a long draught from the bottle, hissed, and slammed the bottle on the desk.

"If I did, I don't know it," she said softly.

"You can go to hell, Miss Amsel."

"I'll be there with the likes of you," she said calmly. "We'll sort it out then. Or now. Is this how you handled the missing girl last year? Beat the nearest cripple mute, and refused offers of help?"

"The dogs will find Titus."

"But they haven't yet. And the trail is only getting colder."

Sheriff Nash didn't reply. He poured himself a glass of whiskey, and sat sipping it, staring at the barred windows in silence. Isobel was restless from confinement, but forced herself to sit on the cot, and breathe. It was hard going. She did not handle confinement well. She cast her thoughts back, to her childhood, trying to recall a younger Nash.

Eventually, a voice interrupted her thoughts. "My little sister looked up to you. Her name was Rachel. She was always pushing at boundaries. Just like you."

Isobel took note of the past tense. "Did I know her?" Isobel asked.

Nash shook his head. "You're a bit of a legend around these parts. Same as Lillie Hitchcock in San Francisco.

Rachel always admired women above their place with too many ideas in their heads."

Isobel bit back a comment, and put on a contrite, listening sort of face that Lotario would have laughed himself into stitches over.

"*You*, and women like you, infected her. You gave her ideas, and at fourteen she ran off and got herself with child. Rachel died in a gutter with acid burns on her lips."

Isobel tried to put herself in Nash's place. But failed. There was a whole lot he wasn't saying. A giant gap in his narrative. "She didn't get *herself* with child. It takes a man, Nash."

Nash jumped to his feet. "If you hadn't infected her with your rebellious ways, she'd have listened to her parents!"

"And then what? She'd have married a man who beat her? A woman comfortable with bruises under the collar? The problem isn't independent women."

"I hope to God your husband beats some sense into you," Nash snarled. He grabbed the door to Samuel's cell.

Isobel tightened her grip on the bars. She didn't relish watching another beating, and felt helpless to prevent it. "Samuel told me what happened, Nash," she said quickly. "Do you plan on sending him to the grave with me as a witness? A drunk sheriff beating a prisoner to death? Think, dammit!" she hissed. "Use your superior brain. Not your fists."

Nash paused. "I hate you."

"I appreciate your honesty. It's a rare trait. But your hate and my reckless disregard for male opinion has nothing to do with Titus Sheel."

His fingers tightened for a moment, and then his hand fell away from the cell door. Isobel let out a slow breath.

"What did Samuel tell you?" It was more order than question.

"Before I came here, I dug a bullet out of Bebé." She fished in her pocket and handed over the smashed bit of lead. "I think John shot Samuel's dog. To be fair, given her coloring, John might have mistaken her for a deer."

"So Samuel had motive."

"To attack John, yes. But he says Titus helped him carry Bebé to his home and bind her wound. Titus was trying to *save* her."

Anger faded from his eyes, and thought entered. Nash fingered a cleft on his chin. "Where'd Titus go?"

"Samuel doesn't know."

Nash glanced at the prisoner in the other cell, and leaned closer. "Or he's lying to you."

"A possibility," she admitted. "But I don't think another beating will shake the truth from him. Why would he lie? Samuel is already set to be hanged by you. And if you let him go now… he'll be lynched. Where are you focusing your search?"

"We started around Samuel's home, and we're fanning out from there."

"What if Titus left Samuel's home, and walked along the road, back to his brother. That's nearly eight miles of desolate road."

Nash frowned at the possibilities. Anyone could have snatched the boy, or he could have fallen off the side of the road in a ditch.

"There's something else," she said. "Samuel said he didn't tie that magnifying glass to the tree."

"Who did?"

"I don't know."

Nash shook his head. "Miss Amsel, you're quick to believe that fellow."

"The bandage on Bebé was tied with a square knot, while the magnifying glass was tied with a bowline hitch. Samuel ties bow knots. That's all he's ever been able to manage."

"You've been reading too many detective novels, Miss Amsel. The real world don't work like that. Stay out of my business." Nash walked back to his desk to sleep.

A KNOCK WOKE ISOBEL FROM SLEEP. FOR A MOMENT, SHE was in a gilded cage with a man towering over her. Gloating. Her heart leapt into her throat. Then she felt the coarse blanket and hard pallet, and remembered where she was. She opened her eyes to a stone and iron jailhouse.

The rising sun teased the sky, promising another sweltering day. Nash hopped from his chair and looked out the window, rifle in hand. He disappeared outside.

Samuel was still curled in a ball. For a moment she feared him dead, but his back moved with each breath.

She dipped her hand in the fresh water bucket, and washed the sleep from her face, smoothing back her hair and pinning it in place. The hairpin was her last resort. But she wasn't there yet.

Julius Bright stepped inside, followed by Mrs. Sheel and her son John. The doctor caught Isobel's eye. Relief was plain on his face. He must have known about her penchant for escaping.

Isobel studied mother and son. Mrs. Sheel was blonde, pale-skinned, and willowy. She might have been the muse for a Gibson Girl poster. While John was black-haired, freckled-faced, and determined, looking nothing like his mother. His gaze was on the man cowering in the corner.

"Titus?" Mrs. Sheel asked.

"I'm afraid we've had no news, ma'am," Nash said.

"Why aren't you out searching for him?"

"My deputy is rounding up another search party. We'll find him."

Mrs. Sheel looked directly at Isobel. "My son tells me a woman found her. Is that her?"

Julius folded his hands behind his back, and waited expectantly.

Nash hesitated. "Erm…yes."

"Why is she in a cell, Sheriff Nash?" Mrs. Sheel's spine was rigid as a board, and her voice was on the verge of cracking. Julius wisely stayed in place. A touch would shatter the woman. As would the wrong answer.

"Sheriff Nash put me in here so I could question the suspect," Isobel said. She thought it a diplomatic answer, but Nash didn't want her help.

"Miss Amsel is a felon, Mrs. Sheel."

"*She* found my son! Let her go, or I'll hold you personally responsible if anything should happen…" Her voice cracked. Tears came. Julius jumped to her side and put a comforting arm around the crying woman.

Nash turned his Stetson in his hands.

"I want to hire you, Miss Amsel," Mrs. Sheel said through her tears.

Isobel arched a brow. "I accept. But as you can see…" She tapped the bars.

"Sheriff," Mrs. Sheel said. "*Please*. For my son."

Resigned, Nash took out his keys and opened the door. "I was going to let you out anyhow. You're more trouble than you're worth," he whispered.

"You're lucky my mother didn't come," she said under her breath.

"Always hiding behind your mother."

Isobel clenched her jaw, and focused on her client. She walked over to mother and son, and shook the woman's hand. "I'll do everything in my power to find Titus, Mrs. Sheel." Isobel didn't bother with trivial formalities. *Every second matters.*

"Julius spoke highly of you, Miss Amsel. And I've heard of you. I followed your trial." Mrs. Sheel glanced at the sheriff. "I think you were wrongly accused under the circumstances." As Mrs. Sheel turned, Isobel caught a faint mark on the woman's neck, peeking just above her high collar. A bruise.

There were men who lost their tempers and struck their wives, and then there was the calculating sort who methodically beat their wives in ways not to leave visible marks. Isobel wondered what those long sleeves and gloves hid. She was eager to meet Mr. Sheel.

"Father won't like the waste of money," John said.

"It's for your brother," Mrs. Sheel said.

"Where is your husband, Mrs. Sheel?" Isobel asked.

"He went away on business the day…" she stuttered. "The day before the boys went camping. He left after we celebrated their birthday. I sent a telegram. Charles is due back any day."

"Father won't come," John whispered. The boy looked down at his shoes, shoulders slumped.

"He'll come, John," his mother assured, but she didn't reach for her son. Only stood rigid.

"Do you have the telegram?" Isobel asked.

The question caught Mrs. Sheel off guard. She fished around her handbag, and produced a yellow slip. It had been sent from San Francisco. Brief and to the point: *I'll return shortly.*

Nash leaned down to murmur in her ear. "Maybe the father isn't really there. It might be a ruse, or better yet, a *conspiracy.*"

Isobel ignored the jab. "Stranger things have happened, which is why I intend to question the train station agents." She handed the telegram back to Mrs. Sheel.

Isobel's professionalism got through to Nash. He had the decency to look abashed. Nash cleared his throat, and adopted an authoritative air. "John, if you're able, I'd like you to see if that's the man who chased you boys."

John nodded. "I'm ready."

Sheriff Nash gripped the boy's shoulder and walked him toward the cell. "Is that him?"

"I can't see his face," John said softly.

Sheriff Nash opened the cell door, and wrenched Samuel's head up by his hair. The moment Samuel saw the boy, he lunged forward. Spittle flew from his swollen lips, and screams of rage tore from his throat. Nash tackled him to the ground. And Mrs. Sheel fainted. Julius caught her.

Isobel grabbed John's arm, and pulled him out of the jailhouse.

"That's him! That's the man!" John shouted. It was early yet, but a few townsfolk had stopped to gawk. Isobel gripped John's shoulders. "It's all right. He can't hurt you."

"That's him," John whispered.

A cell door banged shut. The sound made John flinch. Boots echoed across the wood floor, and Nash joined them on the boardwalk. "You're too trusting, Miss Amsel." He thrust his finger at the open door, where Julius was waving smelling salts beneath Mrs. Sheel's nose, and where only moments before, Samuel had charged a boy in a rage. "Tell me that's a man who wouldn't hurt a boy."

Isobel had no words.

"I'll say it again. G0 back to your crazy house and leave police work to men."

18

A PERSUASIVE PEST

SARAH

Bonk, bonk, bonk. The rhythmic sound was persistent. Sarah Byrne swept the floor with broad, violent strokes. Her nose throbbed, and the skin under her eyes was swollen so badly it hurt to smile. Life was unfair. That's what her Gramma had always told her, and it was as true as the sky being blue. She glanced out a small window. Or the sky being gray, she corrected. San Francisco was an odd place.

Jin had run off, and Mr. Riot had gone after her. She was stuck with the chores for something Jin had started. Sarah should have bolted, too. Then Mr. Riot would be worried about her instead of angry.

Bonk, bonk, bonk. "You know there's floor over there, too," a voice interrupted her fuming. Sarah tightened her grip on the broom. "A whole heap of floor. Unless you got somethin' against the floor over there."

Sarah blew out a breath and refused to acknowledge Tobias White. She slapped a pile of dust she had gathered in his general direction, and was cheered when the boy started coughing.

"Now I know why you're in trouble. You must be havin' some 'women issues'."

Sarah's mouth fell open as she gaped at the boy. Tobias sat on the stairwell, legs stuck through the railing slats, heels kicking the wallboards. His forehead rested on the slats, and all she saw of him was big eyes, a big nose, and ears too big for his head.

"Tobias White, that is not something you should talk about."

"I'm not talking about it. I said it. What's got you all ornery?"

"Don't want to talk about it."

"Did Mr. A.J. give you that nosebleed?"

The question shocked her so thoroughly that she dropped her broom. "'Course not!"

Tobias gave her a cocky grin. And she realized too late that he had asked the question to provoke her. Sarah ground her teeth together. She had always been slow. Not quick like Isobel.

"Maddie says that's what most men do."

"Do what?"

"Hit women."

She couldn't disagree with that observation. Sarah had seen plenty of women with bruises that didn't come from falling down stairs. "Mr. Riot wouldn't *ever* do that," she said with conviction.

"Maybe you haven't got him mad enough. My Ma takes a switch to me all the time."

"A switch ain't a fist. Your Ma is just tryin' to keep you in line."

Tobias rolled his eyes.

Sarah frowned. Worry brought doubt, and doubt brought fear. "You heard Mr. Riot. He won't tolerate a teacher laying a hand on us." Her voice had lost its conviction.

"That's good, 'cause teachers like to hit kids."

"I'd like to take a switch to you, too—'specially now."

Rather than fearful, Tobias looked pleased with himself. Despite her intentions, she had been drawn into a conversation with the pest.

"I'll finish the sweeping if you tell me what happened," he offered.

Sarah blew air past her lips, and winced. She handed over the broom, and as Tobias held up his end of the bargain, she held up hers. When she fell silent, the broom ceased its half-hearted rhythm. "All that over a stupid drawing?"

"It was *my* sketchbook. Mr. Sin…" Sarah caught herself. She wasn't supposed to speak of Sin Chi-Man, the man who had rescued her from her uncle's house. "I mean Mr. Lotario gave it to me after mine was burnt in the house fire." Sarah winced at the lie. She'd be sure to burn now. Eternally. Sarah quickly changed her story. "I meant to say *someone* gave it to me."

Tobias stared at her. No doubt he was contemplating her sanity. But at least Sarah felt better. "*Someone?*"

Caught in a corner, Sarah said the first thing that came to mind. "Is Jin in your fort?"

Tobias rolled his eyes. "Why'd she get so angry?" he asked.

"How the blazes should I know? Does Jin need an excuse to get angry?"

The use of 'blazes' made Sarah feel better. The near curse was proof she was beyond furious.

"Pretty sure she's a wildcat," Tobias said to the floor. "Maybe she's rubbed off on you and that's why you're so ornery."

"Did you just learn the word 'ornery'?"

He scowled, and turned to his work. She watched him struggling with dustpan and broom. Tobias was small and hadn't yet mastered the one-handed sweep into the bin. She finally gave in, and stood to help him.

"Jin's not in my shack. Do you think she ran away for good this time?"

"I don't care," Sarah said.

Tobias thrust his hands in his pocket, and nudged the dustpan with a toe.

"What?" she asked.

He shrugged. "We could go look for her. That way you can say you're sorry."

"She ripped up my drawing!"

"It's just paper."

"It is not. I promised my Gramma I'd fill every page." Tears stung her cheeks. It wasn't the sketchbook her Gramma had given her—that had burned—but the promise was still there. And now she'd never keep it.

"Gawd almighty, don't start crying."

Tobias's plea only made it worse. Sarah dropped the broom and hurried to the water closet. Cool water helped the tears, but not the twisted feeling deep in her gut. She glanced at herself in the mirror, and nearly cried all over again. Puffy-eyed and bruised, she looked horrible.

"You done yet?" Tobias called through the door.

His question sparked anger. She wrenched the door open. Tobias sat on the floor, playing Jacks. "We could do something…" He let the suggestion hang in the air as he tossed up a wooden ball and snatched at the jacks.

Sarah crossed her arms. "What?"

"We could go to the drugstore on California."

"If you say anything more about women issues, I'll wallop you like I did Jin."

Tobias looked up at her with large dark eyes. The wooden ball hit the floor and rolled against a wall. He was as innocent as a boy of eight could look. Angelic even. "Remember Mr. Strata..." He scowled, stumbling over the name. "Mr. Nicholas? The odd man who thought someone was watching him."

"Of course I remember him," Sarah said. "I felt sorry for him."

"Exactly. You heard Mr. A.J.—he's too busy. And what with him now lookin' for Jin, he's even more busy. Your fight likely ruined his plans, so to help Mr. A.J. *and* Mr. Nicholas, we can poke around a bit. See what needs seeing."

Sarah and Jin *had* ruined his plans. He had gone out looking for Jin and never returned. The three of them were supposed to be on a train to Bright Waters. "No. We have chores," she said.

"I figure Mr. A.J. is angry with you."

She bit her lip. It was true. That's where all the tangled mess in her stomach was coming from. After he found Jin, he'd likely tell Isobel what Sarah did, and they'd decide to give her to an orphanage after all. It only took an itty-bitty signature on some stupid piece of paper to get rid of a child.

"Way I figure it," Tobias continued. "If you prove useful, he won't be so angry with you. This way you'll make up for all the trouble you went and caused."

Sarah narrowed her eyes. Tobias White was eight. What did he know?

"Or... you can stay and do the chores. Just remember how pleased Miss Isobel and Mr. A.J. was when I went and

rescued Jin." Tobias jutted out his chin with pride. His ma
had baked him a whole pie after the ordeal, and Mr. Riot
had taken him to that fancy tailor *Stead and Peel* to get fitted
for two new suits. Jin had stolen one, but that was beside the
point. The more Sarah considered his proposal, the more
reasonable it sounded.

TOBIAS WHITE AND SARAH BYRNE LICKED HONEY FROM
their fingers. The children sat on the back of a delivery
wagon with a busted spoke. Their eyes were fixed on a storefront. Detecting was hard work, and the California Market
behind them was difficult to ignore. Hundreds of stalls and
carts bursting with delicious temptations.

Tobias wiped his hands on his trousers. "That doesn't
look like a place that'll tolerate my color. I think you should
go inside."

"This was *your* idea," Sarah argued. "And besides, there's
no sign."

"There's no signs most places in the City. But there's *signs*
all the same."

Sarah frowned. "How come they just don't put 'No
Negroes' on the storefront? I've seen 'No Chinese' signs."

Tobias shrugged. "It's not polite, I suppose."

"Don't know till you try."

"You go," Tobias said. "I'll stay and watch for trouble."

"What sort of trouble are we going to find in a
drugstore?"

Tobias had no answer.

Sarah snatched his hand, and yanked him off the
wagon. "Scaredy cat."

"Am not."

"Then come on."

The pair maneuvered around a grocer's cart, waited for a cable car to pass, and darted in front of a hack to the other side of the street. Sarah pulled him into *Joy's Drugstore*.

The bell dinged, and a man in a clean apron looked up from behind the counter. At the man's scowl, Tobias shrank two inches, and stepped behind Sarah. She jutted out her chin, sniffed at the man, and pulled Tobias over to a display of hand lotions.

A second aproned man appeared behind the barrels. The badge on his shirt said Edwin Joy. "Can I help you, Miss?"

"Huh." Sarah's mind went blank.

"She needs something for her face." Tobias pointed at the bruising.

"My sister punched me," Sarah said.

Mr. Joy's brows shot up.

"She tripped," Tobias corrected.

"After my sister punched me," Sarah explained.

"Perhaps some tincture of arnica for your bruises, and powdered alum in case your nose starts to bleed again."

Sarah nodded, but even that hurt.

The druggist glanced at Tobias, and back to her. "Do you have an account with us?"

"Her mother is coming in. She's looking at hats." Tobias pointed across the street.

"I see."

"I have my own money." Sarah wouldn't lie—not like Tobias. But maybe a small one wouldn't hurt. "There was another druggist here. An acquaintance—Mr. Stratigareas. Is he in today?"

"We call him Mr. Nicholas here. He's working in the back. Shall I have him come out?"

"No, that's all right." Sarah glanced at Tobias, but the boy shrugged. He was no help at all. That thought jogged another loose. Mr. Nicholas hadn't wanted to give out his address. "Erm, I was going to send him a thank you gift—for helping me with something." She blushed. "But my mother lost his address. You don't know where he lives do you?"

Mr. Joy stared down at her. Sarah smiled and fluttered her lashes, tilting her head just so. For a man named "Joy" he was not very joyful.

"You could ask him yourself."

"I wanted it to be a surprise."

"He lives on Leavenworth Street. A few blocks from the University Club. I don't know the number, however."

"That's wonderful!" Sarah caught herself. It was far too much excitement for such a mundane answer. But maybe she'd make a detective after all. Was everything this easy? Before the druggist became suspicious, she turned to flee, but Tobias was nowhere in sight. Not wanting to draw attention to his mysterious disappearance, she walked up to the counter. Mr. Joy gathered the recommended items, and she paid her money.

When she pushed her coins across the counter, she glanced out the window. The glass was tinted, figures obscured behind the bold lettering. "Does Mr. Nicholas close the shop?"

"Every evening, except on Sundays. We're not open." Mr. Joy smiled at her.

"Does he work the counter?"

"You're certainly curious about him. I hope his dealings with you have been respectable?"

"Oh, yes, of course."

Mr. Joy's eyes narrowed behind his pince-nez. She had

roused suspicion. To quench it, she added, "I'm only asking in case my mother would like to speak with him."

The bell saved her. Mr. Joy turned to the next customer. From the corner of her eye, Sarah saw a glint of silver. She nearly fell over. A gentleman dressed for death had walked into the drugstore. Her eyes traveled from his polished shoes, pin-striped trousers, and gentleman's walking stick to the snowy collar that only Miss Lily could manage. She grabbed her things and bolted behind a display of ointments.

"What can I do for you, sir?" Mr. Joy asked.

"A little something for the weekend," Atticus Riot murmured, taking out his billfold.

Mr. Joy reached under the counter and slid a small paper package across. Package and billfold disappeared into Riot's breast pocket. He tipped his hat, and inclined his head towards the window. "Why the tint?"

Mr. Joy glanced at the window in surprise. It was something so familiar that it had been forgotten.

Mr. Joy dredged up an answer. "Discretion is a druggist's bread and butter."

Riot swept a casual gaze over the store. He tipped his hat to the man, and left. Sarah remembered to breathe, and even Mr. Joy seemed to relax. She counted to thirty, and then darted from the drugstore.

The crowd in the market comforted her. She attached herself to two ladies in fine dresses, walking along like she belonged with the pair. It took them a full minute to notice her. They gasped at her bruises, but before they could inquire after her health, or shout at her to leave, she hurried across the street, and sat by a lamppost in front of an oyster booth. Where had Tobias gone?

SARAH CHEWED ON HER NAILS AS SHE WAITED, HER EYES ON the storefront across the way. Twenty minutes passed, and she realized she had ruined her nails. What was she going to do?

But before she had to answer that, Tobias appeared. He strolled from a narrow lane beside a block of stores, pulled his cap low, and darted across the street.

"Where were you?" she hissed when he plopped down beside her.

"In the drugstore."

"I didn't see you. You just disappeared."

"I needed a distraction. You did good," Tobias said.

"A distraction for what?"

Tobias screwed up his face. "I needed to see if Mr. Nicholas was really in the backroom."

Sarah blinked at him.

"You should use that tincture you bought. It might help you not look so bad."

Heat rose in her cheeks. "You should have told me. I was worried about you! I told more lies in one day than I did my entire life. My gramma is gonna skin me alive."

"Your gramma is dead. How's she gonna skin you?"

"The second I get up to heaven she'll kick me right back out."

Tobias made a face. "Don't worry. My Ma will let you back in."

"I don't think your Ma has much say in the matter."

"'Course she does. She's always telling me that the Lord is with her. That makes them friends."

Sarah sighed. What did an eight-year-old know? She fished inside her handbag for the tincture, and dabbed it on. Checking her hand mirror, she frowned. It seemed to hide the bruising more than help it. "Was Mr. Nicholas inside?"

"Yes. I'm never going to be a druggist. Boring job. He just weighs powders and mixes things, and counts pills. The man is all squinty and hunched up. Then he slaps a label on the package, and turns to the next bit. I got stuck under a table, hiding."

"You could have been arrested."

Tobias shrugged. "I suppose. But Miss Isobel gets herself arrested all the time, and she's all right."

A throat cleared nearby. Sarah glanced at the men in front of the oyster booth. She lowered her voice. "How'd you get out?"

"I climbed through a window as soon as he went up front." Tobias dusted off his trousers with his cap. "Glad I didn't wear my new suit."

"While you were hiding, Mr. Riot came into the store."

Tobias choked in surprise. "Did he see you?"

"I don't think so," Sarah said. "He just bought something for the weekend, asked about the tint to the window, and left."

"Not much gets past Mr. A.J."

"That's very perceptive of you," a voice drawled over their heads. The children froze, both hoping the voice would go away. Tobias's eyes slid over to Sarah, asking the same silent question her eyes were asking him: Did you hear that?

Sarah swallowed, and started to turn around, but the voice stopped her. "Don't look at me," Riot warned. "You'll ruin your cover."

She finally located the voice. In her peripheral vision, she noticed a man on the other side of a lamppost reading a newspaper.

"Cover?" Tobias asked.

"I could use a polish." Riot folded his newspaper and fished inside his pocket. He dropped a coin in Tobias's cap.

Catching on, Tobias hopped up and whipped out a hand-kerchief.

"What did you two discover?" Riot asked.

Tobias told him as he polished his shoes.

"Keep an eye on the store, Tobias. Follow Mr. Nicholas when he leaves, but keep your distance. Shine shoes, sell newspapers, but *don't* loiter."

"Yes, sir."

Riot folded his newspaper and glanced down at his shoes. "Maybe stick with newspapers." He handed the Chronicle to the boy. "Sarah, meet me in front of the fruit stall." With that quiet order, he walked off and disappeared into the crowd.

Sarah fidgeted, on the verge of running away. Maybe Jin had the right of it. Tobias made eyes at her. "Told you nothing gets past him." Before she could argue, Tobias ran off to try his hand as a newsboy.

In the end, she trudged to the fruit stall, dragging her feet towards certain doom. Without missing a beat, Riot handed her an apple, and smoothly tucked her arm under his. He raised his stick, and a hack pulled to the curb.

Sarah took a sharp breath. "I knew it. You're going to send me straight to an orphanage!" She tried to free her arm, but Riot pressed it to his side. Gentle but firm. He nudged the brim of his hat up with the knob of his stick, catching her eyes.

His dark eyes were as calm as his next words. "I will do *no* such thing." He opened the door for her, and she climbed inside.

"Leavenworth and Sutter," he called out, before joining her.

Sarah twitched in surprise.

"That's Mr. Nicholas's street."

"It is," Riot said, settling beside her. "While I don't approve of the both of you investigating a case without informing me…" He gave her a pointed look. "I can't ignore your results." The corner of his lip twitched. Hope soared with that small smile. "But, Sarah…" And it quickly deflated. "Please discuss your plans with me next time."

Brows drew together in puzzlement. "Would you have let us go?"

Riot wasn't a man to be rushed. He tilted his head, weighing his answer on a pair of scales. "It depends how persuasive an argument you presented."

Sarah thought him far too lenient, but she wasn't about to tell her adoptive father that. "You saw me in the store, didn't you?"

"I saw you long before that."

She sighed. "I'm real sorry."

A hand came over hers. It blurred.

"I'm not sending you away. No matter what you do. You don't need to be perfect, Sarah."

It was hard to breathe. All she managed was a nod, and then pressed her face against his arm. A hundred questions swirled in her mind. What if Isobel changed her mind? What if something happened? What if Sarah annoyed the both of them? What if one of them, or both of them died? What if they moved away?

Lips brushed the top of her head. That kiss silenced all her doubts.

"A word of advice—don't hit your sister again. Jin's liable to stab you."

It was too much. Sarah snorted against his coat, causing a fresh well of pain. She winced, but looked up at him, a small smile on her lips. He returned the gesture.

"Did you find Jin?" she asked.

A shadow dimmed his eyes. Riot turned the walking stick in his hand. From her angle, she could peer under his spectacles, and the dark circles that ringed his eyes were plain to see.

"I checked the mission first," he explained. "Miss Cameron hadn't seen her, so I checked the shipyard where the Pagan Lady is dry docked." He paused. "Jin was there, and then she wasn't."

"What does that mean?"

Riot gave her a rueful smile. "It means I'm not as small as I once was. She slipped through a fence, and by the time I climbed it, she was long gone."

"She's *really* quick," Sarah said.

"I eventually tracked down a ticket taker at the ferry building who'd spotted a Chinese boy boarding the early ferry to Vallejo."

"Do you think she's headed to Napa Valley?"

"I certainly hope so." Riot looked like his heart was on a spit. "I figured I would only chase her farther away if I kept on her tail."

"I don't think she'd leave without saying goodbye to Isobel," Sarah said. "If I could travel halfway across the United States, then Jin can get to wherever she's going. She's a hundred times more independent than me. She'll be fine."

"She's managed to evade my agents."

"You have your agents looking for her, too?"

"I should say, Tim's extensive army of informants."

"You still look worried."

He arched a brow. "Do I?"

"To me."

"Highbinders are opportunists. They won't hesitate to abduct a Chinese girl traveling alone."

"Most adults don't tell children the truth."

He stared down at her for a blink, looking unsure, and even a little lost. Her gramma would have said he was in over his head. "Would you rather I not?" he asked.

Sarah shook her head. "I always hate it when adults don't tell me when they're sick. Or that there's danger. Makes me worry even more."

Riot ran a hand over his beard. "Noted."

Sarah plucked at some embroidery on her skirt. "If Jin shows up at Bright Waters, will Isobel be angry? We've not been well behaved."

Riot chuckled, a thing felt rather than heard. "Since you like the truth of things, I'll confide something to you."

She waited, holding her breath.

"I don't think Bel would know what to do with well-behaved children."

The hack rolled to a stop.

Before she could ask why anyone would want the two of them, Riot pushed open the door and stepped down. "Shall we?" He held out a gloved hand to her, and Sarah took it. He always made her feel like a proper lady—the kind she had seen at the Palace Hotel.

Riot flipped the driver a coin, and the hack left them standing on a long, straight street that didn't know if it was going up or down. From the length of it, she suspected it cut across the entire city. Homes lined the boardwalk, some pushed so tightly together that they shared a wall. Riot placed his hands on his silver-knobbed walking stick. With his hat at a jaunty angle and his tailored suit, he made everywhere seem fashionable.

"The druggist didn't know his address," Sarah pointed out, dismayed by the long stretch of residences.

"We're close to the University Club," he pointed to a

two-story building with potted palm trees in front. "Any ideas?"

"I suppose we could knock on doors."

"That's a detective's lot." He paused, and cracked a smile down at her. "For the amateur. But there's something called 'process of elimination' that will save our feet a great deal of pain."

Sarah tilted her head.

"What do we know about Mr. Nicholas? What did he tell us?"

Sarah blushed. There was no use denying that she had been listening at the door with the other children. She stared down the street, feeling frustrated. Riot was waiting for an answer. He was patient about it, but she could feel a sort of expectation.

"I don't think he's wealthy." Sarah glanced towards Nob Hill.

"That's a start." Riot offered his arm. She took it, and they strolled slowly down the boardwalk, in the opposite direction of Nob Hill, gazing at houses.

Another thought popped into her head, and she snatched it. "There was a garden window." She glanced at two homes squashed together. "So it's unlikely to be these homes."

Riot inclined his head. It felt like a shout of praise to her. Riot wasn't an expressive man, not in the way of most. It was his small gestures that spoke volumes. The warmth of his voice and the depth of his eyes. Newspapers called him enigmatic and distant, even dangerous, but Sarah thought they were all daft.

"And?" he asked.

"I got the impression that Mr. Nicholas lives alone. With his habits and such, I can't imagine anyone putting up with him." That realization brought another. "He's exceptionally tidy, so that rules out boardinghouses, shops, and run-down buildings. At least, I think. My Gramma said boarding-houses are festering with disease and sin."

"Ravenwood Manor is currently a boardinghouse."

"Miss Lily runs a tight ship."

"That she does." Riot turned his attention to the street. "There are always exceptions, but your Gramma was correct. It was also dark."

"Because the fellow looked through the window at night."

"Precisely." Riot raised his walking stick towards a lamp-post. But not every house had a lamppost out front.

"So we need to find a house with a garden in the back that doesn't have a lamppost nearby. And one with straight lines."

"Well done, Sarah."

She wrinkled her nose. "That still leaves an awful lot of homes."

"I've been told I have the luck of the devil," Riot said.

"Don't brag about it too much. He'll come and take it back."

It took twenty minutes, five houses that nearly matched, and finally an old woman stuck her nose out of a window. "Whatcha doing? I'll ring the police," she warned.

Riot tipped his hat to the woman. "If you like. It would certainly amuse my daughter."

Sarah smiled politely.

The old woman looked both ways down her street, shut her window, and stepped out her front door. She bundled from head to toe. Although it was summer, the rest of the country had not informed San Francisco.

"That's a lovely girl you have—a proper lady," the old

woman said, leaning on her porch railing. "Are you two lost?"

Riot spread his hands. "I'm afraid so, ma'am. A Mr. Nicholas Stratigareas found my daughter's coat. I wrote down the address, but promptly lost it. I only remember his residence was on Leavenworth Street."

The old woman put a finger to her lips. Her rheumy eyes went cross as she searched her brain. "One Ten," she finally said. "Keeps a nice rose, but he's an odd gentleman."

Riot tipped his hat, and they continued down the street arm in arm.

"Mr... Atticus, aren't you worried all your fibbing will get you sent straight to Hell?"

"I figure God is forgiving enough to consider the motivation of a thing."

"So lying isn't bad?"

"I'm a detective, not a preacher. You're asking the wrong man about morality."

"Gramma would have washed your mouth out with soap."

He glanced down at her with a sad look in his eyes. "You're lucky you had someone who cared enough to do that."

"I don't know about that," she said. "Didn't you have anyone?"

Riot didn't answer straightaway. "I suppose I did, but I didn't realize it until he died."

"It wasn't Mr. Tim, then?"

"Tim helped me, but he wasn't much of a guide. Not of the good sort, at any rate. My partner, Ravenwood, cared enough in his own way to steer me right."

"Did he wash your mouth out with soap?"

Riot's eyes danced with amusement. "I'd have shot him if he tried."

Sarah blinked up at him.

"I have a reckless streak in me that would shock you."

"That must be why you love Isobel so much."

"We're definitely of the same mind."

One Ten was a small, neat house with a perfectly straight picket fence. The house sat in the shadows of two larger neighbors. The fence was whitewashed, and had rows of herb boxes along its front pathway. Riot walked up the stairs without pause. Not knowing what else she was supposed to do, Sarah followed.

"Just because there's no one on the street, doesn't mean no one is watching," Riot murmured.

Sarah turned to eye the houses across the way. Had he seen something she hadn't?

"Try not to be obvious." Riot applied his stick to the door. When no one answered, he tried again. She attempted to look into a window, but the curtains were drawn tight. Finally, Riot tapped her shoulder, and walked around back.

"Won't we get into trouble?" she whispered.

"For admiring the roses? I think not."

The garden was small, but perfect. Too perfect, in her opinion. The rose bushes were the closest things to wild in this garden. The flowers broke free, unwilling to be controlled or groomed, their petals twisting in the fog.

Sarah crouched beside a patch of grass, and gently laid her hands on it. It was perfectly square and evenly cut. "I don't see much grass in San Francisco," she said. Sarah missed the green of Tennessee, the fields of hay grass bent by the wind, and the lazy summers spent swimming in rivers.

"Sarah, get behind that tree."

It wasn't a request; it was an order. And she was halfway there before she glanced over her shoulder. Riot had a revolver in his hand. That's when she noticed the broken window. Shards of glass crunched under his shoes as he moved towards the back door.

Sarah ducked behind the tree, and hugged it, squeezing her eyes shut. She prayed there wouldn't be a gunfight. Jin had told her all about the day Mr. Lotario was shot in the courthouse. About the bullet that had whispered past Riot as he lunged for the judge's revolver.

Riot cracked the back door, and stepped inside. The wait nearly killed her. She thought her heart would fly away.

What if someone other than Riot came out? What if he was hurt?

Frantic, Sarah searched the ground around her feet. That's when she noticed two things out of place: a chunk of broken brick and a cigarette stub. She froze. Keeping her feet firmly in place, she looked closer at the ground.

Footsteps tapped on the porch, and she peeked from behind the tree trunk. Riot holstered his revolver. "You can come out, Sarah. It's safe."

"I think you best come over here," she called.

Riot was there in a blink, his gaze taking in her, the fence, and the bushes in one sweep, searching for threat. His revolver was back in his hand. Sarah cringed. "Didn't mean to alarm you." She pointed at the stub and the broken brick. Riot holstered his revolver again, and sat on his haunches.

"I tried not to move," she explained. Riot had been teaching the children in the house how to track. She wasn't near as good as Jin, but she was better than Tobias. Most of the time.

"That's my girl," he murmured absently. "Our burglar

wasn't very concerned about stealth. Hold this, please." He handed her his walking stick.

Riot carefully picked up the stub, and sniffed at it. He brushed the end with a finger, studied it, then tucked it into an envelope. Sarah didn't know anyone else who carried envelopes in pockets.

Riot moved to the fence, took out his magnifying glass, and ran it up a section of wood. He tucked it back into his pocket, and followed the trail up and over the fence. Sarah stared at the empty spot. Were all adoptive fathers so odd? She'd never known her real father—and hadn't known her uncle much at all before he was murdered.

Suddenly aware of how alone she was in the backyard of a house that had just been burgled, she fidgeted with the walking stick, and finally called, "Atticus?"

"One moment," came a distant reply.

"Should I find a call box and ring the police?" It was half whisper and half shout.

"Not yet."

This time his voice was closer. A moment later, he hoisted himself back over the fence. Riot landed in a crouch, and dropped to one knee. He quickly recovered, dusting off his trousers and smoothing his waistcoat.

"Are you all right?" Sarah asked.

"I'm not as small or *agile* as I once was. Thank you." He plucked his walking stick from her hands, and strode towards the house. With a gesture of his head, he indicated she should follow.

"What happened?" she asked. The kitchen was in shambles.

"An Italian bricklayer smoked a cigar while he worked up the nerve to burgle it."

Sarah gasped. "How do you know who he was?"

Riot removed the stub, so she could examine it. "This isn't a cigarette—it's a long, thin cigar, a kind favored by Italians. Do you see this hole?" Sara nodded. "That's the end that's placed in the mouth, and the hole is formed by a straw that's about an inch and a half long. To make the cigar, a broom splint about seven inches long, nearly long enough to reach the lighting end, is run through the straw, and the cigar is formed around that. When the cigar is ready to be smoked, the broom splint is removed, which allows the cigar to draw freely. The straw is a kind of mouthpiece that keeps that end of the cigar from being compressed by the smoker's lips."

Sarah narrowed her eyes. "Maybe it was an Englishman who just likes that kind of cigar. And he might have found the brick lying around."

Riot glanced down at her. "I was trying to impress you."

Sarah bit back a laugh.

"He was wearing railway shoes, however. Steel-tipped. They're popular with laborers." Riot gestured vaguely at the fence. "And the brick. I'd wager it's from the Buckley Brick Yard, near the Italian quarter. All that's a bit too much coincidence for my taste."

She gaped at him. "You know where a brick is made just by looking at it?"

"Each brick is unique to a brickyard, due to the clay it's made from, and the mold. There are only so many brickyards in San Francisco."

"But that means you've looked at every brick."

Riot absently stroked his beard. "Brick connoisseur—the exciting life of a bachelor. I should have had children long before this."

"I think it's the perfect time," Sarah said, nudging a splintered chair with her toe. "I don't understand. Mr.

Nicholas thought someone had already been in his home, and moved his shoes. Why would the burglar return to ruin his home? It looks like a stampede came through here."

Sarah picked up a broken little cat face. She shifted through the wreckage and found the rest of it—a scrimshaw carving broken in two. One innocent eye stared sadly up at her. "Who would do this to him? He's odd, but I think he's harmless."

Riot surveyed the wreckage. His gaze took in every detail, storing it away in a mind that could recall everything—from the glass on the floor, to the angle of the tables, and displaced photographs. It was his curse, and gift. "You bring up excellent points."

"I do?"

"This is more than a burglary. To a man of order, this is an insult."

Sarah imagined poor nervous Mr. Nicholas discovering his home in such a state. Her heart lurched. "We can't let him come home to this."

"He won't be alone," Riot assured.

"Will you call the police?"

Riot shook his head. "Not yet."

"What are we going to do?"

"*You* are going home."

"But…"

He held up a finger. "No amount of persuading will work in this case."

"You didn't give me a chance."

"There's a reason for that."

19

LIES AND MUTINY

ISOBEL

Leave police work to men. Those words rang in Isobel's ears as she stood alone in Titus Sheel's bedroom. They had escorted the Sheels to their home. And presently, Julius was in the sitting room with Mrs. Sheel, reviving her with tea and cakes.

Isobel was angry with herself. For trusting. For believing. For jumping to conclusions. Julius had said that Samuel was incapable of violence, but clearly the alienist had been wrong. And so was she. Had she *wanted* to believe that Samuel was innocent?

Isobel stopped herself. No, she was not the sympathetic sort. Facts. She needed more information. She reined in her thoughts, and focused on Titus Sheel's bedroom. The first thing that struck Isobel were the books. A perfect line of them, sitting within easy reach of the boy's bed.

The bed was made, and the room orderly, but not alarmingly so. Isobel smiled at the Strand magazine sitting by his bed, its pages tattered and smoothed, and assigned a place of honor. Titus struck her as an intelligent boy. A thoughtful one. And if Samuel could be believed, a kind one.

Isobel turned to the desk. The drawers held a treasure trove of trinkets that would rival Tobias White's collection. Feathers, rocks, red cinnabar, a vial of gold flakes, and sketchings of animals found in the valley.

Isobel paused at the chair. It wasn't by the desk, it was by the door. She bent to examine the wood floor. Two feet from the door, precisely aligned, two deep, squared gouges marred the planks.

"What are you doing in here?" a voice asked.

Isobel looked up. John Sheel stood in the doorway.

"Searching for your brother," she said, standing.

John narrowed his eyes. "He's not in here."

"Yes and no," she said. "How are you?"

John shrugged. "I want to look for Titus, but mother won't let me."

"I'd want to look for my brother, too. Where's your room?"

John led the way. It was down the hall, on the far end of the house. John's room was nothing like his older brother's: boxing gloves hung from the bedpost, a baseball bat and ball, and a rifle and boxes of cartridges.

"Are you a really a detective?" John asked.

"I found you, didn't I?"

John wiped his nose on his sleeve.

"Is this the rifle you got for your birthday?"

John wrinkled his nose. "It's only a ninety Winchester short."

"A twenty-two caliber."

He glanced at her in surprise.

"You didn't like your gift?" Isobel asked.

John picked up a cartridge from his desk. "I'm used to my father's rifle. He has a ninety five Winchester. I can shoot fine with it. He let me use it when we hunted. And I was real careful. I cleaned it and everything."

"And it was more powerful," Isobel noted.

The boy nodded. "The one I got isn't good for anything except rabbits and vermin."

"Did you ever take his rifle without asking?" Isobel asked.

John frowned at her. "I'd never do that."

"Why?"

"Because it's my father's."

"Would he get mad at you?"

John looked away.

"John," she said softly. "Does your father strike you or your brother?"

"That's why I don't take his rifle."

"And your mother? Has he ever harmed her?"

John scuffed his boot on the floor. He gave one sharp nod of his head, but didn't meet her eyes. "What's that have to do with Titus?"

"I'm a detective. It's my job to ask questions."

"I don't see much point to it. The sheriff has the man who chased us. That freak knows where my brother is. I know it."

Isobel changed tack. "Did your brother get a rifle, too?"

John snorted. "No, he got a magnifying glass."

"You didn't think much of that?"

"It was a dumb gift."

"Why's that?"

"A magnifying glass doesn't feed you. Not like my rifle. It's useless. It doesn't protect you either. If Titus had a rifle too..." The boy's voice cracked. "That man wouldn't have gotten him."

Isobel touched his shoulder. "John, how did you get that black eye and the bruises on your ribs?"

The boy pressed his lips together.

"Was it your father?"

"I best check on my mother."

"Wait." She squeezed his shoulder. "I need to know what happened. On your birthday."

"What does it matter? Titus is gone."

"Do you want to help your brother?"

"Of course I do," he said firmly.

"Then start at the beginning. What happened on your birthday?"

"It was Titus's birthday," he reminded her. "Mine isn't till *next* week, but Father was going away on business."

"So your parents combined the celebrations?"

John nodded.

"What happened on Monday?"

"Why does Titus's birthday matter?"

"The same reason opening a book and reading it from the beginning matters. You'd never do that, would you?"

"Mother starts past the middle of the bible all the time. She never reads the beginning."

"Does she read to you?"

"Every day," he said sullenly. "It's boring."

"Just so. Why don't you start at the beginning." Isobel stared at the boy with all the authority she possessed, which was considerable—a long line of Portuguese aristocracy ran through her veins.

It loosened his tongue. "We had a small party. And then father left for San Francisco."

"Who was there?"

"Mother and father."

"Servants?"

John made a face. "What do they matter?"

Isobel plucked up a baseball, and tossed it in the air. "How many servants do you have here?"

"A cook, a maid... well, we *had* a maid. And a groundsman." He crossed his arms, and waited for her to ask another pointless question.

"What happened to the maid?"

He shrugged. "She left."

"Why?"

"I don't know."

Isobel sat on his desk, tossing the ball in the air, and waiting for him to go on. John obliged. "Titus and me decided to go camping to try out my new rifle."

"Did you and your brother go camping often?"

John nodded. "We once stayed out five days. I hunted for all our food."

"What did Titus do?"

"Complained."

Isobel smiled. "Sounds like my twin and me. What direction did you walk?"

"Where you found me. Towards the mountains."

"Do you always go there?"

"We go all over. But I thought the hunting would be best out that way."

"Was it good? The hunting?" she asked.

"I shot a deer, but it ran."

"When was that?"

John made a face. "Why's it matter?"

Isobel arched a brow.

John shrugged. "Wednesday, I think. Real early. It was still foggy."

"Are you sure it was a deer?" she asked.

"It looked like one. It was in a meadow. Then out of nowhere that man came screaming at us. Titus told me to run, so I did. Only Titus is slower than I am, and when I stopped... he was gone." Tears welled in his bright blue eyes. He scraped them away.

"Did the man say anything to you?"

"He was hollering something fierce. I went back to our camp 'cause I figured Titus would know to come there. Only he never did." John snatched the baseball out of the air above her palm. He gripped the ball so hard, his knuckles were white.

"Do you like sports?" Isobel asked.

The question restored him. "I'm going to be a batter like Jimmy Ryan."

Isobel picked up a coonskin hat, beside what she assumed was the creature's skull. "Or Davy Crockett?"

"Him, too. Or maybe I'll join Buffalo Bill's Wild West show. I'm a crack shot," John boasted. But his pride deflated. "I should have shot that man."

"A twenty-two gauge bullet wouldn't have done much damage."

"Unless you shoot something in the eye."

"Speaking of eyes, perhaps you should check your eyesight."

His face screwed up. "My eyes are fine."

"You shot a dog. Not a deer."

John blinked. He looked at her in shock. "It *was* a deer," he insisted.

"It was a dog."

John shook his head. "I'm sure of it."

"Are you?"

John dropped his baseball, and stalked out of his room.

"You're lying, John." Isobel called after him.

The voices in the sitting room cut off. Mrs. Sheel appeared in the hallway, and her son drew up short. "What's going on?" Mrs. Sheel asked. She was pale, and used a hand to support herself on the wall.

John turned, and crossed his arms.

"How did you get that black eye?" Isobel pressed.

"I don't want to answer any more questions!"

"Miss Amsel," Julius began, but Isobel put up a hand.

"I know you're lying, John."

"What is going on?" Mrs. Sheel asked again. But this time it was a demand. John stood in the middle of the hallway, equally distant from his mother and Isobel. His fists were clenched.

"You fought with your brother, didn't you?" Isobel asked. "You knew that deer was a dog, and Titus tried to stop you from shooting her."

"Miss Amsel!" Mrs. Sheel cried. "Leave my son alone."

John was staring at his shoes. "It was just a dumb dog. Titus didn't want me to shoot it. We got in a row, and he started punching me. I shoved him away, and I aimed at the dog, and pulled the trigger."

Mrs. Sheel flinched.

"It was Samuel Lopez's dog," Isobel said into the quiet.

"I didn't know!" The boy squeezed his eyes shut. Tears slipped from his eyes. "I thought it was a wild dog," he whispered. "It's all my fault. It's all my fault."

And just like that, Isobel had crushed a child.

"I think you should leave, Miss Amsel."

Mrs. Sheel marched them towards the front door. But Isobel stopped at the doorway to the sitting room. Julius gave her a look, but she ignored his silent plea and ducked inside.

"Erm, Mrs. Sheel. I hope you can get some rest. I can prescribe a…" Julius tried to distract the lady of the house.

"*Where* is Miss Amsel?"

Footsteps approached. Isobel ignored them. A large leather-bound bible that lay on a lectern had caught her attention. The family bible was much handled, and its book-mark was buried deep in the back. But it was open to the front—to Genesis.

"I asked you to leave, Miss Amsel," Mrs. Sheel said. She was the kind of woman who forced authority into her voice. The result was more to reassure herself than to command.

Isobel spun on her heel, and smiled. "Why did your maid leave?"

"She found other work." Mrs. Sheel shook her head. "Why does that matter?"

"Does your husband strike the children, too?"

Mrs. Sheel flinched. "I don't know what you're talking about. Charles is a good man."

"With a temper." Isobel gestured at Mrs. Sheel's neck. "I know those kind of men. I saw the bruises under your collar."

Mrs. Sheel adjusted her collar, tugging it higher. "I don't see what my husband has to do with Titus's disappearance. You should be out looking for my son. I can't believe you recommended her, Doctor Bright."

Isobel cocked a brow at the doctor. Isobel was as surprised as Mrs. Sheel. "We'll show ourselves out."

The door slammed shut on their heels.

Isobel hurried down the steps, and headed to the main street.

"Are you happy with yourself?" Julius asked as he hurried to catch up with her quick strides.

"I had to know."

"He's a child!" Julius bit out.

"Who lied to us," she said.

Julius pulled her to a stop in the middle of the road, and took a deep breath. Anger, it seemed, was something he kept on a tight rein. "Yes," he admitted. "But it's a natural response under the circumstances. You all but blamed John for his brother's disappearance. That kind of guilt won't go away."

"It had to be done."

Julius squared his shoulders. "Did it *really*, Miss Amsel?"

Isobel kept walking.

"You have all the tact of a battering ram."

Isobel gave a sharp laugh.

"This isn't amusing."

"No, it's not. But my methods get results, Doctor."

"My peers make the same claim when they cut out portions of a brain, and lock lunatics in cages, Miss Amsel."

"Noted," she said over her shoulder. "Would you prefer Sheriff Nash's methods?"

"The lesser of two evils is *still* evil."

"I'm well aware, Doctor."

They reached the boardwalk along the main street, and Isobel turned towards Bright Waters.

"One thing is clear," Julius said at her side. "The apple doesn't fall far from the tree."

"I am *not* my mother," Isobel snapped, and instantly caught herself. He knew precisely where to hit. "At least, I'm trying not to be."

"I dread to think what your methods would be if you *weren't* trying."

"Everyone loves my father, but no one forgets my mother," Isobel admitted. "Say one thing about my mother—she's a force to be reckoned with."

Julius grunted his agreement.

"Do you fear turning into your father?" Now it was her turn to poke.

"Yes," he admitted. "It's the reason I started Bright Waters. No one should be locked in a room."

"What about murderers?"

"I'm not the law," Julius admitted. "Can you imagine no reason to kill, Miss Amsel?" His question was asked so casually that it chilled her blood. Isobel stopped, and looked up into his eyes, searching for the truth behind the jovial mask he wore.

Her parents had once taken her to the Japanese theatre. The Noh masks were fixed, but depending on the light, the movement of the actor, and tilt of the head, the featureless mask changed expression. From jovial to sad, from sad to menacing. Julius Bright wore one of those masks. And his ever-present smile now appeared threatening.

Isobel steered away from his question. "I talked with Samuel last night." She told him what she had learned.

"I knew he wouldn't hurt the boy."

"You believe him?"

"Of course," Julius insisted.

"Despite what he did in the jailhouse?"

"I helped him. I… raised him after a fashion."

Fearing the doctor would turn maudlin and she'd be forced to comfort him, she asked, "How did Samuel come to be at Bright Waters?"

"His mother died under my care. Her husband or lover

put her there, and I suspect he was the cause of Samuel's mental stunting. When I finally coaxed Samuel out of the forest, he was whip-thin, and cowered at every noise."

"Why didn't he stay at Bright Waters?"

Julius looked away, down the road to the oblivious white-clad vacationers and tourists strolling under the sun. "Samuel wanted to be independent. To live on his own."

Isobel narrowed her eyes. "You're lying," she said bluntly. "Something happened."

Julius took a deep breath. "Samuel had a puppy. One of the nurses tried to take it from him. He pushed her. But that's all."

"You want to believe he's innocent."

"Of course I do! But he would *never* harm a child."

"This isn't one of your clinical diagnoses, Doctor. You sound desperate."

"Do you blame me?"

"I expected better of you," she said coolly. "Every murderer, every rapist, every brute has a mother and a father. And I'd wager they'd sound very much the same if their child was accused of a heinous crime."

"Not all," Julius insisted. "There are some parents who would be relieved that their child was caught."

"A bad seed?"

Julius nodded. "Some alienists hold to the theory that murderers and rapists are born."

"You?"

"I don't know," he admitted. "I don't think humans fit into a neat mold. We're too messy. But there have been studies. Cerebrum dissections have been performed on some of the most violent criminals. As of yet, there's no explanation, but we ache to find one. To know *why* some men commit the most heinous of crimes."

"And women," she added. "Does your work as an alienist ever answer the why of a thing?"

"In some cases I'm able to guide a person through their own mind. They need to answer that question for themselves. It's often a question they've never realized needed answering."

"Speaking of patients. Don't you have a hospital full of them?"

"I do," he said. "But I have the rare chance to study a reticent patient, so I've cleared my schedule."

Isobel chuckled. They walked in silence for a time, and then she pulled him to a stop under a tree between a blacksmith and stable. "I've been thinking about your question. About why I'm marrying another so soon after Alex."

Julius stood attentive. Listening. He had a pleasant listening face. Not intrusive, but curious. Another trick of his mask. "I asked you if it worried you."

"But you wanted to know the *why* of it."

"I can hardly deny it now."

"Does the ocean call to you?" she asked suddenly.

The shift in topic surprised him. "I find it pleasant, but terrifying."

She nodded. "Can you swim?"

"I can, but I know my limits. I like to think I have a healthy respect for Mother Nature."

"Where you see danger, I see freedom. Storm or sun, in wind and rain, in all its moody glory. I'll jump in that ocean every chance I get. There are no lies. There's nothing but calm surrender. Right down to my bones." She let her words linger. Let him unravel the meaning. And finally, "I never thought I'd find that in a person."

Julius smiled, warmly. "Some call it love."

"Some call love fleeting."

"Not the deep sort," he said gently. "Thank you for sharing that with me, but honestly, I was only worried you were with child and felt forced into marrying again."

Isobel cocked her head, and leaned slightly to the right, looking past his arm. "I *am*, after a fashion." She cursed under her breath, and took off running.

A SMALL, THIN CHILD IN AN OVERSIZED CAP TURNED ON ITS heel, and ran. The child disappeared up and over a fence. Isobel cursed her riding skirt as she scrambled over the top, trying not to trip over the extra fabric. She cut to the right, down a lane, and came out the other side. The child ran straight into her.

Isobel reached for the child as it bounced away. Cap flew off, exposing a long black queue. A revolver skittered across the dirt. Both child and woman lunged for the weapon. The child got there first, and started to raise the revolver.

"What the hell are you doing, Jin?"

Julius Bright huffed around the corner. Sao Jin's eyes widened, and she pointed the revolver at the towering alienist. Isobel growled, and snatched the weapon from her. Before the girl could run again, Isobel grabbed her by the shoulder. "Don't move."

She handed Julius the revolver, and turned Jin to face her.

The girl looked drawn. Her left eye was swollen shut, and dark bruises blossomed along her cheek.

"I'm here to say goodbye," Jin blurted out.

"By pointing a gun at me?" Isobel asked.

"You scared me!" Jin growled.

Isobel closed her eyes. Took a breath, and straightened. "Doctor, meet one of my daughters. Sao Jin."

Julius coughed in surprise.

"Why are you leaving? And what happened to your eye?"

"Din Gau is going to kill me!" Jin's whole body trembled. The girl believed her words down to her bones.

"Who is Din Gau?" Julius asked in concern.

"Riot. My fiancé. Her father," Isobel said.

"He is *not* my father."

"Adopted."

"Ah." Julius busied himself with checking the old revolver chambers. It was loaded. He removed the cartridges, and pocketed both weapon and ammunition.

Isobel considered the girl. Jin was staring defiantly at a wall. Isobel let her go, and picked up the cap, slapping it on her head. "Did you run away and travel all night to get here?"

Jin nodded, as meekly as Isobel had ever seen. "I am sorry, Captain Morgan."

"Have you eaten?"

"I drank out of a trough."

Isobel didn't press her on that point. "And you had money for a train ticket?"

Jin continued to stare at the wall. That explained the black marks on her hands, cheeks, and trousers. "You hitched a ride on the train," Isobel surmised.

"It was easy."

"Well, come on. You can tell me what happened."

"No, I am saying goodbye."

Isobel considered the girl for a moment. "I'm in the middle of an investigation, Jin. I need your help. The doctor here isn't much of a fighter. You can leave afterwards."

Jin frowned at the doctor in thought. Julius smiled back. That decided her. She gave one curt nod.

Isobel thrust out her hand. The child shook it.

"I haven't eaten. Food first." Isobel wasn't hungry. But Jin was a proud child, and Isobel didn't want her fainting in the middle of an investigation.

"Your daughter?" Julius asked as they walked towards a hotel.

"Riot and I are adopting Jin and Sarah," she explained. "He's already signed the papers. I'll sign as soon as we're married."

Julius glanced back at the child. Jin was glaring at his back.

"You certainly jump feet first into everything," he said.

The first hotel refused to serve a Chinese child. As did a tearoom. They finally found a rundown cafe that was only concerned about the color of cash.

"You traveled from San Francisco alone?" Julius asked.

Jin had a mouthful of biscuit. She chewed, and glared at the doctor. Isobel took a sip of black coffee. "We're working on her manners," she said. "Aren't we?"

"Yes." The girl said, spewing crumbs out of her mouth. Isobel suspected it was done intentionally.

"Those are delicious, aren't they?" Isobel asked. Jin nodded, and reached for a second, but Isobel placed a hand over hers. "First, what happened?"

Jin blew out a breath, and sat back. "I punched Sarah. And now Din Gau is going to kill me. She is his favorite."

Isobel tilted her head. "And how did you get that black eye?"

Jin pressed her lips together.

"Riot's not going to kill you, Jin."

"He will kick me out!" Her nostrils flared.

"So you left before he could do that?"

Jin gave a jerk of her head.

"I see." She took a sip of her coffee. "Why did you punch Sarah?"

A muscle in Jin's jaw twitched.

Isobel blinked. "Sarah punched *you* first, didn't she?"

Julius cleared his throat. "You sound rather excited by that prospect."

"I didn't think Sarah had it in her," Isobel said.

Jin snorted, and quickly stiffened back up like a statue.

Isobel cracked a smile at the girl. "I bet you were shocked."

Jin tried to reach for the biscuit again.

"Not yet. Why did Sarah punch you?"

Jin deflated. "I tore out a page in her sketchbook. She drew me without my permission."

"Ah." Isobel handed her the biscuit. "Jin, your sister—"

"She is *not* my sister!"

"You certainly sound like sisters. At the very least she's your crew mate. And I'm your captain. So no abandoning ship on my watch, is that clear?"

"Yes, Captain."

"Right. Stay here. I need to send a telegram."

"Please do not tell Din Gau I am here."

"Riot was likely searching for you all of last night. Stay here. And don't hurt Doctor Bright." She gave the girl a pointed look. "One more thing... where did you get that revolver?"

"From the attic."

Julius folded his hands over his waistcoat, watching the two interact He looked as if he were dissecting something interesting.

Isobel pointed at her daughter. "I don't suggest picking apart this one's brain."

Jin froze, and swallowed, her eyes sliding to the smiling alienist.

"I don't dissect brains," Julius said. "Well, not in the living. What does Din Gau mean?"

"Rabid dog," Jin said, proudly. "He has killed many boo how doy."

Julius looked to Isobel in question.

"That's enough, Jin. *Stop making up stories.*" Isobel raised her brows at the girl.

Jin clicked her mouth shut.

"You're lucky boo how doy didn't catch you," Isobel said.

"I would have killed them," Jin hissed.

Isobel didn't doubt it. The revolver in Julius's pocket was proof of Jin's violent streak.

20

LOST AND FOUND

"WHAT ARE WE LOOKING FOR, MISS AMSEL?" JULIUS Bright asked.

Isobel stood in the center of what counted as Samuel Lopez's front yard. Trampled grass, a splintered door, and logs from the wood pile were scattered every which way. The mob of searchers had taken out their frustrations on the man's humble abode.

"I don't know."

Jin stood by her side. Quiet and attentive. Her eyes taking in the scene.

As a child Isobel had loathed adults and their tendency to keep information to themselves. It was demeaning and dangerous, in her opinion. So on the road there, she had filled the girl in on the pertinent details. Her purpose was twofold. If she involved the girl, Jin would stay. She also had a sharp mind, and sharper eyes.

Jin stepped into the shack, and Isobel followed. The girl crouched by the dog bed, but her eyes didn't stay on it for long. She stared at the fire poker leaning against the fire-

place. Jin touched it, and shuddered slightly, before wrap-
ping her hand around the iron.

Jin tapped her foot on the floorboards. Moving methodically around the shack.

"There are sometimes boards where people keep things.
Sometimes they are large enough for a child."

Isobel clenched her jaw, and gave a sharp nod. She did
not press the girl for information, or ask how she knew. The
answers were plain as the scars on Jin's face.

When they found a promising board, Isobel applied the
poker to a crevice. The board popped loose easily. The dark
cavity underneath was hollow. Isobel took out her candle, lit
it, and put it in the hole. It looked like a magpie's nest: a
polished bell, a shiny silver button, a pair of cracked spec-
tacle frames, a cufflink, and a mirror wrapped in heavy
leather and tied with perfect little bow knots.

Jin gazed into the mirror for a moment, and quickly
wrapped it back up. Isobel could well imagine Samuel doing
the same. Isobel wondered what Jin saw in her reflection.
Memories of pain and torture? Or self-loathing? And what
of Samuel, who lived with a visage that brought nothing but
scorn and abuse? If only living with disfigurement were as
simple as covering a mirror.

"Have you found something?" Julius asked.

Jin spun at his voice, poker in hand.

His shadow filled the doorway. He raised his hands, and
smiled.

Jin muttered something under her breath in Cantonese,
but Isobel didn't catch the words.

Isobel plucked out a cufflink, and studied it. "Samuel
seems to have a fascination with baubles. Isn't this yours,
Doctor?"

Julius started with surprise. Then leaned in to study it.

"So it is." He plucked the cufflink from her fingers. "Samuel must have found it at Bright Waters. Everything shiny is a treasure to him. He loves the idea of finding treasure." It was the match to the cufflink in his office.

"Isn't that everyone's dream?" she asked.

"Finding what's hidden?" the doctor mused. "I suppose it is."

"Not metaphorically," she said. "I mean actual buried treasure."

"I can't say that was ever a fascination of mine, but then I don't name myself after pirates." His eyes twinkled.

Isobel stood without comment. She walked around the property, but anything she'd hoped to learn had been destroyed by the search party. There was nothing but ruin.

"Jin." Isobel said as she watched Julius rifle through the toppled lean-to. "What did you say in the shack?"

"I said he smiles too much."

THE COTTAGE FELT SMALL WITH THE PRESS OF PEOPLE. Lotario was propped on a divan, and surrounded by cushions. Marcus Amsel sat on the edge of a plush chair, his long hands folded together and looking pleased as his wife fussed over their youngest son. Mr. Hop stood in the corner, sipping tea. He looked amused, but then he often was.

All eyes turned to Isobel and Jin.

"Jin!" Lotario exclaimed. "You're looking far more murderous than usual today."

"Mr. Amsel," the girl inclined her head.

"Lotario," Catarina hissed. "How dare you." She focused on her soon-to-be-granddaughter. "Is Mr. Riot here, too?"

"No. Jin was just missing me," Isobel said.

"Where were you?" her mother asked.

"In jail."

Marcus Amsel looked at the ceiling, and Catarina frowned. "What did you do now?"

"Mrs. Sheel hired me to find her son."

"Don't dodge my question, young lady," Catarina said.

"I didn't dodge it."

"Please." Marcus made a calming gesture with his hands.

Isobel took a breath, gripped Jin's shoulders and pushed her forward. "Ari, I need you to watch her."

Jin bristled. "I do not need a child minder!"

Husband and wife shared a brief look, and a laugh. "You are exactly like Isobel," Catarina said, taking the girl's hand. To Isobel's relief, Jin did not attack. Truth be told, Isobel was more worried about Jin than her mother. "Isobel used to scream that very thing at us all the time. Poor Mr. Hop heard it daily. You remember our butler?" Catarina asked.

Mr. Hop bowed deeply. But Jin stood straight, staring at him with suspicion.

Catarina arched a sharp brow. "Have you no manners?"

"No." Jin replied.

Isobel gave Jin's shoulder a squeeze. But the girl remained rigid.

"Ah, well. Respect is earned, isn't it?" Marcus said. "Come, come, sit down, and you may listen to Lotario be exasperated with us." His warm enthusiasm lured Jin over to a plush chair, but she stopped short of sitting.

"Won't you sit, *mein Kind*?"

Jin glanced at Catarina. "I do not wish to take Mrs. Amsel's chair."

Isobel heard a faint grunt of approval from her mother.

"You will have an eventful life with this one," Catarina said in Portuguese.

"She's *your* grandchild," Isobel replied under her breath.

"I know." There was a trace of warmth in those words. And to Isobel's shock, Catarina brushed Isobel's arm before taking the vacant chair.

"I'll be back," Isobel said, making to leave.

"Where are you going?" Four voices said as one.

"I have a child to find. Doctor Bright will be with me."

Jin hurried over to stand by Isobel's side like a stubborn shadow.

"You haven't slept all night. Stay here," Isobel ordered.

"I will run away," Jin threatened.

Marcus clapped and chortled. And Jin slowly turned on the couple. She stood on her toes to whisper in Isobel's ears. "What is wrong with your parents?"

"They had me for a daughter. I ran away every week. They think you're adorable."

Jin shut her mouth, and studied Isobel under a different light. Before the girl could dig her heels in further, Isobel planted a kiss on her head, and left Sao Jin in equal parts shocked fury and bewilderment.

Isobel was ten feet from the cottage when Lotario caught up to her.

"Where are you going?" he asked.

"The mines. I may not return tonight."

"Hmm. Have you discovered anything?"

"Samuel claims Titus came to his home to help bandage Bebé. But when John came to identify him in jail, Samuel charged him."

Lotario whistled low. "Why the mines?"

"Despite the evidence…" She hesitated. "I don't think Samuel harmed Titus."

"The dogs haven't picked up his trail?"

"They've been sniffing in circles. The animals are either anosmic, or—"

"Titus hitched a ride," Lotario said.

Isobel nodded. "And he disappeared miles from Samuel's shack."

"On my way into town, I hopped on a wagon myself. A miner by the name of Finneas O'Conner was driving. He used to work for father."

The name sounded familiar.

"O, you wee devils are goin' somewhere other than 'eaven. Mark my words," Lotario crooned, with an Irish lilt.

"Finn!"

"You remember him?"

"He used to give me cigarettes."

Lotario laughed. "I always assumed you pinched them."

She lifted a shoulder. "Occasionally. Are you feeling up to doing something for me?"

He narrowed his eyes.

"I need you to question the station agents. Find out what time Charles Sheel boarded a train for Vallejo. And whether he was alone or not."

Lotario gripped her arm with his good hand. "Only if you don't leave me with mother and father."

"I'm giving you an excuse to leave."

"They'll insist on coming with me."

Isobel patted her twin's hand. "That's why I'm leaving Jin with you."

"You're a wolf in sheep's clothing. You know that, don't you?"

Isobel showed her teeth.

"You know I'm having regrets about coming to Bright Waters for recuperation."

"You're back in the fold. Although I have to admit..." She glanced at the cottage when a burst of laughter came out. "It *is* unnerving."

"They're just happy you're alive," Lotario said.

"They're happy you are, too. Enjoy their good graces."

Lotario's lips pressed into a line. "I'm still a stain on the family name. It's not like I can profess my love for a dashing detective, the way you can."

"I know, Ari. But for now, for whatever reason, mother has extended an olive branch. Don't throw it in her face."

Isobel felt him sigh, and she gripped his hand. "Besides, you'll never find another dashing detective like mine." She kissed him on the cheek, and left.

As she was walking away, Lotario called out, "Are you sure he doesn't have a brother?"

21

OAT HILL MINE

Barren, baked ground, and an unforgiving sun beat on the miners from above and below. Dusty, unwashed men milled like ants, with pickaxes and hammers and grim faces. Trees and shrubs gave the area a wide berth. Steam hissed from giant, open kettles where cinnabar was being refined into quicksilver. The air reeked of rotten eggs.

Miners stopped to stare as Isobel and Julius wove their way through crude wooden dwellings, canvas tents, and fire pits. Isobel pulled her horse beside a group of men. They tipped their hats, but it didn't stop them from leering.

"Ma'am." One of the men stepped forward to take her reins, but she nudged her horse back.

"Who's your foreman?"

The fellow pointed with his tin mug. His fingers were raw and pink under the dust. "You look set to raise hell."

Isobel gave a sharp laugh. "You have no idea." She tipped her Stetson and clicked her horse forward. The men parted slowly. Julius cleared his throat, but it didn't quicken them any.

When they were clear, Isobel glanced over at her companion. "You appear nervous, Doctor."

"This is hardly a place for a lady."

Isobel had debated disguising herself as a man, but in the end she had kept her blouse and riding skirt. Sometimes there were advantages to being a woman.

"Those ladies over there seem content." She nodded at several women leaning against a crude shack. Their shoulders were bare, and their skirts were tied up on one side, revealing soft thighs. They looked bored. And drunk.

"Prostitutes live dangerous lives."

"And I don't?" Isobel asked with some amusement. "Don't worry, Doctor. I can see to my own honor. Though a knife or a revolver would put my mind at ease. I don't suppose you brought the one you confiscated from Jin?"

"I still have it, but it's not loaded."

"Well, don't shy away from loading those chambers if I stir things up."

"I'd rather you not."

The foreman was a thin fellow with a crisp collar and immaculate fingernails. His manner reminded Isobel of a razor—one that had never touched a chin. He wore a frown, even after the doctor nodded in greeting.

The foreman didn't bother with pleasantries. "Why are you distracting my men? If it's whoring you're looking for, talk to Mrs. Gold. She's the madam here."

"I'm here on behalf of Sheriff Nash," Isobel lied. "This is Doctor Julius Bright. I'm his nurse. We need to know which of your men visited Calistoga in the past five days."

The foreman stared at her. The word 'sheriff' seemed to be foremost on his mind. He eyed the doctor's chest, searching for a badge. "Why are you here?"

"There's a syphilis outbreak in town," Isobel explained.

"Doctor Bright needs to make a few discreet inquiries to see if any of your men are infected."

Julius coughed, and cleared his throat. "We don't want it spreading."

"The infected men won't be of any use to you, anyway."

The foreman blanched. "Most of them go into town on Sundays. Why the last five days?"

"We believe we've pinpointed the source," Isobel said suggestively. "Have any of them gone to town for deliveries?"

The foreman gestured towards the wagons. "Mr. O'Conner handles those. You can question him, but I want to know if any of my men were visiting whores on company time."

"Of course," Isobel said.

The foreman returned to his logbook. "And let me know if any of them are infected. Paying an undertaker cuts into profits."

"We wouldn't want that."

They left the foreman to his business, and Isobel headed for a cluster of shacks.

"I can't believe that worked," Julius said under his breath. Although his whisper tended to carry.

"Anyone will believe anything if it makes them uncomfortable."

"Ah, I see. They're less likely to ask questions."

"Precisely."

"But why didn't you just tell him about Titus? I'm sure word of the boy's disappearance has reached here."

"That would have been like accusing one of his men of abducting the boy. Inquiries cause delays, and that is the last thing a mine foreman wants."

"Indeed." Julius sounded impressed. "Do you know, Miss Amsel, you would make an excellent alienist."

"For Titus's sake, let's hope I make an excellent detective, too."

Isobel headed straight for a woman who was lounging on the steps of a dilapidated shack. The woman was rough and worn, and *perfume de gin* wafted from her lips. The woman eyed Julius up and down, and then settled on Isobel. "I don't want savin'. Your kind, with your charity—" The woman finished her sentence by spitting on the ground.

"We're not here on charity. I want information," Isobel said.

"You payin'?"

"Depends on how sober you are."

The woman cackled, showing off toothless gums. Another woman stepped out from a shack, adjusting a shawl over her shoulders. Her dark eyes were downcast, her hair was pulled into a neat bun, and the lace at her bodice shone white under the sun. A sharp contrast to her skin.

"Is your friend always drunk before noon?" Isobel asked.

"No sabe, señora."

"I wouldn't bother with Maria," the drunk woman slurred. "That gibberish of hers don't make no sense, and her high and mighty ways drive me to drink."

Julius surmised a distraction was needed. He quickly settled himself beside the drunk woman on the step, and engaged her in conversation. He was clearly the more interesting of the newcomers, so the drunk tugged down her blouse a dangerous inch and ignored the others.

Isobel introduced herself in Spanish, and the woman's eyes lit up.

"Maria Garcia. Don't mind Lacy," she said in Spanish. "She's had a rough life. And that's saying a lot here." Maria pulled Isobel away from Lacy and Julius. The doctor must have asked Lacy a question, because she began shouting about all the people who had done her wrong.

"Saavedra," Maria murmured in thought.

"Portuguese. I'm afraid my Spanish doesn't sound much better than her English."

Maria laughed, and shook her head. "No, it's fine. Why are you here?"

"A Spanish man was accused of abducting a boy. Do you know Samuel Lopez?"

Maria's eyes widened. "Not Samuel."

"Is he a client of yours?"

Maria immediately shook her head. "No. Never. He's simple; he has the mind of a child. But he's kind. I sometimes knit him socks and mend his clothes. Some of the others do too."

"Does Samuel visit here often?"

"He occasionally brings us letters from town, but the men treat him badly."

"Who?"

Maria looked toward the kettles. "It's mostly the Irish. They lord it over everyone in camp. A few Mexicans do, too. The Negros and Chinese keep their heads down."

"Anyone in particular?"

"Finneas O'Conner is the ringleader. Nice enough fellow, unless your skin is on the dark side. And then there's José. But it's nothing brutal. Mostly heckling. It's been going on as long as I've been here. Do you think Samuel did something to that boy?" Concern shone in her eyes.

"I wouldn't be here if I did," Isobel replied. "Have any of the men mentioned picking up a boy on the road? To give him a ride?"

Maria shook her head. "I haven't heard. But if anyone

knows, it'd be Finneas. He never stops talking, but somehow he knows everything."

"Do you get the impression that any of these men would hurt a child?"

Maria frowned in thought. "These men do a lot of a horrible things. But they're a pack, and they wouldn't tolerate someone like that."

Isobel thanked her, and fished around a hidden pocket, but it was empty. She had forgotten—she wasn't allowed currency while at the asylum.

Maria put a hand on her arm. "Don't. It's for Samuel."

"I'll do my best to find out what happened."

Maria nodded, and hugged her shawl to her shoulders.

Isobel hesitated. "If you ever need help." She presented a card stamped with a raven. "You'll know where to find me."

Mist swam in Maria's eyes. She accepted the card and tucked it away, turning quickly to disappear inside a shack.

Isobel turned to find Lacy in rapt conversation with Julius. It was mostly one-sided, but he appeared captivated. Isobel struck off, and Julius hastily excused himself, peeled the woman off his arm, and hurried to catch up.

"Attempting to escape?" Julius asked.

"You looked to be in the midst of a talking session."

"After a fashion." He shook his head. "It's really quite useless to speak with an inebriated individual. I've tried... but drunkenness is a strange, ravaging affliction."

"A slow, cowardly death," she murmured.

"I wouldn't call it cowardice. To you, perhaps. I thought you intended to question the miners?"

"Those women know the miners best. They know the brutes, and the kind-hearted. And they know the desires and dreams of them all."

"True," he agreed. "Men will tell a prostitute anything. I've always thought they were akin to alienists."

Isobel chuckled.

"I'm quite serious," he defended.

"The truth is ironic. What does that say about your profession, Doctor?"

"That we have much to learn," he said.

They found Finneas O'Conner leaning against a wagon cleaning his fingernails with a knife. Finn looked her up and down, then twirled his knife, sheathing it in one smooth motion. "I would've thought you wee devils might have diverged a bit."

"I could say the same of you and your ways." She thrust out her hand, and he bowed over it with a flourish, brushing the air above her knuckles.

"I can't be shaking the hand of a beautiful lass like you, Miss Amsel."

"This is Doctor Bright."

"Is he your keeper?"

She smiled. "One in a long line."

Finn laughed. "And we all know what happened to those." He winked.

"Thanks for giving Lotario a ride into town the other day."

"That lad looked in a bad way."

"That'd be my fault, as usual."

Finn grinned from ear to ear, and hooked his thumbs beneath his waistcoat. She remembered the man from her childhood. He was the kind of man that took a penny from her ear, and laughed at mischief. She also remembered why her father fired him.

"Wasn't it always?" Finn laughed.

"I've reformed my ways."

"That's what a little bird told me. A bona fide detective now. Are you here to turn those lovely eyes on me?"

"I'm afraid not."

Finn clutched his heart. "By my sweet mother's grave, she'll roll over to hear I've reformed and mended my ways."

"I doubt it. But I was hoping you could help me."

"How may I assist the devil herself?"

"I know you have ears everywhere."

"That I do." He crossed his heart.

"Have you heard of the missing boy?"

"Rumors flit to my ears like wee fairies. It's good you found him."

"I found *one* boy."

Finn looked confused. "There's two missing boys?" he asked in surprise.

She shook her head. "I found John. But the older boy is still missing."

"I did not know that."

"Did you happen to see a boy walking along the road, or give one a ride?"

"I haven't given anyone a ride into town," he said quickly. "Except your brother. He's close to a boy, I suppose."

"He's hardly a boy," Isobel said.

"Could'a fooled ol' Finn." He flashed another lopsided grin. But he quickly turned serious, squinting at the sky in thought. "I haven't heard anyone mention giving the Sheel boys a lift. But we do see those boys from time to time lurking around the mines. They're a pair to rival you wee devils. Leaders, they are."

"Why are the boys lurking around the mines?"

"Gah. I don't know." He paused to spat. "Lookin' for gold in the shafts, I suppose."

"Look, Finn, someone is already in custody. None of the men here have to worry about being accused of any wrong-doing," she lied through her teeth.

"Yeah, I heard about Samuel." Finn took out a cigarette, and struck a match against his trousers. "I'll tell you one thing," he said, putting flame to the end. "I always said Samuel Lopez was a creep."

"Why is that?"

Finn took a drag on his cigarette. "Caught him watching those boys. Out by Holm's place. It's about time Samuel gets a noose around his neck."

"Watching hardly calls for a noose."

"That girl last year. She ran with those boys sometimes, and I caught that idiot following her once, too."

22

AN ORDERLY MIND

NICHOLAS

Nicholas turned the sign around on the door. He straightened it so it wasn't tilted, and when he was satisfied, he wiped the glass with a clean cloth.

"Thank you, Nicholas. Any plans tonight?" Mr. Joy asked.

"Plans?"

Edwin Joy was a severe man, but he had a ready smile when he was relaxed. "Headed to a restaurant? Taking a young lady to the theater?"

Nicholas glanced down at his shoes. "Er, no, Mr. Joy. I don't think any woman would put up with my habits." The question had caught him off guard, and when he was surprised his stutter returned. Nervous now, Nicholas turned the key, lest a late customer should come inside. But once was never enough. To be sure he turned it again, and then once more to be satisfied.

Mr. Joy chuckled. "Well, I appreciate your habits, Nicholas. You're well suited to the profession. I never have to worry with you. I know all our mixtures and tinctures will be spot on. A misstep in this line of work can kill." Edwin Joy patted Nicholas's back, as he did most nights. Nicholas wasn't sure if the compliment was sincere or if he was being mocked. Nicholas did not understand people.

"Goodnight, Nicholas."

Nicholas stood straight as a board. "Goodnight, sir."

Mr. Joy stepped out onto the boardwalk. Gaslights shone like beacons in the mist. Across the way, the California Theatre glowed with promise. A line of theatergoers stood under the bright lights. None of it interested Nicholas. He turned to the shop, and picked up the broom, sweeping again, and then polishing the counter until it gleamed under his skilled hand.

By the time he was satisfied with his work, darkness had thickened and the lights outside had turned ominous. He glanced out the tinted windows, his face centered in the shop's 'O'. Figures drifted by like ghosts. He should have left with Mr. Joy.

A large shadow stopped, and looked directly at him. Nicholas jerked away from the glass. He had left a smudge. Heart galloping, he stood frozen for a minute, torn between wiping away the smudge and hiding from the face outside the window. Mind warred with body, until he thought he'd be ripped apart.

Nicholas grunted as if struck, and sat on his haunches, covering his ears, and squeezing his eyes shut. He listened to his heart, to the blood rushing through his veins. *Whoosh, whoosh, whoosh.* It was so loud. He counted to ten, but somewhere between the three and four, he stuttered on his count and it wasn't symmetrical, so he started over again. On the third time, he was pleased with the pause between numbers, and opened his eyes.

The shadow was gone. The smudge remained. His choice was obvious now. Nicholas hopped to his feet, whipped out a cloth, and set about cleaning the window with his favorite cleaner—rubbing alcohol. It had a soothing smell. When he was finished, not a streak remained.

Nicholas checked his pocket watch. He made three circuits of the drugstore, and then stepped outside, putting his key into the lock. He turned it once, twice, three times, then tucked the key in his pocket, patting it to make sure it was snug. He straightened his cuffs, and walked out into the dark night.

The evening rush was ebbing, though a few devout businessmen still trudged home. He glanced over his shoulder. Two men walked behind him. One pushed a cart: a chimney sweep. The second had his hands in his pockets; the flare of a cigarette glowed beneath his cap.

Nicholas smacked into something solid. He reeled backwards, and hands clamped down to steady him.

"Whoa, now. Take it easy, son." Shiny badge, tall cap, and uniform. A police officer. "Where are you going in such a hurry?"

Nicholas ducked his head. "Sorry, sir. I'm clumsy." Keeping his eyes on the ground, he quickly rushed past the officer. He wished he could hide like a turtle.

Nicholas hopped on a cable car, and watched the city roll by. Saloons were lit and theaters glowed. San Francisco shifted at night from businesses to pleasure, leaving the financial district quiet. He disembarked at Leavenworth Street, and comforted himself by counting boards on the walk home.

He stopped at a curb and tucked the number into his mind, before glancing over his shoulder. A boy with a newspaper bag strolled down the street, a block away. Relieved,

Nicholas continued his counting. At five hundred and seventy three, he stopped, and looked up. A man stood in front of his house.

Nicholas scrambled a few steps backwards. Badge, shiny buttons, a bullseye lantern, and a billy club. Another police officer. He could never bring himself to look at the eyes. There was too much complexity in those organs—intricate vessels, the pupils constricting and dilating, and the colors— the colors were mesmerizing. Nicholas would lose himself in wonder, and it made people uncomfortable.

"'Cuse me, sir. You live here?"

The man spoke to him.

Nicholas glanced at the officer's shoes. And groaned. They were not shiny at all, but scratched and muddy. Nicholas's fingers twitched.

"You've had a break in, sir."

"Wh—what?" Nicholas stuttered.

The officer gestured with his billy club. "Do you live here?"

Nicholas glanced at his house. It was dark, but everything appeared to be order. "Yes, I do."

"I'll show you, then. You can make a report, and tell me what's missing."

The word sent a panic through Nicholas. He opened his gate and ran up the steps, forgetting to count them. As he fished out his key, he looked back and mentally counted. They were all there. But so was someone else. Just outside his front fence stood a gentleman with a silver-tipped walking stick. Nicholas noted the man's polished shoes with approval. He followed the shoes up the man's trousers, to a crisp suit and a snowy collar. A trim beard on the man's jaw calmed Nicholas. And so did the voice.

"Is everything all right, Mr. Nicholas?"

"Mr. Riot," Nicholas said, more to himself than in greeting. "It appears I've been robbed. H...how did you—"

"It's fortunate this officer arrived to help you," Riot said.

Nicholas glanced at the officer's badge. "Yes, I suppose."

With hunched shoulders, Nicholas put his key into its lock. It slid in perfectly. The door *was* locked. There was that. So why was the officer claiming he'd been robbed?

The officer shifted. Voices droned behind him. Introductions. Why did everyone want a name? It made no sense to Nicholas. But then little did. He opened his door, and reached for the gaslight. Light illuminated his haven, but instead of comfort he found chaos.

Nicholas cried out, but quickly put a fist to his mouth to stifle the sound. A hand touched his arm. He flinched, and the hand fell away, but even in his distressed state, he noted the orderly fingernails.

"Is there anything missing?" the officer asked.

Everything was out of place. Shards of glass and wood littered the floor. Nicholas bent and righted his coat stand. He picked up an umbrella stand next, and moved it to the right, five inches away from the coat stand. He turned it just so. One thing at a time, and all would be well again.

"Mr. Nicholas!" the officer's shout barely registered. "Shouldn't you be checking on your valuables?"

Nicholas swallowed, gazing at the chaos he would have to pass over. But he *had* to know. Were they safe? Nicholas took a breath, closed his eyes, and bolted over the mess. He knew his home by heart. He stopped at the back door, and without daring to look at the broken glass, wrenched it open and shot down the back steps.

They were there. Nicholas exhaled. Beneath the moon and silver mist, he could just make out the familiar, wild shapes of his rose bushes. He ran a hand over a petal, brushing velvet life.

"My darlings," he breathed. "You're all right, aren't you?"

"What the devil!" the officer spat out.

"Who reported the break in?" Riot asked.

"Who are you to him, Mr. Riot?" the officer returned.

"A friend."

"A neighbor rang the call box. Found a broken brick," the officer grunted, and took out a notepad and pencil. He licked the tip. "Mr. Nicholas. I have other pressing crimes to be investigating. Can you tell me if anything were stolen?"

Nicholas glanced at the officer's broad chest. "No... nothing."

"But you haven't checked."

Nicholas titled his head to the side. He glanced at both men, shying away from their eyes. "Everything is here," he said softly.

The officer spat. Nicholas flinched, gaze drawn to the dark ground. Unfortunately, it wasn't dark enough. His cheek twitched at the thick wad of saliva staining the earth.

"It's fortunate nothing of value was stolen," Riot said.

Nicholas couldn't take it. He donned his gloves, scooped up the saliva and dirt, and carried it to a compost pile. He hesitated, glancing at his gloves. Resigned, he stripped them off and let them fall into the compost pile, along with the dirt and saliva.

"Look 'ere. I need to write my report. Can you *please* check if anything were stolen?"

"My roses are here," Nicholas said. The officer stared at him. Nicholas tucked his head down, and hurried up the stairs. The kitchen. He groaned. To comfort himself, he picked up a chair and righted it. Then replaced a pot on its hook, and reached for a dust bin.

"Sir! You can clean afterwards!"

"Officer Jones, he doesn't appear to be concerned with anything other than his roses. I think you can move on," Riot said.

"Let me do my job."

Riot tipped his hat, and stepped back. The officer grabbed Nicholas's arm and jerked him to his feet. "Valuables, *sir*."

Nicholas winced at the tone of voice. The officer's skin was red above his collar, but Nicholas never made it farther than his scruffy chin.

Riot stood casually by, hands on his walking stick, watching the men. "You can clean up later," Riot suggested.

"Yes, of course," Nicholas said.

The officer let him go. He tucked his hands in his pockets, and picked his way over the ruins of his life. Every crack, every crunch, made him want to curl into a ball and hide. He glanced at the detective. Mr. Riot. The one who hadn't believed him. Why was he here now?

Nicholas asked the question out loud.

"I'm here to help you, Nicholas, as your friend," Riot replied.

Nicholas puzzled over the answer. When had Mr. Riot become his friend? Had visiting his home been the beginning of friendship? Nicholas shook his head. Social complexities were beyond him.

The officer nudged Nicholas. He stumbled forward. "What should I check for?" Nicholas asked.

"Money. Gold. Jewelry," the officer bit back.

"Yes, right." Nicholas searched for his cash box—a

carved scrimshaw box. It was lying open on the floor, his savings gone.

"Forty seven dollars and twenty-nine cents was taken," he informed the officer. But Nicholas didn't care about money. He only cared about his roses and books. Nicholas dropped to his knees, clutching at their torn pages—his own flesh and blood. "Who would do this?" he choked out.

All his memories. Journals, photographs, every day of his life chronicled. It was too much. Nicholas curled into a ball on the torn pages, and pressed his palms over his ears, blocking out the world.

23

A PECULIAR CASE

RIOT

ATTICUS RIOT REGARDED THE YOUNG MAN AT HIS FEET. AND then he looked to Officer Jones. The man was gruff, heavyset in a strongman's way, with roughened hands. His uniform strained over his chest. Jones stabbed his pencil at the paper, and snapped his notebook shut.

"Do you have everything you need?" Riot asked.

"Yes. Doubt we'll get his money back."

"I think that highly unlikely," Riot agreed. He waited, tapping a finger on the knob of his stick. The officer looked around the room, and blew a noisy breath past his lips. With a muttered oath, he stomped out. The door slammed shut, and Riot continued to wait. After the echo died, he moved to the hallway and listened for a few moments. But the only sound was Nicholas's harsh breathing.

He went back to his client and patted the young man's shoulder. "I'm sorry, Nicholas." The man seemed to curl into an even tighter ball. Riot frowned down at him. The man seemed to want to hide. Riot located a blanket in the mess, and laid it over him.

"I'll get you something to drink." He didn't know if Nicholas could hear anything in such a distressed state.

It didn't take long to find a drink. Nicholas kept no alcohol in the house, only a pitcher of water with lemon slices inside the ice box. Riot carried a glass back to the study. Nicholas had roused himself. He was sitting upright, sorting through torn pages and placing them in neat stacks, as he murmured under his breath.

Riot held the glass out to him. "Drink this."

"I need to fix this."

Riot set the glass on a side table. He righted a chair, and sat, crossing his legs. He had failed Mr. Nicholas. Riot had been too preoccupied with the present and haunted by his past—one where a murderer had entered his own home. Fear had blinded Riot—fear that Nicholas was another assassin. Another threat. But the man was no such thing. He was only sensitive and misunderstood. Possessed of a peculiar mind.

Riot toyed with his beard as he watched the strange young man. After a time, he shifted and leaned forward, intertwining his fingers. "Nicholas, you asked for my help the other day. I'm here now. Someone appears to have been looking for something in your home. Do you have any idea what that might be?"

No answer.

Riot was about to try another angle when Nicholas spoke. "I don't understand people. I don't know why they do what they do," he said without looking up from his methodical sorting.

"You and me both."

Nicholas paused. He repeated Riot's words under his

breath, and shook his head. He reached for the water and drank it in one long gulp, then took a handkerchief out of his pocket, and wiped the glass carefully before setting it back.

"You visited me in my home. You asked for my help," Riot said gently.

"It was foolish."

"No, it wasn't. I think you're in danger, Nicholas."

"Why?" Nicholas looked at the chaos. "I'm a druggist. And... a freak. That's what you thought. I know you did. In your house."

"Out of my own fear. I did," Riot admitted.

"I don't need your help anymore. They did what they did." Nicholas focused back on his papers.

"You're still in danger."

"Why?" Nicholas asked again.

"I intend to find out. But I need your help."

"I can't." Nicholas swallowed, and dipped his head. "I need to sort this. I have work on Monday."

Riot picked up a pressed flower from the rug, and studied it. Nicholas thrust out his hand, fingers twitching. "That goes in May of 1894. Not there in your hand."

"Of course." Riot surrendered the pressed poppy. "Do you like flowers?"

"Yes. I know. It's not... manly," he stuttered.

"If only more men took an interest in flowers," Riot mused. "I might be out of a job."

Nicholas focused on Riot for the first time. His pale gaze was intense, critical, and all-seeing. Nicholas looked like a madman. "Poison. There are poisonous flowers."

Riot inclined his head. "Have you dispensed poisons?"

"Most medications are derived from poisonous plants. In minute doses. Wormwood, nightshade, arsenic..." Nicholas rattled off every such plant he knew at an alarming rate. Riot sat stunned by the man's knowledge. When Nicholas had run out of poisons, he fell silent.

"Do you keep poisonous plants in your home?"

"As I said, Mr. Riot. Most plants are poisonous."

"Do you have any rare plants?" Riot asked.

Nicholas shook his head. "Would that matter?"

"It might." Although it was a long shot. Riot tried waiting to see if Nicholas would divulge anything else, but silence didn't work with this man. Nicholas seemed oblivious to such things. "I'd like to place an agent in your home. To guard you."

Nicholas shook his head without glancing up. "They would make a mess."

Riot couldn't argue with that. "Why did you choose me?"

Nicholas stopped, and looked at him—right in the eyes. Riot held his gaze, but the man kept looking, even tilting his head. Nicholas was looking *into* Riot's eyes, not the center of his nose, or even at one, but into both eyes.

"I saw your photograph in a newspaper. You were clean and orderly." Without breaking eye contact, Riot waited for more. Nicholas's stare wasn't posturing, but something else. There was an openness to Nicholas—an unmistakable innocence and curiosity. "You have nice eyes, Mr. Riot. But your spectacles need cleaning." Nicholas went back to his sorting.

Riot cocked his head, the edge of his lip hitching upwards. He followed Nicholas's suggestion and cleaned his spectacles, wondering what Isobel would make of this odd young man. The thought brought a pang of longing that he couldn't ignore. The sooner he helped Mr. Nicholas, the sooner he could visit her. But that brought another question: how to help a man who didn't want it?

24

WHERE THE HEART LIES

Riot and Tobias walked up the side lane to Ravenwood Manor. Light spilled from the windows and laughter pushed through the walls. It sounded like a celebration.

"What's going on tonight?"

Tobias shrugged. "Some party."

As Riot had hoped, there was a light on in the carriage house. One wide door was cracked open. Tim was home. "Head inside, Tobias," Riot said. "I'm sure your mother saved us dinner. There might even be cake for you."

Tobias had done a fine job watching the drugstore, and following Mr. Nicholas home. He had kept his distance and waited for the police officer to leave. The boy had excellent instincts.

"I'd rather stick with you, sir. It's late, and I don't want to face my ma alone."

Riot grimaced. He had forgotten about that. Tobias followed him into the carriage house.

"You look like shit," Tim said by way of greeting.

Riot paused in the doorway, and sniffed. "You smell like it."

Tim's white beard was matted and dingy, and his clothes had a dubious color to them. He was pulling off a pair of boots that were caked with muck. Judging from the smell, Riot doubted it was mud.

"I found that ring," Tim said.

"Sewers?"

"Sewers," Tim confirmed.

"Had a hell of a time chasing the damned thief. I'm not as young as I'd like to be."

"I still can't catch you, Tim."

The old man cackled. "This one gave me a run for my money. He was slippery in more ways than one."

Riot glanced down at Tobias. "Next time I'll send you with Tim."

"I could 'ave used some help." Tim eyed the boy. "Are you quick on your feet?"

Tobias took a step back. "No, sir. I trip over my own. Barely managed to tail that fellow home."

"How'd you get that shiner?" Tim asked.

"I ran into some other newsboys."

Tim glanced at Riot. "Miss Lily is going to skin your hide."

Riot cleared his throat. "Why don't you get inside, Tobias."

"She's gonna whip me, isn't she?"

Tim flashed his gold teeth. "Blame it all on A.J. and you'll be fine."

The boy looked up at Riot, lips twitching. "You're gonna get it, sir."

Riot flipped Tobias twenty-five cents. "For your work today."

Overjoyed, Tobias darted towards the main house. Apparently the boy still believed that Tim was capable of telling the truth.

Tim stripped off his sodden clothing, and dropped it on some dirty hay. He stomped upstairs, and the sound of rushing water came a moment later. "Haven't had a bite all day, and I can't eat until I'm clean," Tim hollered down the stairs. "Come and talk."

Riot followed him upstairs.

"A telegram came for you," Tim called from the bathroom.

"Where is it?" Riot asked.

Tim poked his head from the doorway, and pointed at the missive. "I took the liberty of opening it. Your wayward daughter found her way to that wildcat you call a woman."

A knot unwound between's Riot's shoulder blades. He snatched up the telegram from a table, and read it.

I found your missing mutineer. She claims a certain gunslinger tried to kill her. I suggest disarming the attic. -B

Riot stared at the words. It explained why Jin had run when he tracked her to the dry dock. But why would she think he'd kill her? He'd find out soon enough in Napa Valley—if he ever untangled himself from this latest case.

Water splashed, Tim sighed, and Riot moved to the doorway, crossing his arms. "I need you to check on a police officer. I have his badge number."

"I'll put Matt on it." Tim dunked his head and came back up. Deprived of the fluff of his white beard, Tim was all muscle, bone, and sharp edges.

"You'd best hurry, Tim. You're likely to starve to death in that bath."

"I'm hurrying." Tim renewed his efforts with the brush. "Miss Lily has high standards."

"Higher than you're used to," Riot murmured.

"What was that?" Tim called over the splashing water.

"Nothing." Riot told him about his day.

"Sounds like a simple burglary," Tim said.

"Maybe so.

"What has you on edge?"

"I'd like to know who called the police."

"I thought you said a neighbor called it in," Tim said.

"That's what the officer said. After I dropped off Sarah, I went back to Leavenworth Street, and ingratiated myself with a Mrs. Pavel—an elderly woman across the street with a convenient view of Nicholas's home."

Tim guffawed. "Using a poor elderly woman. You've sunk low, A.J."

"Officer Jones came to the house at 7:50 p.m., went around back, and then loitered outside the fence until Nicholas returned from work."

Tim grunted. "Fishy. I'll look into the badge. Anything else you want?"

"I need to look into Nicholas's family, university, friends… He must be getting help. He's so focused on minutia that I can't imagine him signing up for university, or even settling a grocer's bill by himself."

"Gotcha. Do you want this Nicholas watched?"

"I think our time would be better spent digging into his past. He doesn't want anyone in his home. And if there is someone watching him, then we'll only chase them off."

"Do you think he's in danger?"

Riot removed his spectacles, and ran a hand over his face. "I don't know. I need to sleep on it."

"No, you need to sleep. Period."

"I had a long night."

"Heart's not in it?" Tim asked.

"My heart is in Napa Valley." He gave his friend a rueful smile.

"With a woman whose instincts rival Ravenwood's," Tim said. "Question is: do you attract that sort or do they attract you?"

"The latter. I got stuck with you, didn't I?"

Tim threw a sponge at him, and then relaxed into the dirty tub. "Don't suppose you could bring an old man dinner?"

"I'll be back in a tick." Riot turned to leave.

"And A.J.?"

"Hmm?"

"I was serious about Miss Lily."

"I'll tread quietly."

THE KITCHEN WAS FILLED WITH THE DETRITUS OF celebration. Sarah stood at the sink up to her elbows in suds. A mountain of pots, pans, and dishes waited to be cleaned, while Watson sprawled under her feet, lazily batting at her apron string. The smell brought Riot up short in the doorway. His stomach growled in response.

"Atticus!" Sarah beamed at him. There was relief in her voice.

"How is your penance coming along?" he asked.

Sarah flicked some suds at him. "Well enough. What happened with Mr. Nicholas?"

"The police came," Riot said, looking towards the dining room. "What's going on?" Dinner at the manor was generally served at eight o'clock—buffet style.

"Mr. Löfgren is getting married. It's his engagement celebration."

Riot tried to recall the man's face.

Seeing his thoughtful expression, Sarah nudged his memory. "The Swedish man." She frowned at him. "Don't you know anyone in your own house?"

"As a general rule I try to avoid the other boarders."

She rolled her eyes. "Some detective."

"I'm far more concerned with what's inside these pots." He lifted one lid, and made appreciative noises. And then another. Pot roast, carrots, mashed potatoes, gravy, and biscuits that looked like clouds. He heard a hopeful purr, followed by a furry head butting his shin. Riot ignored the cat.

"And you should see the cake," Sarah said, drying her hands. "I'll make you a plate."

"Make it two, if you please. Tim's not presentable for the kitchen."

Sarah wrinkled her nose. "We smelled. When will you and Isobel have an engagement party?"

"Is that something people generally do?"

"You *have* to have one."

"We do?"

"Of course you do."

"If you say so."

"*Really?*" Her eyes widened. "You'll have a party then?"

"Everything is on hold until Isobel is free."

"Why?"

He started to give an easy answer, but paused. "Why indeed?" he murmured.

A wave of voices pushed into the kitchen, along with the door. Maddie carried in a tray, followed by her mother. Lily frowned at Riot.

Sarah leaned in close. "You're in trouble," she mouthed.

Lily set down her tray, and turned on him. "Mr. Riot, is it true you used my son to spy on a drugstore?"

"I did," Riot said.

"But, Miss Lily, me and Tobias were already..." Sarah started, but one look from the woman silenced her. She handed Riot a plate of food.

"I do apologize for not asking first," Riot said.

"Asking forgiveness instead of permission doesn't work with me." Lily grabbed a knife, and started sawing at the roast, placing lean cuts on Maddie's fresh tray. "I don't care what you and yours do, but when it involves *my* children, I want a say in the matter."

"Yes, ma'am," Riot said. "It's easy to forget your children's ages. They inherited their mother's intelligence."

Lily glanced at him out of the corner of her eye. "If your voice were any smoother, I'd use it to honey the biscuits."

Riot plucked a biscuit from his plate, and bit into it. "You're right, no honey needed."

Maddie laughed, eyes alight. Lily looked heavenward, but that same twinkle was in her own eyes.

"I suppose this would be an inappropriate time to ask if Grimm could work for the agency?" The motor by his feet got louder, along with a strong body twining between his legs. But Riot wasn't about to give up his biscuit.

Lily sighed. "Is it ever the right time?"

"Would you poison my food if I asked now?"

She gave a pointed look at his biscuit. "Who says I haven't already?"

The girls snickered, and Lily shooed them both out with fresh trays. She wiped her hands on an apron before turning to him.

"I should have asked," Riot said more seriously.

"Yes, you should have," came her firm reply. "Apology accepted. And no, Grimm's better off here."

"Can he drive the carriage?"

Lily sighed. "He has been, hasn't he?"

"But you're worried about him."

"I can't explain. I'm sorry, Mr. Riot." She turned abruptly, staring out the kitchen window at the dark yard.

Riot studied the set of her shoulders. "I may be able to help. Whatever it is."

Lily's back stiffened. It was obvious she wanted to say something, so Riot waited. But she didn't vocalize whatever was on her mind. Instead, she shook her head.

"I thank you, Mr. Riot. But my business is my own. And while Grimm is his own man, I don't want him involved in police work. Same goes for Tobias."

Miss Lily must have heard his faint sigh, because she took pity on him. "Maybe the occasional errand," she relented. "But Mr. Riot," she leaned closer, "We can't draw attention to ourselves. Not even here."

"My offer stands. When you're ready."

Lily nodded, but kept her lips sealed.

"Do you do this sort of thing often?" He gestured to the kitchen as he took a seat. "I didn't realize celebrations were part of the rent."

"They're not."

"That's kind of you, Miss Lily."

"I didn't say I'm doing this for free." She handed him fork and knife. The roast didn't need a knife. He took a bite and nearly missed her next words. "Miss Dupree inquired about the teaching post."

"I need to speak with Bel first."

Lily nodded with approval.

"What would you prefer, Miss Lily?" he asked.

"I'd prefer a qualified teacher who wasn't a prostitute. And I'd prefer not to have to worry about the color of my skin every time I leave this house."

"Anything else?" he asked.

"I'd like the past to stay where it belongs, and I'd like my employer to stop using my youngest son as a spy." She paused. "A mountain of gold would be nice, too. What do you prefer?"

"To be in Bright Waters." He took another bite. "This is delicious."

"Buttering me up doesn't work either, but you can keep trying."

"Noted." Riot started in on his mashed potatoes, ignoring the claws that had hooked themselves into his trouser leg. "I've been giving some thought to what you told me… regarding the state of my finances. Investing takes time."

"*And* it's a gamble," she reminded.

"Which is why I intend to take more interest in Ravenwood Agency. I haven't paid it proper attention for years." He watched the gravy run down the side of his potatoes, pooling like a lake on the plate. "I've wanted to put the past where it belongs, too. And the agency suffered because of it."

She ignored his double meaning. Agency could easily be replaced with family. *Her* family.

"Would you like me to give the boarders their notice?" Lily asked.

Riot glanced towards the dining room. Joyful voices and laughter filled the house. It was a pleasant sound. Riot shook his head. "Not yet. I'll fix the attic up for Jin, if she returns. We'll sort the rest out once Isobel is free."

"You're busy as it is, Mr. Riot. I'll have Grimm clean the attic and crate everything. You can go through the boxes at your leisure."

"I appreciate the offer, but it's something I need to do myself."

Lily didn't argue. She sat down at the table across from him. "What if people can't pay your agency? From what I understand, Mr. Tim has been very generous with the poorer clients."

"He is. And so am I. We'll start accepting reward money."

Lily tilted her head. "Why wouldn't you? Isn't that part of the business?"

"Not always. Call it professional pride. There's a fine line between an investigator and a bounty hunter, and reward money pushes that line. Clients willing to front a reward aren't always concerned about justice. They're usually more concerned with their own interests. The Pinkertons don't accept reward money either."

"I don't want you to compromise your principles."

He gave her a small smile. "I'm a gambler. I don't have many."

"You're not fooling anyone, Mr. Riot."

"I do my best." He nodded to the dishes. "In the mean-time, I doubt you'll have much time to look into suitable investments with all this going on. Have you thought of hiring outside help?"

Lily gave him a look. "I'm particular about my kitchen. And I have to cook for my own anyway."

"Thank God for that," he said, and then took another enthusiastic bite. It gave his mind a firm nudge. "Tim." He had all but forgotten the old man. Riot quickly swallowed, and started to rise. "I promised I'd bring him dinner."

Lily placed a hand over his. "I'll take it."

"He's not fit for ladies."

"Is he ever?" Lily stood, and plucked a plate from the counter. "Seeing that man turn brick red is always amusing."

"You'll be blinded today."

Lily laughed as she placed a napkin over the plate. "Sit, eat, and take your time. Miss Isobel will never forgive me if those cheekbones of yours get any sharper."

"Yes, ma'am." As soon as Miss Lily left, he tossed a piece of roast to Watson. "Don't tell anyone."

CARDS FLUTTERED UNDER RIOT'S FINGERTIPS. THE BLUR reminded him of hummingbird wings flitting from one hand to the next. Hypnotic. Soothing.

A soft knock inserted itself into his contemplation. Watson looked up from where he was melting in front of the hearth.

"Yes?"

"It's me."

"Come in," he called.

The fat cat rolled onto his other side to watch the door. Sarah poked her head in the room, and Tobias slipped under her arm. He skipped over to land in Ravenwood's chair. The boy wore striped pajamas that had been let out to the threads, and that stopped at his shins. He was growing like a weed.

Riot tucked his cards away, and stood. "Stand for a lady, Tobias."

The boy glanced at Sarah, blew out a breath, and slid off the chair.

Sarah was wearing her nightclothes, too. Robe, night-gown, and slippers. "Would you like some tea?" she asked.

Riot pointed to a snifter with his forgotten brandy inside. "No, thank you. Take my chair."

"She's just using tea as an excuse," Tobias said. "We want to know what happened."

Riot sat on the ottoman, and reached for his brandy.

"You can take my seat," Tobias said.

"I've never much liked that chair," Riot said.

But Watson did. The cat roused himself to jump up on the throne. He sat and began cleaning his claws.

Tobias frowned at the thief. "Why not?"

Rather than argue with the cat, Tobias sat on the floor.

"That chair never did fit me right." Riot drained his snifter. "I suppose Tobias told you about his day?" he asked Sarah.

She nodded. "It was boring up to where the other news-boys chased him off."

"You mentioned a police officer on patrol," Riot said.

"Two different ones. A fellow with a mustache and a straight back. Maybe around your age, Mr. A.J. And another one."

"What did the other one look like?"

"Mean enough to steal the coins off a dead man's eyes," Tobias said.

"You can't just say 'mean'," Sarah said. "Lots of folks look mean."

Tobias stared at his slippers. "He was white, and had long sideburns, no neck, and big hands."

"What time did you see him?" Riot asked.

"He came round a few times during the day. Even looked in the window."

"Right before Mr. Nicholas left?"

Tobias nodded. "There was a fellow in a peacoat following Mr. Nicholas, too, but he cut out towards the docks."

"And did anyone follow Nicholas from the cable car?"

Tobias shook his head.

"Did you summon the police after you took me home?" Sarah asked.

Riot squared his deck. "I did not. The officer was waiting for him at home. He arrived a few minutes before Mr. Nicholas returned. I believe he's the same officer who Tobias described as looking mean."

"That's strange," Sarah said.

"I thought so, too."

"I saw the time sheet while I was in the back room," Tobias said. "Mr. Nicholas comes in every morning at seven, and he leaves every evening at seven, too. Except on Sundays. It's closed."

"It's infinitely easier to burgle the home of a reliable gentleman than an unreliable one," Riot said.

"But who summoned the police? And why'd they wait so long?" Sarah asked.

"I don't think the police were ever summoned."

Both children looked at him, puzzled.

"Maybe the policeman saw the cracked window," Tobias said.

"I suspect something more," Riot said.

"What's that?" Sarah asked.

Riot stood. "I'll tell you when I've confirmed it."

Tobias perked up. "We'll help."

"There is something you can do."

Two expectant faces waited.

"Go to bed. Both of you."

Sarah slumped back in the chair, and Tobias blew out a breath. "We don't get no fun."

"Any," Sarah corrected. "I should have run off with Jin," she mumbled.

Riot placed a kiss on top of her head. "Knowing Bel— Jin's likely regretting her choice." He glanced at the ever-present sketchbook in her hand. Sarah seemed to need it, to find comfort in it, like a child with a favorite stuffed toy. He tilted his head at her current drawing. It was Mr. Nicholas. "Sarah, can you draw someone from a description?"

She frowned up at him. "I don't know."

"You can always try."

"I suppose there's no harm. Who do you want me to draw?"

Riot pointed at Tobias. "The second policeman he saw. The mean-looking one."

"Tobias isn't very good at describing things."

"Then ask a lot of questions. But do it in the morning. *Goodnight.* Both of you."

25

ADRIFT

ISOBEL

Isobel tapped on the shutter before opening it. Moonlight streamed through, illuminating her sleeping twin. It was like looking into a pond's reflection.

Lotario opened his eyes, and yawned. "It's late."

She crossed her arms on the sill. "How's Jin?"

"Not even a 'Hello, my dearest brother, how I've missed you?'"

"Hello, my dearest brother, how I've missed you," she repeated dryly.

Lotario rolled his eyes, and eased himself up, leaning against the headboard. His bed was directly beside the window, as were all the beds at Bright Waters. Julius Bright believed nature healed: fresh air, sun, and stars. And a soft breeze. There were far worse treatments, in Isobel's opinion.

"Forced praised isn't praise at all." Lotario reached between headboard and mattress. He came up with a bottle. "*Schnaps*? You look as though you could use a stiff drink."

"I thought you weren't supposed to imbibe while here?"

"Father brought it to celebrate." He looked suspiciously at the bottle. "I don't precisely know *what* he was celebrating, but nonetheless I pinched it as he was leaving."

"I'll have a glass." She began climbing through the window, but Lotario made a hissing noise at her. She froze. Balancing awkwardly on the sill, she unlaced her boots, tugged them off, and tossed them on the floor. When she plopped on his mattress, a glass was waiting for her.

"Where's Jin?" she asked.

"She insisted on sleeping in your room."

"How did she get on with the grandparents?"

"I have no idea. When I tried to go into town, mother threw a fit. She finally sent Hop and father off to question the station agents. Then, while I was resting, mother took Jin out for a walk. When they returned, Jin demanded to know where your room was, then stormed out. I couldn't get a word out of her, but then she doesn't trust me."

"What did Mother do to her?"

"Who knows. Mother said they had a 'pleasant walk'."

"Hell," she murmured.

"I'm sure that's what Jin thought. Mother and Father are staying at the *Magnolia*."

"What did Hop and Father uncover?"

"That Mr. Sheel boarded a train bound for Vallejo on Monday. He had a single bag, and was alone."

It was a six hour train ride. And Mr. Sheel certainly had enough time to make a return trip.

"And, no. No one saw him return," Lotario said, reading her mind.

Isobel sniffed at her glass, and took a sip. It burned down her throat, and she coughed. "Has father been dabbling in distilling again?"

"Hmm. He's searching for the perfect *Schnaps*."

She wiped water from her eyes.

"I did warn you." Lotario studied the glass apprecia-tively. "Although I think *burning water* makes more sense in Portuguese than *fruit brandy* in German. Father should call it *aguardente*. How goes the hunt?"

She told him about her conversation with Finn.

"Do you believe him?"

"I don't know," she said. "It could explain why he went out of his way to pick on Samuel. But I also remember why father dismissed him."

Lotario sat up a little straighter.

"Finn had a cruel sense of humor, and didn't much care for Chinese."

"That could be said of about half the population of America."

Isobel couldn't argue the point. "You know how protec-tive mother and father are of Hop…"

"Did Finn do something to Hop?"

"Finn wouldn't take orders from him. I remember that much."

"*We* didn't take orders from Hop very well either."

The edge of Isobel's lips quirked upwards. "We don't take orders from *anyone* very well."

Lotario touched his glass to hers. "Amen, sister."

"Julius and I interviewed every miner. A few of them admitted to chasing the children away from the mines at one time or another, but most couldn't tell one child from the next."

"Scruffy heathens."

"The miners or children?" she asked.

Lotario smiled like a cat, but didn't answer.

"No one admitted to giving Titus a ride, or seeing him in the past week."

"Someone is lying."

"Or they are telling the truth. I have to consider the possibility that my instincts are wrong—that Samuel *did* do something with the boy on his way home."

"But the bandages on Bebé. Samuel can only tie one knot."

"So says Doctor Bright, who is protective of Samuel. I think he views him as a son, or at the very least he feels responsible for him. Samuel may have tied those bandages. He learned one knot, perhaps someone took the time to teach him another."

"How do you account for the tracking dogs running in circles?"

"Maybe they're senile."

Lotario snorted. He took another sip. "I like your theory —that Titus hitched a ride on a wagon or horse."

The words sparked an idea. "A wagon..." She took a long swallow, and let the burn ignite her mind. "How many times did we hitch a ride on a wagon without the driver knowing?"

Lotario waggled his brows. "I was wondering when you'd think of that."

Isobel cocked a brow. "Really?"

"I am the smarter brother."

She gave a sharp laugh. "So what's my next move, *Mycroft?*"

Lotario looked extremely pleased with himself. "Track down everyone on holiday in Calistoga, and lay your horse-whip on them."

"That's your fantasy," she quipped.

Lotario ignored the comment.

"Before I take such drastic measures, I'll stop by The Giant's Fortress. He wasn't at his homestead today." As children, she and Lotario had roamed the valley whenever their family stayed at the vineyard. The twins had dubbed a large Finnish hermit, *The Giant*. Mostly for his habit of chasing them off with axe or shotgun.

"You should take Jin with you."

Isobel stared into her glass. "There's a child missing. I'm fairly sure taking a child along to look for a possible child murderer is irresponsible."

"Oh, come now. She needs it, Bel."

Isobel looked up at the serious note in his voice. Her twin was rarely serious.

"Why do you say that?"

"Because if you don't, I think she'll take off for good."

"Riot and I can't keep her against her will. We wouldn't be any better than the people who put those scars on her."

"She's adrift. You need to anchor her."

As always, Lotario knew just how to make her see the light. Isobel swallowed his words, and let them sink deep inside her heart. "I will."

Isobel walked into her room at Bright Waters. It was cozy rather than small. Moonlight streamed through the open window, along with a refreshing breeze. The bed was empty. Dread clutched her throat for a moment before she squashed it. An open window didn't mean Jin had left.

She poked her head outside, and searched the ground. And then the trees. A foot dangled from an oak branch. Isobel changed into simple shirt and trousers, and plucked an apple from a bowl. She tucked it in her shirt, and climbed over the sill. She held onto the beam jutting from the adobe, then dropped, landing softy on the ground.

Jin lay on an oak branch, staring up at the sky. Without a word, Isobel climbed up the tree, and put her back to the trunk. She followed the girl's gaze. Stars. Too many to count. Too vast for a logical mind. It made her dizzy to contemplate.

Isobel shook away her unease, and took comfort in the simple things. An apple. She sank her teeth into it with a crunch.

Jin glared at her.

"I'm hungry," Isobel said. "Did you eat today?"

"Mrs. Amsel kept trying to stuff food in me."

"Whatever my mother did, I'm sorry."

Jin raised herself on her elbows. "We went for a walk."

"And?"

Jin didn't answer.

"Lotario said you stormed out."

"Mrs. Amsel did nothing."

"That's shocking," Isobel muttered. She ate the apple, core and all, and tossed the stem onto the ground. She was on the verge of leaving when Jin spoke.

"Your parents are nice."

"You may be the first person to ever utter those words about my mother."

Jin did not reply.

"So what happened?" Isobel asked.

Jin lifted a shoulder. "They are *too* nice."

Isobel tilted her head, trying to unravel the girl. "Would you rather they scream at you?"

Jin sat up, nostrils flaring. "Yes," she bit out. "They are being nice because they feel sorry for me." She gestured violently at her face.

Isobel held up her hand. "That could be. *Or,*" she paused, but the words got stuck. "By God, I'm about to defend my mother." Isobel raked her fingers through her hair.

"You do not usually?"

"No."

Isobel scooted closer, and let her bare feet dangle over empty air. "My father would be kind to the devil himself, but my mother could try a saint. Lotario and I don't get on with my mother very well."

"They were very nice to Lotario today."

"*Exactly*. For what's it's worth, Ari and I are suspicious, too, but..." Isobel rubbed the back of her neck. "They've lost children. My sister died, and they lost a granddaughter, too. One of my brothers is missing. Another was... He died earlier this year. And they believed I had been killed. I think my mother is trying to change—but maybe she's just angling for something."

Jin pondered her words. "Loss can turn to bitterness. I did not think it could turn into kindness."

"Mei is a good example of that," Isobel said.

Jin looked down at her hands.

"You can still go, Jin. If you want to." Her voice was rough.

"Do you want me to go?"

"No," Isobel said truthfully. "But I want what's best for you."

"I will miss her."

Isobel nodded.

"But I would miss you, too."

"You'd get over me," Isobel said lightly.

Jin shook her head. "I *still* miss my parents."

Isobel didn't know what to say. She searched for some comforting words, but there weren't any. "Is that why you ran off after the walk with my mother? You remembered what it was like to have a family?"

Jin didn't answer, not straightaway. Isobel let her be, until the faintest of whispers rasped into the night. "My mother smelled like jasmine and honey." Jin shook herself, visibly hardening. Her hand went to the opposite arm. Nails dug into flesh. Physical pain was far simpler than an empty heart.

Isobel took Jin's hand. "My mother smells like fire and brimstone."

Despite herself, Jin snorted, but it was clipped short by a choking sound. The brief crack in emotion was quickly filled with anger. "I've ruined everything again!"

"What do you mean by that? *Again*?"

Jin pressed her lips together. There was no breaking that stubborn wall. The silence only deepened, but the girl didn't snatch her hand away. Progress, Isobel thought. She knew Jin didn't like being backed into corners—physically or conversationally. So Isobel let the subject die, and changed tack.

"Riot isn't going to kill you. And we're not tossing you into the street for hitting Sarah. Sometimes sisters and brothers fight. I terrorized my older brothers all the time, and my parents kept me."

Jin pulled away. "And what happens when you have a child? You will toss me to the gutter because I'm not the same as you. I am Chinese."

"A captain does not abandon her crew. And I don't take kindly to mutineers. And..." Isobel shifted. "I very likely can't have children of my own, so I picked the ones I wanted. You are one of them. What's more binding—choosing a child, or being saddled with an accident?"

Jin looked up in surprise. "Why can't you have children?"

Isobel looked to the stars, wishing they held answers. "It doesn't matter," she said after a while. "And I'm happy for it. I've always preferred grown cats over kittens. They're more temperamental."

Words were on the tip of Jin's tongue, but they never made it past her lips. The girl swallowed them back down, and the two sat in silence.

"Would you like to come with me tomorrow? To look for the missing boy?"

Jin nodded.

"Good. You found that loose floorboard. I need a pair of sharp eyes with me. And speaking of sharp eyes—how is Riot?"

Jin considered her question. "Besides angry with me?"

"He's not angry. Trust me."

"You were not there."

"Exactly. Tell me how he is."

"Since we returned to Ravenwood Manor we have not seen much of him. He's always busy. And I don't think he is sleeping very well."

Isobel nodded. She wanted to scream at injustice. But then she was not entirely without blame.

Isobel climbed down, and she watched as Jin fell backwards off the branch, caught her legs, and swung, landing on her feet in a neat drop.

"What did you mean about the doctor? That he smiles too much?"

Jin lifted a shoulder. "I do not trust men who smile."

And once again, Isobel was reminded of Noh masks. Creating illusion with a trick of the light.

26

HOLM'S PLACE

HOLM'S PLACE SAT AT A FORK IN THE ROAD—A QUAINT cabin miles from another soul. Solitude. Isobel stopped to appreciate the homestead. It reminded her of a ship at sea. But this one was surrounded by trees.

Jin poked her head around Isobel's arm. "Who would want to live there?"

"I would," Isobel said.

"Wouldn't you grow bored?" Julius asked.

"It would take at least a week." Isobel clucked her horse forward. "Doctor, you said you taught Samuel how to tie a bow. Is he capable of learning another knot?"

"I've never seen him tie anything else."

"But you don't know for sure?"

"It's possible," Julius conceded.

They followed a rhythmic chopping noise coming from around the corner of a barn. A large man stood cutting wood. His axe rose and fell, splitting logs with one powerful sweep. A log was split in two, pieces tumbled to the ground, and another set in place. One after another. Precision and power. As they rode closer, the man stopped and looked up. He was large, blond, and had quiet eyes.

"Hello there," Isobel called.

The man raised his axe in what she hoped was a greeting. Isobel had never formally met The Giant, but he had chased her off his property plenty of times.

Isobel dismounted, and handed her reins to Jin. "Ride and get help if anything should happen," she whispered.

"I don't know how to ride."

Isobel stared at her, then reached up and pulled the child off the saddle. She set her on the ground. "Then run for help. For now, hold the horse."

Jin looked at the reins in her hands. "What if the horse bites me?"

"Be nice to her and she won't bite." Isobel gave the horse a friendly pat.

"What is this?" the big man growled. "Has the doctor come to take me away?"

"Hardly, Karl," Julius called back. "You are likely the sanest man here."

Karl laughed heartily, and the two men shook hands.

"This is my associate, Isobel Amsel."

Karl's grip staggered Isobel. "It's a lovely piece of land here," she said. It was surreal, standing in front of The Giant as an adult on equal footing.

"It's my kingdom. A man doesn't need much."

"Man or woman," Isobel said.

"You look familiar. Amsel…" Karl tasted the name. "I have heard that name. Even out here."

"My parents owned a vineyard not far from here."

"Ah, yes." He slapped his thigh. His Levis were threadbare and straining over muscle. "You are the maker of trouble."

"I didn't realize I had left such an impression," she said. It was difficult being a detective when everyone remembered you as a little girl.

Karl chortled. "You left a world of aggravation."

"I'm told I'm still aggravating."

Another laugh. "Is she, Doctor?"

"Certainly intriguing."

Karl grunted. "She used to be a terror."

"It must have been my brother."

Karl waggled his finger at her. "It was you. Coffee? And what about that one?" He pointed to Jin.

Isobel motioned Jin over, and made introductions. Then she showed her how to hitch the horses to a post, and they walked inside Karl's cabin. The cabin's decor was sparse, its space cluttered with necessities. Every item earned its place.

When they were settled at the table, Karl poured coffee. Jin sniffed at her tin cup, wrinkled her nose, and politely set it back down.

Karl busied himself with his pipe. "What brings you here? I hope it is not to move my things around, and make me think I go crazy."

"We only did that because you kept chasing us out of places," Isobel said.

"Places children had no business going," Karl huffed.

"Speaking of children. Do you know the Sheel boys?" she asked.

Karl made a face. "Gah."

"I'll take that as a yes."

"The youngest, John, is a *kakara*."

At their puzzled glances, Karl explained. "A erm…" He tapped the table, searching for the word. "Bad child. Unruly."

Isobel took a sip of coffee. It was strong, and as bold as

the man across from her. "And the older boy?"

Karl tilted his hand. "He followed. Yes. Like your brother."

"Did the Sheel boys ever bother you?"

"You are bothering me now." It was said harshly, with the same voice he used to holler at Isobel when she was younger, but a smile cracked the tension. "Same as you. I chase them out of places."

"Have you seen them recently?" Isobel asked.

"I saw the smaller boy. On Wednesday, I think. He was walking down the road, and waved."

"Was his brother, John, with him?"

Karl shook his head. "Not that I saw."

"Did he seem frightened?"

Karl sucked on his pipe for a moment. "His nose was bloody, but he seemed fine. He was far away, though. I was heading out to hunt along the Palisades Trail."

"Which way was he walking?"

"Towards the mine."

"Do you have a map of the area?"

Karl did not, but he produced a rough sketch. His homestead sat in the crook of a Y. To the left, the Oat Hill Mine Road diverged into the Palisades, and to the right, it headed towards the mine and Aetna Springs, a popular resort. That left seven miles of wilderness.

"We found John's camp here." She placed her finger on a spot along the Oat Hill Mine Road. "Where did you chase the boys from?"

"There are old prospecting mines here." Karl sketched them out.

"I do recall."

"And it's a good thing I chase children away. The younger ones follow the older ones."

"Where was Gabriella Banker found?"

Karl sniffed. "Sad. Very sad." He marked a spot on the map. It was closer to his homestead than the mines, and not far from where she had found John. "It was here, at this one. But that little girl wasn't a follower."

"She wasn't?"

"No. She put those boys to shame. They were like her shadow."

"What were the children doing up there?"

"I don't know. Likely same as you. Why did you go as a child?"

Isobel felt her cheeks warm. "I was looking for buried treasure."

"Did you ever find your treasure?" Julius asked.

"I'm still looking."

"I'll add 'delusional' to my notes."

DEEP IN THOUGHT, ISOBEL STOOD IN THE FORK OF THE ROAD. Her horse nuzzled her hand, and she shifted the reins to scratch his forehead.

"Now Karl can prove that Samuel didn't harm Titus," Julius said with relief. "Titus was alone, *with* the bloody nose, walking on this road."

Isobel nodded.

"Should we get the Sheriff?" Julius asked.

"Maybe Mr. Karl mistook Titus for John," said Jin.

"That is precisely what Nash will argue," Isobel said.

"But Karl said it was the smaller boy," Julius said.

"To Karl, everyone is small," Isobel pointed out.

"All the same, we have to let the sheriff know." Julius put his foot in the stirrup.

"Wait a moment, Doctor." Isobel looked down the lonely stretch of road, and the seven miles that lay between there and the mines. She had to narrow it down. "If we fetch Nash it will cost us another day. Time Titus Sheel doesn't have."

"What are you suggesting?"

"You can get Nash while Jin and I go on."

"But I'm responsible for you."

"I'll claim I held you at gunpoint."

Julius shook his head. "I'll ask Karl to go."

Isobel gave a slight nod.

NATURE AND TIME WORKED HAND IN HAND. A SETTLEMENT was slowly being pulled down by bramble. A sapling sprouted from the ruins, and rusted wagon wheels and ribs poked from the grass like bones. The hills and valley were littered with old prospecting camps. Isobel and Lotario had explored them all as children. But ruins were all the same— abandoned dreams and wasted lives.

"Why are we here?" Jin asked.

"A suspicion." The carcass of a burnt cabin remained.

Jin slid off the saddle. "What is your suspicion?"

Isobel didn't answer. She handed the reins to Jin, and made her way around back, searching the ground. A mark made her heart leap. And a crushed carpet of chaparral quickened her steps. Isobel fought her way through the thorny bushes to a hole in the ground. Two planks had been pulled away, and tossed into the bramble.

With a trembling hand, she struck a match. The flame wavered, and she let it fall. For a brief moment, it touched on a pale face.

"Doctor!" Isobel called. "Titus! Can you hear me?"

No answer.

"Help me with these boards," she said to Jin. But the girl didn't move. Sao Jin stood frozen, staring into the black slice between boards. She shook from head to toe. Isobel gripped her shoulders, and Jin jerked, murder in her eyes. Slowly, Isobel backed her up a step, then another. "Stay back," she said softly.

Julius came crashing through the bramble.

"Titus is down there," Isobel explained.

"Is he alive?" Julius asked, bending to help.

"I don't know."

When the final plank was pulled away, they were left with a black square ringed by rotting timber and crumbling stone.

Julius frowned at the hole. "You won't fit."

"You can't go down there," Jin blurted out.

Isobel bent to unlace her boots. "I'll be fine, Jin. I need you to fetch the lead ropes from the horses. Have the doctor help you tie them together."

Jin tugged on her shirt, trying to drag her away. "Don't go down there."

"Jin. Get the ropes. Now."

The girl stumbled back, and fled from the hole in the ground.

Isobel took a calming breath. She tried not to focus on the darkness, or on what she might find at the bottom. Carefully, she lowered herself into the well.

Darkness closed around her. Stone pressed on her from all sides, slick with moisture. She moved slowly, testing each foothold as she shimmied her way down. A sharp scent mingled with damp earth. Blood.

"Titus?" she called again. Her voice bounced alarmingly.

Dirt trickled on her head, and something slithered in the dark. Isobel stopped, hands and feet braced on opposite sides of the well. She waited for a warning rattle. One breath, two, and nothing.

Isobel felt like she was drowning in darkness. Her throat clutched with the press of earth. "Damn Sheriff Nash," she hissed. Anger burned away fear. Every shift of hand and foot ticked another wasted second. Her anger grew. At Sheriff Nash, at the boy's parents, but mostly at herself.

The well opened, and she nearly lost her footing. The darkness was absolute, save for a distant square of light far overhead. Bracing herself against either side of the wall, she took out match and candle. Isobel had learned early on to never be without a light source.

Warmth illuminated the tight space. She directed the flame towards the ground. Titus Sheel lay at the bottom of the well, his leg bent at an excruciating angle. She stuck her candle in a crevice. Careful not to land on him, she gingerly stepped between his body and the rock wall, and pressed fingers against the side of his neck. A thready beat whispered against her fingertips. He felt like a stove.

"He's alive!" she called. "Barely."

She shrugged off her coat, and wrapped it around the boy. His head was matted with blood. "Stay with me, Titus. I'll get you out of here." And to the slice of light above. "I need water."

Shortly, a canteen was tossed down. She dribbled water onto his lips. Titus swallowed.

"We're working on the ropes," Julius called down.

"Is there something I can use to fashion a splint?"

The head vanished from above. Isobel ran the candle over Titus's face. His left eye and cheek were bruised. Blood stained the front of his shirt. One of his fingers was broken, wooden splinters were buried under his nails.

As Isobel searched the boy's pockets and person, she tried not to look at the innocent face. Tried not to think of the days he had spent here, screaming his voice hoarse. Not yet. Not here.

Steeling herself, she turned to his broken leg and carefully palpated it. Bone grated on bone. Titus moaned.

"I'll drop the things," Julius said.

Isobel straightened. "Go ahead." She caught one stick, and then another, and a leather belt from the saddlebags.

"Injuries?" Julius called down.

"Broken leg. Head wound. Broken fingers. Maybe ribs. And a fever. I don't know if he'll survive being moved."

"He'll die if you don't."

The words fell like a rock into the well, and Isobel felt the full force of them. She stared down at the dying boy. The doctor was right. But did she trust Julius Bright? Would he rather Titus Sheel died down here?

Isobel gazed at the distant light. A chill passed through her bones. It felt like a grave. What would become of Jin? With that thought, Isobel shook herself.

"I need to straighten out his leg. Any advice, Doctor?" Her voice echoed in the grave, and the seconds ticked by without answer.

A head appeared overhead. "What was that?" Julius asked.

Relief rushed through her veins. She repeated herself.

"Gently pull on the bone below the fracture, and hold the top steady. It's easier with two people."

"You definitely won't fit down here."

Isobel laid out the sticks and belt along Titus's leg. She gripped his shin, hands on either side of the break. She took a breath, and pulled. The bones shifted, and scraped as the limb straightened. Titus groaned, and she stopped. The leg wasn't perfect, but it would do for now. Isobel pushed the branches firmly against either side of his leg, held them in place with one hand, and wrapped the belt with her other, pulling it tight with her teeth.

Isobel checked his pulse again. Still thready. She gazed up at the square of light far above. A snake slithered out of a crevice near her candle's flame. It was a harmless black snake, but there'd be others.

"There's an issue with the rope," Julius bellowed. "The closest tree trunk is ten feet away, and I don't trust the bushes to support you. I could brace myself—"

"Never mind the rope," Isobel quickly said. She was not about to place her life and Titus's in the hands of a man she didn't fully trust. What better way to get rid of the both of them.

"I'll get help then, and a longer rope," Julius called.

Could Titus wait until dark?

"I don't think he'll survive that long," she called up. "I need your suspenders, Doctor."

"You can't possibly carry him up."

"Waiting is not an option," she said.

"You could both fall."

"Or we could both survive, and I could trip over a root topside and crack my head open."

She heard a faint mumble, and then, "Watch your head."

Isobel caught his suspenders. She tied them around Titus's wrists, and crouched low to put his arms around her neck. Testing his weight, she used her coat to fashion a kind of sling, supporting his rear.

The boy was older than his brother, but half the size. A

delicate boy with hardly any weight on him. She lifted her arms, and hopped, testing her crude support. Hardly a shift.

She glanced at the candle sputtering in the dark. There was no way to carry it. She'd have to climb blind. Isobel took a breath, braced one leg, and then the other, and searched for her first handhold. She had to pinch each hold on the slick rock. Slowly, she moved upwards. One foot, then the other, pausing to blindly search the darkness with her hand. For long minutes there was only the sound of Titus's labored breathing in her ear. Her arms began to ache from the extra weight.

A sharp hiss, the sinking of teeth, and Isobel braced herself like a cat over a sink. "God dammit," she growled.

"What happened?" Julius yelled down.

"Snake."

"Rattler?"

Had there been a hint of hope in his question, or had she imagined it? Isobel swallowed. "Let's hope not." The little bastard was still clamped onto her heel. It released, and struck again. Isobel shook her leg towards the stones. But it only tightened the snake's jaws. She cursed again, and kept moving.

The moment light touched her head, Julius reached for her. But her foot was slick with blood. She slipped. Isobel flailed for a handhold. She caught herself on a wooden support, but the wood turned to mush in her hand. For a moment she was falling, and then was jerked to a stop.

The load on her back was being pulled upwards. Julius grunted. He had Titus by the makeshift harness. Braced over the opening, he fought to keep them both from falling.

Isobel stretched out her hands and feet, bracing on all sides of the well. With the doctor's help, she climbed the last few feet.

She crawled onto the discarded well planks. Shaking and drenched in sweat, she untied Titus. Julius lifted the boy from her back.

Isobel rolled onto her back and stared at the darkening sky.

Jin's face hovered over her own, as pale and grave as the hole Isobel had just climbed from. Isobel gently gripped the back of Jin's neck, and gave a reassuring squeeze.

Jin pulled her into a sitting position, and Isobel checked her foot. A dead black snake was latched onto her heel. She pried its teeth free and tossed it down the hole. A dozen little red pinpricks dotted her skin.

Julius frowned down at Titus as he checked his pulse.

"Is he alive?" she asked.

"For now."

"I don't suppose you have some restorative brandy?"

"That won't help him," Julius said.

"I meant for me."

Julius met her eyes. "I'm sorry. I don't."

"Where's Watson when you need him," she muttered.

"At home. Probably sleeping in front of the stove," Jin said.

"Not that one."

"Who then?"

"I see I'll have to introduce you to the Great Detective. Come on. We need to get Titus to Bright Waters."

When Julius was in the saddle, she lifted Titus up to him. "You're right, Miss Amsel," the doctor said. "He wouldn't have lasted until nightfall."

"He's not out of danger yet."

TIRED AND RAGGED, ISOBEL SAT OUTSIDE TITUS SHEEL'S ward room with Jin. The girl hadn't said much, but then she rarely did when she wasn't cussing up a storm. Doctor Bright and a nurse were inside with the boy.

"I am sorry I froze," Jin said. The sudden words jerked Isobel out of her daze.

"You did fine, Jin."

The girl shook her head. "I should have climbed down there. Not you."

Isobel gave her arm a squeeze. "I wouldn't have let you go down there. And before you start swearing at me, I wouldn't have let Riot climb down either."

"I do not think you are his captain."

Isobel chuckled. "No, I'm not. But his size would have made a difference."

"He is not very large for a man."

"The well wasn't large either."

Jin dug around her pocket, and pulled out a length of twine. "I do not know if this matters, but I found this tied to a bush in the thicket near the edge of the well. It was stuffed under the branches." Isobel noticed the scratches on Jin's hand for the first time. Not the deliberate nail marks that usually marred her skin, but paper thin, random ones made by thorns.

Isobel studied the length of twine. It was covered in dirt. One end had been cut by a sharp knife. "Do you remember the knot?"

"I don't know the name." Jin picked up one end, and after a few attempts, she managed to reproduce the knot. A bowline hitch.

"You are one of the brightest people I know, Jin." Isobel tucked the length of twine away. "This is very important."

"What does it mean?" Jin asked.

A commotion at the end of the corridor brought her around. The Sheels had arrived with Sheriff Nash. Charles Sheel was slick, and rich, and fuming. He had the look of a self-made man. Hard work and grit had earned him his place in the world. He was of average height, but as strapping as a man half his age.

Isobel climbed to her feet. "Let's see how things play out," she whispered to the girl at her side.

"You found my boy?" Mr. Sheel asked.

Isobel nodded. "He was in a dried-up well."

"Is he—" Mrs. Sheel began, but no parent could finish that sentence.

John braced himself, and Mr. Sheel finished for his wife. "Is Titus alive?"

"He is alive," Isobel said, motioning to the door. "Doctor Bright is with him."

Mrs. Sheel slumped against her husband. And John closed his eyes, nostrils flaring. When he opened them, his bright blue eyes were misty.

Mr. Sheel placed a firm hand on his younger son's shoulder. "Stay here, John."

"I want to see him."

"Not yet."

Mr. Sheel knocked on the door.

A nurse poked her head outside, and gave the family a sympathetic smile. "One moment."

Not long after, Julius stepped outside.

"I want to see my son," Mrs. Sheel said.

"You can, but don't disturb him," Julius said. "He's not out of danger."

Mrs. Sheel paled. She clutched her husband's hand for support. "What's wrong with him?"

"Fever," Julius said. "He has a fractured leg, cuts, bruises, and dehydration."

"You said he was in a well." Mr. Sheel looked to Isobel. "Why was he down there?"

"We don't know," Isobel said.

"He's currently incoherent," Julius said.

"Which well?" Sheriff Nash asked.

"I want to see my brother," John said.

"I don't want to crowd the room. Your parents first." Julius opened the door for them. Through the brief opening, Isobel glimpsed a pale child lost in blankets and bedding.

John turned away from the sight.

"You did everything you could," Julius said, patting John's shoulder. "Miss Amsel found him in time. Now all we can do is wait."

Sheriff Nash pulled Isobel to the side. "What well was he in?"

"The same one Gabriella Banker was found in," Isobel said.

"I personally nailed that shut," Nash growled.

"I don't doubt it," Isobel said. "Now that we've found him, you need to release Samuel."

"How do you know Samuel wasn't involved? He could have shoved the boy down there."

"Because Mr. Holm saw Titus walking towards the mines. Alone, with a bloody nose. Titus seemed cheerful and waved in greeting."

"That sighting might have been *before* Samuel chased those boys."

Isobel shook her head. "This fits with Samuel's story. I'll wager John gave his brother that bloody nose right before he shot Bebé."

"I'm not releasing Samuel until that boy tells me what

happened."

"Why are you so set on Samuel Lopez as a criminal?" Isobel asked.

"Why are you set on defending him?"

"Examine the facts, Sheriff Nash, and you'll come to the same conclusion."

Nash's jaw worked. "I thank you kindly for your assistance. I cannot deny that. But this is my town and my investigation."

Isobel swept her arm out in invitation, and stepped back.

Sheriff Nash ran a thumb along his jaw, and shook off her silent sarcasm. He focused on John. "Any idea why your brother would head out that way?"

"Titus likes snakes. There's a whole lot of them in that well."

"Did you boys remove those planks?"

John had his hands in his pockets. He nodded sullenly. "So the snakes could get in and out."

"John, it's all right if you want to change your story. Did you see Titus after the incident with the dog? After Samuel Lopez chased you both?" Isobel asked.

John shook his head. "I thought that man had him."

Mr. Sheel stepped out. "You can go in, John, but don't disturb your brother." Through the open door, Mrs. Sheel dabbed at her eyes.

"We'd like to thank you, Miss Amsel. And you, Sheriff. I've told those boys not to go near those old homesteads."

"I'll take some men out that way and fill that hole for good," Nash vowed.

Mr. Sheel nodded. "The boy is clumsy. He likely slipped down there."

Isobel looked into the room, to John Sheel's back, and his mother holding the hand of his fever-ridden brother.

27

THE DOOR

Isobel sat on the windowsill in her room, one leg
dangling over air. Smoke twined around her fingertips and
ash fell from the forgotten cigarette. Titus Sheel was alive,
for now. Questions buzzed between her ears. Facts slid into
place. And a single nagging detail robbed her of sleep: the
magnifying glass.

A soft whimper drew her gaze. Sao Jin lay on a cot by
Isobel's bed. The girl had avoided questions, reassurances,
and attempts at conversation. And now she was tangled in
her blankets. Jin was an entirely different kind of puzzle.

Isobel smashed her cigarette into an ashtray, and
brushed the ash off her trousers. She glanced at her empty
bed, but was too tired to drag herself over there. She closed
her eyes, only for a moment, or so she thought.

A scream jerked her awake. Disoriented, she started to
roll out of her bed, only it was open air. At the last moment,
she caught herself on the sill. Cursing her exhaustion, Isobel
pulled herself back into the room, and crouched, feeling the
reassuring rug under her toes. Confused, she searched for

the source of the scream. Had it been real? Or had she dreamt it?

A breeze stirred the curtains. She moved across the room on silent feet, and turned on the gas. The mantle caught and dim light filled the room. Jin's cot was empty.

Then she heard it—a small, panting breath.

Isobel looked under the bed. Jin was curled in a tight ball, her face buried against her knees.

"Jin, what happened?"

The girl didn't answer.

Isobel checked the room again. It was empty. Unless someone was hiding in the wardrobe. Ever thorough, she checked. There were no murderers lurking inside.

"Jin?" she asked again. She reached for the girl, and slowly dragged her out from under the bed. Jin's nightgown was drenched in sweat, and fresh scratches marred her cheeks.

Without warning, Jin wrapped trembling arms around Isobel's neck. Stunned, Isobel froze, unsure what to do. She was acutely aware of a bird-like heart fluttering against her own. Of how small she was. For all her fierceness, Jin was a child—frightened and fragile.

Isobel's first instinct was to hand the child over to a more qualified adult, even her own mother. But no one else was present. The girl's shaking body melted something in Isobel, and she returned the girl's fierce hug, holding her tightly.

When Jin's trembling lessened, Isobel untangled her arms and set her on the bed. She poured a glass of water from the pitcher, and turned to the little ball huddled under the bedding. She sat down on the edge. "Drink this."

At her firm order, Jin gulped down the water. As soon as the glass was drained, Jin returned to her fetal-like position. After a moment of hesitation, Isobel placed a soothing hand on her head. Jin's sleeve had fallen back, exposing fresh scratches and a myriad of scars. Purposeful, and very deliberate. Some were from cruel hands, and others clearly self-inflicted. Isobel's heart twisted.

"I've tried to be strong most my life, too," Isobel whispered. "But strength isn't what I thought it was. We all have our own demons. I have nightmares. So does Riot. Only they're not nightmares. They're memories. And those are the worst kinds of dreams." Isobel's words trailed into a painful rasp. She cleared her throat. "Sometimes it helps to talk."

Jin rolled away from her touch to face the wall. "You will not want me if I talk."

"I'll be the judge of that."

Silence. Long enough that Isobel started to wonder if Jin had fallen asleep. Then the worst kind of whisper broke that quiet. "I killed my parents." The words were torn from some dark place and forced into the light.

Isobel stifled a question, and waited.

"I was playing outside with my wooden duck. I saw men coming. *Boo how doy.* I should have run inside and locked the door, but one of them smiled and patted me on the head. I watched them walk into my father's shop. The men—" Jin cut off, nails digging into her arm.

Isobel reached over the girl, and took her hand. "*This* is what strength is. Saying those words stuck in your throat," she whispered.

"The men used hatchets," Jin gasped, nostrils flaring. "I hid. I did nothing!"

Hatchets. That word churned in Isobel's overactive mind. The implications sunk deep into her psyche, and burned a haunting image. The screams of the mother. The cries of the father. The smell of blood and terror, and a little girl clutching a wooden duck. Isobel took a shaky breath.

"I wager you weren't more than five years old."

Jin said nothing.

"Did you have a gun in your wooden duck?"

Jin sat up, eyes furious. "I should have thrown it at them! I should have closed the door and locked it! The men would not have killed my parents!"

There was no arguing with regret. So Isobel didn't try. When the fury of Jin's words had faded into the room, Isobel held up their intertwined hands. She pointed to the tattered bracelet on her wrist—the bracelet Jin had gifted her during the trial. It had given Isobel strength when she'd needed it most.

"I hope you don't mind, your bracelet was about to fall apart, so I added a bit of leather to reinforce it. We can't make it new again, but we can give it a second chance."

Jin stared at the beaded bracelet. And then a sob shook the girl, unleashing a flood of pain. As the choking tears kept coming, Isobel sat and stroked the child's hair until the storm passed.

When Jin was drained and limp, Isobel leaned closer. "I'm not going anywhere. Death will have to drag me kicking and screaming away from you. I swear it on the Pagan Lady."

Jin hugged Isobel's hand to her, and curled around it, holding on tight. After a time, her breathing evened, and she relaxed into merciful sleep. As the night deepened, Isobel stayed by Jin, and stared at the door. What was worse... blaming oneself or living with the knowledge that doors don't stop monsters?

That thought triggered another: that lone chair sitting

by the door in Titus Sheel's room... Isobel took a sharp breath, and shot out of the room.

Titus Sheel lay on a bed surrounded by pillows. A nighttime breeze sneaked through shutters. The door was cracked. A nurse dozed outside his room as the boy's chest rose and fell, shallow but steady. It was the veil between night and morning. The critical hours for the sick, and the desperate hour for murderers.

A shadow crept towards his window. Quiet. Careful. Cautious. The shadow paused beneath the shuttered window, and cocked an ear. A rustling of leaves, interrupted by a flap of wings. But no voices. The shadow edged forward, and pressed its eye to the crack between shutters. It took out a vial, and squeezed a few drops onto the hinges. Slowly, patiently, like the hunter it was, the shadow opened the shutter. Moonlight touched Titus Sheel's face.

Titus shifted. The nurse slept. And the shadow slipped inside. It crouched on the sill, gazing down at the prone boy. Carefully, it stepped onto the bed frame and lowered itself to the floor. It picked up a pillow from the bed, and pressed it over Titus Sheel's face. Silent, and deadly.

A lantern flared in the room. Isobel stepped from behind the wardrobe. She lunged towards the murderer, grabbed his wrist and snatched the pillow from his hand.

John Sheel screamed in pain.

"Let me go!" John begged.

Isobel pushed the large boy into a nearby chair. "So you can finish what you started, and kill your brother?"

Tears welled in his bright eyes. "I wasn't. I only wanted

to visit him." John sniffled, and wiped a sleeve across his freckled nose.

"I know what happened," she said.

"You're crazy. Nurse! Nurse!" John called frantically.

"She won't help you."

The boy shut his mouth.

"I knew you'd come. Tonight. You couldn't take the chance that your brother would recover."

"I don't know what you mean."

Isobel placed herself between the boys. Without taking her eyes from John, she placed a hand on Titus's chest. It continued to rise and fall. "Shall I tell you what happened?"

"You're just a stupid girl. You don't know what you're saying."

"Do you want to tell me yourself?"

John crossed his arms.

"Where to begin... I think this has been going on for some time, but for the sake of current events, I'll start with the most recent trigger. You had to share a birthday with your brother. You, the pride and joy of your father—how dare he leave before *your* real birthday."

"It's just a dumb birthday."

"But Titus was *so* excited about his magnifying glass. And all you got was an inferior rifle. What a sting. A great hunter like you with a peashooter that couldn't even kill a dog properly."

John curled his fists.

"You shot that dog on purpose. And Titus, your mother's favorite—sweet and gentle—tried to stop you." Isobel pointed to John's fading bruises from the resulting brawl.

"So what," John said. "I told you that already. It was a dumb dog. And our father taught us to fight it out like men. You wouldn't understand, but Sheriff Nash will."

"But during the fight, Titus dropped his magnifying glass. Then Samuel Lopez interrupted the fight, and you ran like a *coward*."

"I'm not a coward!" he screamed.

Titus stirred fitfully.

"Eventually you returned and picked up the magnifying glass. You knew your brother. You knew he'd help Samuel and Bebé." Isobel brought out the length of twine from her pocket. "You knew he'd be back, and he'd want his magnifying glass. But you were jealous of him. Of your mother's affection. Of your father's attention. You were upset that he got a better present than you, so you tied up his gift, dropped it down a well, and buried the twine. And when he came back, you told him that you'd dropped it down the well." She leaned forward, staring into his eyes, knowing she had the right of it with every word. "You used his treasure as a lure. And when Titus peered down that dark hole, you…" Isobel shoved her hands at the air. "…you pushed him. Just like you pushed Gabriella Banker."

"You don't know anything."

"What was it about her? Could she hunt better than you? Or were you angry that she could keep up?"

John smirked.

"Ah, no. Of course not." Isobel smiled. "It was because she and Titus ignored you. They got along, and you were cast aside."

"The fall didn't kill her, and she begged *me* to help," John said. There was no remorse. Only pride. "No one will believe you. You're just a crazy girl in a madhouse who attacked a child. It's your word against mine."

Isobel pointed to Titus. "And his."

"Titus is too yellow to say anything."

"You bully him. That's why he has a chair by his bedroom door. To keep you out."

John stood up. For a child he was solid and tall.

Isobel stood, too. There wasn't a hint of fear in the boy's eyes. "Do you bully your mother, too? Is that why she keeps her distance from you?"

"She's weak. Same as you. No one will care what you say."

"I know," Isobel said. "That's why I brought a witness. He's been sitting outside this whole time."

Doctor Bright stepped into the doorway—shocked, appalled, but mostly grieved.

John Sheel lunged at her with youthful speed and ferocity. For a moment, his hands locked around her throat. He squeezed. There was glee in his eyes, and power. It shocked her.

The boy was yanked backwards, his hands clawing at her. Julius Bright had the boy by his collar. He swept his leg, and sent John face first to the floor.

"Don't you dare get up," Julius warned.

John wiped the blood from his lip, and stared defiantly back at the towering doctor.

"I think you should come with me now," Julius said softly.

28

LOVE BLINDS

"WHAT'S THE MEANING OF THIS?" CHARLES SHEEL AND HIS wife stood in front of a doorway to a padded room. They gazed through the slat in the door. A single window let in a beam of light, shining on a boy in a chair. His lips were firm, and his arms crossed.

"Why is my son in there?" Mr. Sheel asked.

Sheriff Nash squared his shoulders. Isobel and the doctor had summoned him first. "I had to put him somewhere secure, until I can transfer him to a cell."

Mr. Sheel stiffened with outrage. "What on earth?"

Nash held up his hands. "Hear me out. There have been some... developments."

Mr. Sheel glanced at Doctor Bright and Isobel. His jaw worked slightly. "What happened?"

Nash cleared his throat. "Your son was erm... That is John tried to kill Titus last night. Early this morning."

Mr. Sheel's fists curled, and his wife placed a handkerchief over her lips.

"I did not!" John shouted from inside the room. "I told you, I only wanted to see my brother!"

"These are serious accusations, Sheriff. I'll take my son's word over some half-cocked theory. I want him out of there. *Now*." The father wrenched opened the door, and John walked out.

"It's not a theory, Mr. Sheel." Isobel said. "John sneaked into Titus's room last night, and placed a pillow over his mouth. The doctor and I were there, and saw him do it."

Mr. Sheel laughed. "Some playfulness between brothers. That's all." He patted his son's back.

"John confessed to pushing Titus into the well. And to doing the same to Gabriella Banker," Isobel said the words without emotion. Each word a blow, one after another. But both parents only shook their heads.

"I can confirm every word," Julius said.

"Impossible. He was distressed. Isn't that right, son?"

"It is, Father. They misheard me is all. I said I tried to *help*. That I once *pretended* to push Titus in. But it was only a game."

Mr. Sheel nodded. "There you have it."

Nash held up a small, hinged pocket mirror. "We found this in his pocket. It was Gabriella's. It has her initials on it."

"She gave it to me," John said.

"That girl fell down the well. It was an accident," Mr. Sheel said. "And you didn't fill that death trap in. Your incompetence nearly killed my boy, Nash."

Nash's fingers tightened around the mirror.

Isobel looked to the mother. "Mrs. Sheel. How did you get those bruises around your neck?"

"I don't remember," she said with a shaky breath.

John smiled at his mother. "The doctor shoved me to the ground."

"Because you attacked Miss Amsel," Julius said.

"That woman was scaring me. She's crazy."

Isobel ignored the boy. "Mrs. Sheel," she said softly. "Titus is in danger. *Tell* Sheriff Nash the truth. How did you get those bruises?"

"I gave them to her," Mr. Sheel said quickly. "It's my right as her husband. It's not against the law for me to discipline my wife."

Isobel stifled a growl.

Mrs. Sheel stayed silent.

"Titus will be able to clear up this accusation," Mr. Sheel said. "Meanwhile, I want you out of here." He pointed at Isobel. "You're not getting a dime out of us. Not after this… After these *lies*."

John turned slightly, so Isobel was the only one who could see the small smile on his face. Every fiber of her body bristled with rage. Julius placed a hand on her shoulder and drew her a step back.

"I think that's best, Miss Amsel," Sheriff Nash said. "Titus will clear things up when he wakes."

"I should check on him," Julius said and turned to leave, but Mr. Sheel was shaking his head.

"No, I don't want you near my son either. We'll take him home with us, and get a real doctor."

Heels clicked down the hallway. A nurse in a blue dress hurried their way. "Doctor Bright. I was on my way to find you." She smiled at the Sheels. "Your son is awake." She beamed. But the hallway was silent. And her smile fell.

Julius cleared his throat.

But Nash beat him to it. "I'll talk with him."

"And me," Mr. Sheel said.

Julius shook his head. "I don't recommend upsetting Titus. It would be best if the sheriff spoke with him first."

"He's *my* son, Doctor. I'll speak with him," Mr. Sheel said.

"Sheriff," Julius implored.

Nash shook his head. He gripped John's shoulder, and they followed after Mr. Sheel towards Titus's room.

Isobel fell in step beside Mrs. Sheel. "You have to tell him," she hissed.

"John is my son," Mrs. Sheel said faintly.

"He tried to *kill* Titus."

"I don't believe it. It was a mistake to hire you." Mrs. Sheel quickened her pace. And Isobel followed, feeling helpless.

The parents went inside. Nash ordered John to wait with the doctor and Isobel, then he too stepped into the room. Grimly, Isobel watched and listened, and was not at all surprised.

"Titus." Mrs. Sheel sat on the bed, and hugged her son. He was pale and weak, but recovering. The young were resilient.

The boy hugged his mother back, taking refuge in her arms.

"Father," Titus said, when he pulled away from his mother. His father nodded, but didn't reach out to his older son.

"Titus, I'm Sheriff Nash. We've met before."

"Yes, sir."

"I'd like you to tell me what happened," Nash said in a deep, gentle voice.

"There's a detective who claims your brother pushed you into that well. But that couldn't…"

"*Mr. Sheel*," Nash cut in. "Let Titus tell the story."

Mr. Sheel ignored the Sheriff. "It couldn't be the truth, now could it, son?"

The boy stared at his father. He seemed to shrink, and pale even further. He looked like a ghost.

"Surely it was an accident," Mrs. Sheel said. There was a note of begging in her voice.

Silence. And then with a faint, wavering voice he sealed his fate. "I slipped."

John Sheel looked up at Isobel, and smiled.

———————

"THAT LITTLE..." ISOBEL FUMED. BUT WORDS FAILED HER. There wasn't a fitting word for that boy. John Sheel was a murderer. After the Sheel's had left with their sons, Nash and Isobel had joined Julius in his office.

And now Isobel paced like a caged tiger.

"That child is a psychopath," Julius stated.

Sheriff Nash turned his Stetson over in his hands. "Are you sure you heard correctly?" he asked. "You both were run ragged, working on very little sleep—"

"John tried to choke me," Isobel growled. She unbuttoned her collar, and brandished her bruises. "You need to throw that boy into a cell."

Nash held up a hand. "Look, Miss Amsel, I appreciate you finding Titus. I do. But I can't do anything else. Unless Titus backs up your story... my hands are tied."

"I heard every word, too," Julius said.

"And I don't doubt you."

"The facts are proof enough." Isobel began ticking off her fingers. "The knots. The magnifying glass. John Sheel tried to kill me with a reflection when I was climbing the Palisades. He nearly did me in."

"A boyish prank," Nash said. "That's how the courts will see it. Without Titus's testimony we don't have proof."

Isobel cursed under her breath. "John admitted to his crimes!" she fumed. Silence followed her sharp outburst.

"And now he's denied them. As did the victim."

Isobel took a breath.

"Sheriff, this boy is... deeply disturbed. He'll kill again. Or try to," Julius said.

"And I'll be watching him," Nash said. "Trust me. I'll sit down with Mr. Sheel, and have a good long talk with him. The father will watch his son. You can be sure of that."

"*How?*" Isobel growled. "After he murders someone else? After his brother dies in a convenient accident?"

Sheriff Nash was silent. But the firm set to his jaw made it clear his silence wasn't the thoughtful sort.

"Sheriff," Julius said, catching his attention. "When you speak with the Sheels, I'd strongly suggest that they allow me to treat the boy. I may be able to reach him."

"Before something bad happens? How can we risk that?" Isobel asked. "I'll press charges for his attack on me. With the doctor as a witness..." But even as she said it, she knew it would fail. She was a woman in an asylum convicted of a crime. And she'd be testifying against a wealthy man's son. Her only witness was another outcast of society: an alienist whose methods were frowned upon by his own peers.

"Miss Amsel," Sheriff Nash said. "I'll scare that boy senseless, and I'll watch him like a hawk. I promise you that."

"And when he's grown?" she asked.

"I don't have any answers. But maybe he'll straighten out."

"I'm not one for optimism when it comes to humankind."

Sheriff Nash dipped his head. "I can understand that. And for what it's worth—"

Isobel cut him off. "You're not the first man incapable of looking past my gender, Sheriff."

"Well, you don't make it easy. Just so. I'm sorry for doubting you."

"I'm not the one you should be apologizing to. There's an innocent man in your jail, and you have his blood on your knuckles."

Sheriff Nash turned his hat in his hands. "I'll make it right with Samuel. You have my word." He slipped on his Stetson and walked out of the office.

Isobel sat down on the settee. Her mind grappled with failure, with a situation so far removed from logic that she had no words. "The parents are fools," she muttered.

Julius lowered himself into his consultation chair. His smile was gone. The laugh lines had reversed, showing their true nature—the marks of a hard road.

"As disillusioned as they may be, John is still their son. And they love him. Would you let yourself believe it?" he asked. "That one of your daughters was a murderer?"

Isobel thought of Sao Jin. Of her violent streak, of the revolver she had pointed at the doctor. She met Julius's gaze, and when she spoke, her voice was hoarse. "I wouldn't have allowed it to get to this point."

"How?" Julius wasn't asking about John Sheel.

"I'll find a way," she vowed.

Julius leaned forward. "So will I. With that boy. I *have* to believe a child like that can be helped."

"And if he can't be?"

"It doesn't mean we won't try."

Both retreated into their own thoughts for a time. It was a comfortable sort of silence.

Eventually, Julius roused himself. "Did you know it was John who would be coming through that window?"

"I did."

"But how?"

"John was always one of my suspects."

"One?"

Isobel gave him an apologetic smile. "The last murderer I caught was a coroner. I was working on a case with him. And you did cross my mind, Doctor. Your protectiveness of Samuel and the cufflink under his floorboard were suspicious."

"You thought I harmed Titus?"

Isobel raised an eyebrow in a kind of shrug. "Trust doesn't come easily to me. At the very least, I thought you might have helped Samuel cover up a crime."

Julius folded his hands over his waistcoat. But he wasn't upset, only thoughtful. "I can understand why you'd think that. But why did you suspect John?"

"Why not?" she countered.

"Most wouldn't suspect a child. I certainly didn't."

"I'm not most." Isobel twitched her lips in a quick smile. "I don't shy away from uncomfortable truth and call it coincidence. John's story never set well with me. There were inconsistencies at every corner. When we found him he claimed he had been paralyzed with terror. Instead of running home to tell someone about his brother, he shot a quail and cooked it. The ashes in the fire were still hot."

"Some fall back on the simple things when faced with tragedy."

Isobel acknowledged the observation with a nod. "It wasn't one thing, but a culmination of clues that became hard to ignore." She counted off her fingers. "The type of knot used on the twine discounted Samuel, and told me that whoever was aiming that glass at my face was also present at the well. Jin found a length of twine tied to one of the bushes. The two pieces of twine matched. Hunters use lures all the time to attract prey. And what boy wouldn't stand at the edge of the well to look for a cherished gift?"

Another finger ticked. "The birthday celebration. When I questioned John it was clear he was angry at having to share a birthday party with his older brother. And on the wrong day, no less. Not only that, John is a hunter. He considers himself equal to Daniel Boone and Wild Bill, and he was gifted a peashooter. That would wound anyone's fragile ego. By themselves, these don't make a murderer, but John has a cruel streak. Fighting with a brother is one thing, but fighting with a brother who is trying to stop you from shooting someone's dog is quite another."

"And the mother's distance," Julius pointed out.

Isobel nodded. "Mrs. Sheel was stiff with her younger son. Hesitant. He didn't want her comfort. When I questioned her about the bruises on her neck, she became defensive. Now I know she was protecting her son despite his abuse of her."

"Why did you pause in the Sheel's sitting room. You looked at their family bible."

"John claimed his mother read to them every day from the bible. But he said that she never started at the beginning —the Old Testament. Most mothers don't read that part to their children. It's too brutal. Too graphic. When I looked, the bookmark was buried in the New Testament, but the pages were open to Genesis."

"And that is significant how?"

"Cain murders his brother Abel. Joseph is thrown down a well by his jealous brothers."

"I didn't take you for a churchgoer, Miss Amsel."

Isobel smiled. "I'm not. But that doesn't mean I don't read. Beheadings, floggings, a woman driving a tent peg through a man's head, and prostitutes saving the day. It's like an ancient penny dreadful."

"You think John read it?"

"The exciting bits," she said. "What child hasn't? Given John's cruel streak, it isn't a stretch to imagine he'd be drawn to such stories. And maybe get a few ideas of his own. There was also Gabriella Banker. Both boys knew her. They explored together. And from what Mr. Holm said, she outdid them. A boy's ego will generally be hurt when a girl outperforms him. I left a string of fuming boys behind me as a little girl. But the final straw was the chair in Titus's room."

"What of it?"

"It wasn't by his desk. It was by his door. There were deep gouges in the floor that matched the chair's legs. Titus used it to jam the door shut. To protect himself."

"Titus might have done that to keep his father out."

"He might have, but in this case, Mr. Sheel wasn't anywhere near the boys. My father and Hop confirmed that. If it hadn't been for the strange circumstance of the magnifying glass, I might have suspected a random traveler or a miner. But it was too convenient. And it didn't explain the rest. The only piece that fit into the jumble of clues was John. But I barely realized it in time. And when I did I knew he'd be back to make sure Titus never uttered a word."

"Impressive."

Isobel felt her cheeks warm. "Thank you."

Julius cleared his throat. "If I recall my Sunday School correctly, Joseph's brothers lowered him into a well and sold him into slavery. Out of envy."

Isobel frowned at the rug. "Envy has a powerful bite. Joseph's brothers eventually felt remorse, but I'm afraid John Sheel will never feel that."

"We can hope," Julius said.

"Never a strong suit of mine."

"And yet you hold out hope for Sao Jin."

Isobel said nothing.

"May I ask, Miss Amsel…"

"Probably not."

He harrumphed, and she arched an impatient brow for him to continue.

"Why are you adopting those girls? Have you considered the implications?"

Isobel was quiet for a time. It was a good question. A powerful one. And she didn't take it lightly. "I probably haven't," she admitted. "I can't, because life is as unpredictable as the sea. Riot and I will try to keep our heads above water, and we'll help Jin and Sarah do the same until they're able to strike out on their own. I think that's all any parent can do. The rest will be up to them."

Julius pondered her words. "Do you know, Miss Amsel, you may be the sanest person I've ever met."

"Insults are beneath you, Doctor. But given what you just said, I hope these past days absolve me from future talking sessions."

Julius only laughed.

"I thought not." Isobel climbed to her feet. She felt old and tired. And fragile. "Now if you'll excuse me, I'm going to fall into my bed."

"I believe I'll do that very same thing. Sleep well, Miss Amsel. You did everything you could."

The words stuck with her. Despite everything, she felt a failure. And with every step that feeling intensified. Her mood spiraled into a hole as dark as the well she'd pulled Titus from.

29

THE TROUBLE WITH RINGS

RIOT

A throat cleared. "So."

Riot glanced up from his desk. Tim stood in the door-way, rocking back and forth on his heels. "Badge number checks out." But the grin on the old man's face said otherwise.

"But?"

"Issued in 1897 to an Officer Clemens, who went to a saloon to celebrate his new job. He was promptly killed in a drunken brawl. Him being one of the drunks. His badge was stolen somewhere between the saloon and the grave."

"Where it appears on a man three years later. Any idea who the other fellow involved in the fight was?" Riot asked.

"It was a woman," Tim corrected. "Mad Meg had a mean left hook, and the inebriated new officer hit his head on a spittoon, just so. No charges were pressed due to embarrassment."

Riot leaned back in his chair. "I hope you'll do me the same favor, Tim."

"Already planned to. I suspect that wildcat of a woman you're fixin' to marry will be the death of you."

Riot ignored the twinkle in the old man's eye. "The house?"

"Inherited after Nicholas's grandmother died of cancer last year. Nicholas graduated with honors in chemistry from the University of California. He's been working for Mr. Joy for the past four months."

"Who was taking care of the house while he was across the bay?"

"It was being rented to a distant relative, who recently got married and moved to Sacramento."

Riot frowned at a missive on his desk. He hadn't heard from Isobel since that single, brief telegram about Jin.

Tim knew him well enough to know where his mind was. "She can take care of herself," Tim said.

"Bel is in a precarious situation." As a convict and a woman with a ruined reputation—society was stacked against her. Any dealings with local law enforcement put her at risk.

Tim shrugged. "I suspect she's used to that."

Riot reined his thoughts to the matter at hand. "You've confirmed my suspicion—that Officer Jones was looking for something more. He was keen on Nicholas checking his valuables. That, and the state of the house. It was too deliberate."

"But why?"

"There's the rub." The possibilities were endless. "Whatever our fake officer's motivations, he may have a connection with Buckley Brick Yard, or he may be a bricklayer."

Tim sucked on a gold tooth. "I have a friend with the Bricklayer and Stonemason's union. I'll show Sarah's drawing around." After interviewing Tobias and Riot on

Sunday, Sarah had managed to capture the likeness of the man. Riot wasn't at all surprised.

"I'll canvas the local pawn shops," Riot said. "It's time I reacquaint myself with San Francisco's criminal element."

"Isn't that what you've been doing?" Tim asked.

"Indirectly."

"You always did manage to make their lives miserable."

———

ATTICUS RIOT STEPPED OFF THE RUNNER AND WALKED across an empty street. The dingy pawn shop would be his eighth of the day. It was a small, cluttered place squashed between two brothels, its single window framed with broken hopes and shattered dreams.

A bell chimed as Riot stepped inside. A man in a bright waistcoat smiled. His eyes took in Riot's fine clothes, and he instantly looked over Riot's shoulder.

"I'm not a police officer," Riot said.

"I know who you are." The pawnshop owner had a thick Greek accent, bushy brows, and shrewd eyes.

Riot studied the man. "I don't know your name."

"Kafatos. Alex Kafatos."

"Your father was Demetri?"

Alex slapped his hand on the counter. "*Is*. He retired. I take over the shop."

"You've grown a bit." In the waist and jowls. Such was the plight of young men who grew up.

Alex grinned. "You do remember me, then. I will never forget you."

Riot inclined his head. "It's hard to forget a man who threatened your father."

"Well, maybe he deserved it. He's not so good when he's

in his cups." Alex gestured to the items in his shop. "Are you buying or selling today?"

"Asking." Riot slid a dollar across the counter.

"Why did my father ever hate you?" Alex snatched up the dollar.

"Did a police badge with the number seventy-one find its way into your establishment?"

Alex crossed his arms. "I would never sell police things."

"It is illegal," Riot agreed, pushing another dollar across the counter. "But I'm running out of cash and patience."

Alex scoffed. "You own a big house on the big hill. I am not a stupid man."

"Foolish, maybe." Riot watched him with a steady gaze.

"Eh, you would not shoot an old friend."

"The son of a scoundrel," Riot corrected. "But you're right, I won't shoot you. It's too much hassle."

"I am feeling generous." Alex leaned forward. "A woman sold it to me. She said it was her husband's."

"Doubtful," Riot said. "But I'll accept your lie as long as the next is the truth. Who bought it?"

"I don't ask names." A noise came from the backroom, and Riot casually unbuttoned his coat.

"It's my boy," Alex explained quickly. "He helps me in the shop like I helped my father."

Riot left his coat open.

"I don't know the man's name. It was two weeks ago."

"What did this man look like?"

"Gruff, grizzled, rough hands. I think he was Italian."

"Had you seen him before?" Riot asked.

Alex smiled. "There are so many people in this city. The mind, eh, it's rattled."

"That's probably why you sold an illegal item that could land you in jail."

"You said you're not police."

"I need to find that fellow, Alex."

"I've seen him at The Strassburg, but don't tell my wife. I only go for the pool."

"Of course you do." Riot tipped his hat, and paused over a glass case behind the counter. Alex turned to see what had caught his attention: a tray of rings.

"Are you in the market for a wedding ring? I have many fine rings." Before Riot could say no, Alex set the case on the counter under his nose, and opened the glass top. Riot tilted his head at a large diamond set in gold. It could poke an eye out. Isobel might like that.

"Where did you get this one?" he asked, tapping the diamond weapon.

"A widow sold it to me. It's real." Alex waggled his brows. "You can bring an appraiser if you doubt me."

Riot frowned at the rings. Sapphires, emeralds, diamonds—every ring had some sad history. "I don't suppose a happy divorcee sold any to you?"

"Ahh, yes, of course. This one."

Sarcasm was lost on the eager merchant. Alex plucked a sapphire and diamond encrusted ring from its nest. Naturally it was the most expensive.

"I'm afraid it's not to my taste."

"Of course it's not to *your* taste. It is for the lady."

Riot cocked a brow at the ring. "Definitely not to hers either." He plucked his walking stick from the counter.

"I get rings every day. And I take trades."

Riot knocked a fist against his thigh. "Did this Italian fellow trade anything for the badge?"

Alex turned, and took a scrimshaw box from a shelf. It was intricately carved with crashing waves and rising peaks.

"How much?" Riot asked.

THE BELL RANG, AND RIOT NODDED TO THE SLICK YOUNG man behind the counter. It wasn't Mr. Joy and it wasn't Nicholas.

"What can I do for you, sir?"

Riot searched the drugstore, worry niggling at his mind. "Is Mr. Nicholas in today?"

"No, sir."

"Is it his day off?"

"No…" the man hesitated.

"Has something happened?"

The slick man nodded. "Mr. Joy said he needed a personal day." The assistant looked confused.

"Has Nicholas ever taken one before?"

"No, sir. Would you like me to get Mr. Joy?"

Riot shook his head, turned and left. Had he misjudged the situation? Was Nicholas in danger? He hopped on the California cable car line and rode to Leavenworth. While it was still climbing, he stepped down and strode briskly towards Mr. Nicholas's home. The house seemed in order. He applied his stick to the door. No answer.

Riot's hand flexed and tightened on the silver knob of his walking stick, thoughts racing to the difficult task of tracking down a missing man in a city of strangers. He could do it. He had done it before. But the end usually led to a corpse.

Clenching his jaw, he hurried down the narrow path that led to the backyard. Relief washed over him. Nicholas was bent over his rose bushes, talking softly to the petals and stroking each one.

"Nicholas."

The sound of Riot's voice didn't faze the man. Riot

neared. But it wasn't until his polished shoes invaded the young man's line of sight that Nicholas looked up. "Oh, Mr. Riot." Nicholas's gaze didn't reach past Riot's beard.

"Are you well?"

"Yes, fine," Nicholas said vaguely. "Everything is in order."

"Is it?"

"Mr. Joy gave me leave to clean my home. I suppose you've come for your payment," Nicholas said absently.

"Nicholas," Riot said softly. "The case isn't over."

Startled, the man looked up briefly. "It isn't?"

"No."

Nicholas ran a nervous hand through his hair. "But Mr. Joy said that the man only wanted to burgle my home. That's what the Watcher wanted, wasn't it? To rob me."

"I don't think so. I think your stalker was searching your home. He thinks you have... something," Riot finished lamely.

"Something?"

"May we go inside?"

Nicholas tucked away his clippers, and headed for the back door. When Nicholas had said everything was in order, he hadn't been exaggerating. Riot stopped in the doorway. The kitchen sparkled. Every canister, every pot, every surface gleamed. But it wasn't just that—every item in the kitchen was uniform to the extreme.

"By God," Riot murmured.

Nicholas gave a little chuckle. "God didn't do this, Mr. Riot." He stood in the middle of his kitchen looking unsure and uncomfortable. "I'd offer tea, but I'm afraid with my... condition... it takes an unbearable amount of time for most people. Not that I've had many people for tea. I don't... have friends. Not for long, at any rate." Nicholas stumbled over the words. The longer Riot was present, the more anxious he appeared.

"Did you look at the policeman who was here?"

Nicholas shook his head. "I have… trouble. With faces… eyes mostly."

"I thought as much." Riot fished inside his pocket, and placed Sarah's sketching under Nicholas's nose. "This is the policeman who was here."

Nicholas took the sketching and laid it flat on his table. He sat down, straightened the edges, and placed his palms flat on either side of the paper. Riot watched Nicholas's eyes. Darting from line to line, tracing every curve and detail. A clock ticked from the hallway. Birds sang outside, and a fruit seller hauled his cart down the street, ringing a bell. And still Nicholas stared.

"Do you recognize him?" Riot finally asked.

"Who drew this?"

"One of my daughters. Sarah." The foreign words had come so naturally that Riot felt like the world had tipped him over. He quickly pulled out a chair, and sat.

"The detail is extraordinary. It's alive," Nicholas whispered.

"I'll let her know," Riot said. "Do you know that man?"

Nicholas twitched, brushing the air over the sketch. "He *seems* familiar."

Given that the man had been in Nicholas's house and talked with him for considerable length, that came as no surprise. But then Nicholas had trouble looking at faces.

Nicholas closed his eyes. He always sat with his spine perfectly straight and his shoulders square, but there was an unusual stiffness to the strange man. When Nicholas opened his eyes, he was positively energized. He shot out of the chair and rushed into the library.

Riot found him running a finger over a long line of slim leather journals. They were all exactly the same size, and each was labeled in a tight script that looked painfully square. Nicholas selected a journal and flipped it open. He pointed to a grainy old photograph.

"He's younger here, but that's the man in the drawing, isn't it?" Nicholas asked.

Riot took the book from his hands, and studied the photograph. Two men in their twenties stood on a rocky shore. Each had a basket balanced on a shoulder and wore a shirt with a large pouch. Riot adjusted his spectacles, and leaned in closer. Eggs. Their shirts and baskets bulged with eggs.

"This is my *papou*. Theodoros." Nicholas pointed to the second man in the photograph. "He died shortly after this photo was taken." Although younger, the first man was unmistakable: the wide set to his eyes, flat nose, and an expanse of forehead that had only been emphasized with age. The fake police officer, Mr. Jones.

Riot flipped the photograph over. The sloppy cursive was faded with time, but still legible: Leonardo and Theodoros, 1862.

"Eggers," Riot said.

"That's right. *Yiayia* told me he collected eggs on the Farallones."

Riot was familiar with the eggs. Having been born sometime in the late fifties or early sixties, he knew first-hand how scarce food was during the Gold Rush. Gold fever left little time for farming, and eggs were an expensive luxury. The Farallon islands had plenty of murres—a penguin-like bird. Blue-speckled eggs with deep red yolks and no whites—just clear and gelatinous. To a starving street orphan seeing those eggs was like seeing gold. When

Riot first saw a chicken egg some years later, he hadn't known what it was.

"Did they work for the Pacific Egg Company?" Riot asked.

"I don't know. Wasn't that who collected the eggs?"

"There were a number of independent entrepreneurs."

"*Yiayia* didn't talk about my grandfather very often. He died so long ago."

The edge of Riot's lip quirked. Time stretched on for the young, while it passed in a blink for the old.

"Was your grandfather a scrimshander?"

Nicholas stared at him.

"A carver of scrimshaw?" Riot nodded towards Nicholas's cash box. It had been repaired with glue.

"Oh, yes. How did you know?"

"A popular pastime of sailors." Riot unwrapped a package in his hand. He placed the scrimshaw box on a table. "Does this look familiar?"

Nicholas studied it, and then reached for his cash box. He compared the two for long minutes, and finally straightened. "The style is the same. Where did you find this?"

"At a pawnshop. I think it's your grandfather's work. You're welcome to keep it."

Nicholas sank into a chair. "I don't understand any of this."

Riot tapped the sketch. "This man, your grandfather's partner in the photograph, isn't a policeman, Nicholas."

"But he had a badge."

"That badge belonged to an officer who died in a saloon brawl. I believe the man in uniform, Leonardo, who was waiting for you, was the same man who ransacked your home."

Nicholas twitched, and instantly went about straightening his cuffs.

"Nicholas." Riot touched his hand, drawing his gaze to his own. Nicholas stared at him with the same scrutiny he had examined Sarah's sketch. "The false policeman, Leonardo, ransacked your home because generally a person checks on what he values most. Leonardo wanted to see where you'd go."

"Roses." Near to frantic, Nicholas jerked out of his chair.

"No, Nicholas." But the man was single-minded, and he rushed to his backyard. Riot followed him and stood watching as he examined every petal, assuring himself that his roses were safe.

"Will he come back for my roses?" There was a dangerous edge to the young man's voice.

"I don't know what he'll do. Desperate men do desperate things. But I do know that he's looking for something." The question is, why now? And what?

30

THE DEVIL'S ACRE

Atticus Riot walked bold as brass down the middle of Kearny. The fog had lifted around noon and hadn't returned, leaving the night warm and lively. Driven by heat, throngs of men poured into the Barbary Coast—sweaty, restless, and in the mood for pleasure.

Young men ignored Riot, and oblivious gawkers paid him even less mind. But the regulars took note. It was the way he walked. He wasn't there to gawk, and he wasn't there for vice. To discerning residents that only meant one thing—he was a dangerous sort.

Their wariness might have had something to do with the pint-sized man at his side. Wild white beard to match his blue eyes, gold teeth, and a strut born from the saddle. In the Barbary Coast, men got old by killing everyone else.

Tim took a deep breath. "Ah, that air. Sweat, piss, and lust. Brings back memories."

Riot glanced at the old man by his side. "Reminiscing about the good ol' days?"

"They were, weren't they?"

A tipsy young sailor staggered straight at the pair. A grin

split the sailor's face, and Tim flashed his gold teeth. The sailor's eyes widened, and he tripped over his own feet. Tim picked the fellow from the ground, and sent him on his way with a pat on the back.

"It's tamed down." Tim clucked his tongue at the fellow. "That boy would have been on his way to Shanghai by now."

"The night is young."

"Do you recall Big Louise?"

Riot started in surprise. "I do. Did something happen to Miss Marshall?"

"Last year it did. You know how she used to crush anyone who irritated her?"

"I remember seeing you under three hundred pounds of her."

Tim guffawed. "I should have given her a dollar for that."

"You nearly suffocated, Tim."

He tugged his beard. "I don't know about that. Cracked my back though. Needed it."

"Back to Miss Marshall."

"Right. Well, last summer there was this dancing girl, Little Josie Dupree, lithe little thing, about the same size as Miss Bel. Big Louise and her had a falling out. So Big Louise grabbed her, as was her wont, hugged her to that bosom of hers, and fell on top."

"A tried and true tactic of hers," he agreed.

Tim nodded. "Only this time, the girl she tried to squash was a spry thing. She squirmed her way free, climbed up on Big Louise's back, and hit her over the head with a beer mug."

Riot winced.

"The physician had to shave off Big Louise's pride and

joy—her blonde hair."

"I do recall she was fond of that mane."

"Fond is one word. She was so ashamed she never returned to the Eureka."

"I sincerely hope Miss Marshall is living a quiet life in the country somewhere."

Tim snorted. "I don't think Louise was ever quiet a day in her life."

The edge of Riot's lip quirked. "San Francisco certainly knows how to make a woman."

"Spirited and ornery as a virgin porcupine."

A mass of men were gathered below a row of buildings known as Battle Row. They were gawking at the second story windows. One eager fellow gave a hoot and three others broke out of their trance to join the lines of men crowding into the bagnios, deadfalls, and cheap dance halls.

Riot didn't look up. He knew what was there—windows without curtains, and a glimpse into the illuminated rooms of prostitutes. Mostly with their johns of the moment.

He did, however, glance at the opening of a cavernous stairway. Men eyed him from beneath their low caps, and he stared boldly back. The Morgue—a den of macks, thieves, and drug addicts.

A commotion, a shift in the crowd, and two women screamed profanity as they clawed at each other. The combatants tumbled into the street. As men gathered to watch the women fight, enterprising fingers dipped into careless pockets.

Riot kept walking. And Tim cursed under his breath. "Idiots."

Tim pulled Riot to a stop when he discerned their destination: The Strassburg. It was on the fringes of The Devil's Acre—the lowest of the low in the Barbary Coast. Red lanterns lit the recessed doorway, where a large bouncer stood with his arms crossed.

"So, ah, did you ever make good with Spanish Kitty?"

"I did not," Riot said.

"Shit."

"Why do you think I asked you along?"

"For my amiable company?"

"And your charming friend, Mr. Bowie."

Tim cackled. "It just so happens I brought along another friend."

Riot glanced at him sidelong. "Please tell me you didn't bring dynamite?" he asked out of the corner of his mouth.

Tim only smiled.

The bouncer patted down Riot's hips and let him through. But his new No. 3 sat snuggly under his arm with a spare in an ankle holster. While Tim hadn't brought his customary shotgun, he had his bowie knife. The bouncer let them through.

The cramped entryway gave way to a hallway. Music and voices warred as Tim and Riot strolled down lit stairs into the dance hall. It was a large rectangular basement filled with crude tables and chairs, and billiard tables. A fiddler and pianist plied their craft in a corner beside a wooden stage, with a space cleared for dancing. The dancing involved men pawing "pretty waiter girls" who wore unbuttoned blouses and short red skirts.

Tim elbowed Riot in the ribs. "Remember, you're a soon-to-be married man." Before Riot could reply, Tim dipped into the crowd and disappeared.

A woman with a warm smile sidled up to him. "Beer and cigar?" she asked, her voice warm and sultry against his ear. He placed a twenty-five cent piece on her tray. "Have

you seen an older Italian fellow by the name of Leonardo?
He's a regular here."

The waitress eyed him. "Sweetie, I know lots of men by
that name."

"It is unfortunately common," he agreed. "But he's a big
fellow. Wide-set eyes, flat nose, harsh jaw, and rough hands."

She gave him an easy smile, trained and practiced, but it
didn't touch her eyes.

"It's only business," he assured.

"Most men come for pleasure," she said, running a hand
down his waistcoat. He could feel a tremor in those fingertips. Fear. Either Leonardo was a dangerous customer, or
she recognized an infamous gunfighter who likely had a
price or two on his head. Damn the newspapers, Riot
thought.

"Yes, I am," he said.

She started in surprise. "I… You are, aren't you? That
detective?" It was a breathless question.

Riot didn't bother smiling. It wouldn't put her at ease.
Women of the underworld knew fake when they saw it, and
they sensed danger long before.

She pressed against him. "I'm paid to get you soused, up
those stairs, and—"

"Part me from my cash."

"The best money you'll ever spend…" Her hand drifted
downwards.

Riot stopped her short, and placed her roving hand back
on her tray. "Undoubtedly."

"If you change your mind…" Her eyes slid to a stairway.
One that led upstairs to a honeycomb of small, partitioned
rooms.

"I thank you kindly for the offer, but I'm here for
business."

"We can't talk about our customers." She glanced at the billiards table.

Riot placed another coin on her tray.

"Clara has a loose tongue. You might pump her instead." Her eyes danced with amusement as she sauntered away. But the woman's good humor was far from reassuring.

Riot moved through the crowd, avoiding the billiard tables. He kept his brim low as he questioned two more waitresses, then ran into an old gunfighter who he'd put a bullet through twenty years before. The man bore him no ill feelings.

Cheers went up around the tables, and a man stomped through the crowd, while the audience jeered at him. A tall, dark-haired woman tucked her winnings in her bodice.

"Anyone else?" she challenged.

A fool stepped up, and the game began again.

Spanish Kitty hadn't changed in the past five years. Dark-haired and tall, she bent over the table, and caressed her cue stick. Her focus was absolute, and so was the focus of the men behind her. But the last man who'd put a hand up under her short skirt left The Strassburg a eunuch.

When Riot finally found Clara, the first waitress's amusement became clear. Clara was sitting on the lap of an inebriated man who was all hands and no class. The woman had a look Riot knew well—sickly sweet smile, a fake laugh, and eyes full of disdain for the man pawing at her.

Riot caught her eye. "Miss Clara?"

The man looked up. "Bugger off."

"Are you paying?" Riot asked.

"I'm sampling."

Riot held up a gold dollar between his fingers, and inclined his head towards the stairway. Clara whispered in the man's ear, and started to rise. But the man fished in his pocket and stuffed a dollar between her ample breasts. "Had her first," he said.

"And last night, Brett," she nibbled on his ear.

"I'll only be a few minutes," Riot said.

"Find another whore," the man growled.

Riot didn't take his suggestion.

"Gentlemen, please," Clara said into the mounting tension. But Brett ignored her plea. He stood, knocking her off his lap.

"Do you know who I am?" Brett asked.

"Should I?" Riot countered.

Brett bristled. "Are you aiming for a fight?"

"If you swing, you'll be kicked out."

Brett grinned wildly. "They don't kick *me* out."

Riot cocked his head. "You must be the local copper with a greased palm."

"You cocky little——" Brett swung.

Riot ducked under the drunken fist, and took a step back. He held up his hands, walking stick loosely dangling from his fingers. "I don't want trouble."

Brett charged. What Riot lacked in size, he made up in speed. Riot sidestepped the drunken attack and tripped Brett up with his walking stick. Brett fell to his knees. But the scuffle had attracted attention. The crowd had cleared a space, and large toughs were coming their way.

Riot stepped up to Clara, and calmly asked, "Do you know an Italian named Leonardo? A big fellow, about sixty, wide eyes and rough hands?"

She blinked at him, her gaze sliding over his shoulder. "He's a bouncer here."

It was Riot's turn for surprise.

"Back off. He's mine!" Brett growled.

Four men surrounded Riot, from dark to light, to young and old, but all similarly large.

"I'm afraid not, Mr. Brewer. Miss Kitty wants to see him," said a bouncer with a scarred smile etched onto his cheeks.

Brett fumed, but kept his mouth shut. A second bouncer locked a hand over Riot's shoulder. He was missing two fingers. With little choice in the matter, Riot was escorted towards a billiards table.

The five men stopped a few feet from the table. Spanish Kitty was bent over, her long body stretched on the green mat, arms poised. She didn't look up. The cue stick slid between her fingers. White hit black, and the eight ball rolled into a pocket. Her opponent slapped a stack of cash on the table.

"Search him," Kitty said without looking up.

The bouncers did a more thorough search of Riot's person than the doorman. In a matter of seconds, he was freed of his No. 3 and his Shopkeeper.

Kitty plucked the black ball from its pocket. "The last time you visited my establishment you brought the police, cost me two nights of business, and left a man bleeding on my dance floor."

"Not the first blood to stain these floors."

"Cocky as ever." Spanish Kitty took her time looking him up and down. "The white hair looks good on you. Nice touch." She made a slashing gesture across her temple. "You know there's a bounty on your head."

"There usually is," he said. "But most are smart enough to realize the money isn't worth crossing me."

Kitty laughed. "Life is cheap. Men kill for pennies in this part of the world."

"So I've noticed."

"I should shoot you myself," mused Kitty.

"And ruin your floors?"

"It would be worth it."

"Have you been dreaming of killing me for the past five years?"

A bouncer hit him in the lower back. Riot grunted, and his knees buckled, but he managed to stay upright.

"Easy, boys," Kitty said. She pointed the cue stick at him. "I haven't given you a single thought since that night. Not until you walked into my turf with your same song and dance."

"Trouble wasn't my aim tonight. Mr. Brewer swung at me."

Kitty tossed the cue ball on the table. "Set up another round," she said to a nearby gentleman. He jumped to obey, gathering the balls in a wooden triangle.

"You owe me money, Atticus Riot."

At the sound of his name, conversation died. The music stopped, but the women on stage kept dancing. A desperate kind of pantomime of scuffing and high kicks. Not a single eye was on their exhibition.

"I'm looking for one of your bouncers. Leonardo. He's been spooking a client of mine."

Kitty's hands tightened on her cue stick. "You. Owe. Me. Money."

"The man bleeding on your floor was responsible for that trouble five years before."

"He's dead."

"Hanged, if I recall. By the Justice Department."

"I don't give a damn. You owe me six hundred dollars."

"Not as I see it."

Kitty arched a brow, and positioned the cue ball. The triangle was removed. "How do you see this ending?"

Riot glanced around the dance hall. "At this point?" He removed his spectacles and tucked them away. "I see it ending in blood. But I warn you, Kate, I'll cost you a great deal more if you make an issue out of this. I only came to talk to one of your bouncers."

"You can talk to four of them."

The cue stick slid through her fingers. The ball struck, and so did the first blow. Only it wasn't the fist aimed at Riot. He had leaned back and dodged the swing. Scar Face rushed in, and Riot twisted, thrusting his walking stick. The tip caught Scar Face in the solar plexus. Another blink, and the weighted stick slammed against Eight Finger's throat.

Number Three lunged for the stick, and the fourth bouncer attacked simultaneously. Riot moved into the blow. The fist connected with his face, but the blow lacked power. Riot drove his shoulder into Number Four's gut. The bouncer staggered back. Riot wrenched free his stick, gave it a quick twirl, and the heavy silver knob connected with the man's head.

Number Four dropped to the floor.

Scar Face slammed into him from the side. Riot hit the billiards table, and a large dark fist pounded his face. Riot grabbed a smooth ball and drove it into the side of Scar Face's skull. Scar Face reeled to the side. A hiss insinuated itself into the buzz of combat. Smoke came next, and burning.

Screams erupted, feet rushed, and a stampede headed for the exits. Riot was blind, his eyes full of fire. But he was well used to the lack of sight. Wheezing, he wrenched his revolver from Scar Face's waistband and rolled off the table. Riot coughed and gagged, slipping on rolling billiard balls. Blinking past the sting in his eyes, he stumbled to his feet and joined the surge.

A hand clapped his back, and Riot spun. Bright blue eyes stilled his fist. Tim had a handkerchief tied over his nose. "Git goin', boy." He gave Riot a shove, and goaded him into the street, and then into the mouth of an alley.

Riot doubled over, and coughed up the burn in his throat. He tried to wipe his eyes, but it only made the sting worse.

"Stay still."

Riot did as ordered. Tim grabbed him by his hair and bent back his head. Water splashed over his eyes. It lessened the sting. "What the hell did you do?" Riot wheezed.

Tim cackled. "I made a slight improvement to those smoke bombs. I added cayenne and pepper. Though I may have added a mite too much."

Riot wiped the blood from his nose. "Couldn't you have come to my rescue *before* the beating?"

"I was reacquainting myself with an old friend. You were fine."

"Until I wasn't." Riot eased his spectacles back on. No cracks in the lens. Small blessings. He smoothed his hair and glanced back at the street. Drunks were convinced they were dying, whores were retching, and the fire brigade bells were ringing like mad.

"Our man is a bouncer upstairs."

"Gawd dammit," Tim said, slapping his hat on his knee.

Riot narrowed his eyes at the hat. His own had fallen off in the fight.

"Why'd you have to go and antagonize Miss Kitty?"

"I did not antagonize her, Tim." Riot put a hand to his lower back. There'd be a bruise in the morning, and he'd likely be pissing blood.

"Yer losin' that smooth tongue of yours."

"We seem to have different memories of the past twenty years. Have you been drunk all these years?"

"Maybe so. Not near as amusing as it used to be."

Riot checked his revolver, and clicked the chamber shut before holstering it. Determined, he strode back towards The Strassburg with stick in hand.

Tim hurried after. "Where you going?"

"To get my hat."

"Look here, boy. I aim to keep you alive long enough to make Miss Bel a widow."

"I don't plan on making her a widow for a good long while," Riot said as he pushed his way into the crowd. He grabbed a beer from a gawking man, and poured it over a handkerchief. Before Tim could argue, he tied the handkerchief around his face, and slipped back inside the dance hall.

THE DANCE HALL WAS IN RUINS FROM THE STAMPEDE, BUT IT was generally left that way nightly. A stinging smoke lingered. Scar Face was slumped in a far corner, he appeared to be breathing. Riot picked up his hat, knocked it back into shape, and placed it on his head. Just so. A gunshot barked, and his hat flew off again.

"I'll kill you, Riot!" Kitty screamed.

Riot drew and fired. A bullet splintered the bar that Kitty hid behind. Two bandana-wearing toughs came through a side door and Riot bolted for the stairs, taking them two at a time. A rush of footsteps followed. He ran through the first open door with a window, and climbed straight out onto a fire escape. Another bark bit the metal near his head, and a *ping* sparked by his hand. Riot didn't stop. He rushed down the escape, gripped the last rung, and dropped to the ground.

Riot hit the muck of the alleyway, and fell to his knees. Half-dressed women and men crowded around him. A rough hand reached out, and Riot took it. "Thank you kindly." He looked up to find a large man with wide-set eyes and a flat nose looking down at him. The last time Riot had seen the man he had been wearing a police uniform.

"Kill 'im, Leo!" Kitty yelled from the upstairs window.

Recognition lit Leonardo's eyes. The man clamped down on Riot's hand, and reached for the knife on his hip. Riot jabbed upwards with his stick. The knob caught Leonardo under the jaw, and he staggered back a step. A gunshot ricocheted through the alleyway. The crowd fled, pushing towards wider streets, and Leonardo bolted with them. The big man scattered whores and johns, shoving them out of his way.

Riot gave chase. The two men broke free of the crowd, and Riot shot down the boardwalk in pursuit: through a narrow lane with huddled forms, past a dozen brothels and saloons, and into a crowded street. Electric lights blinded him, and everywhere he looked, rough men stared back.

"Damn." Riot leaned against the closest wall to catch his breath. He ripped off his handkerchief and dabbed at the blood on his nose. He was glad he couldn't smell the cheap beer soaking it.

"You look worse for wear."

Riot glanced at a woman who shared his wall. Makeup caked her wrinkled face, her bodice was unlaced, and her skirts tucked up to the hip.

"I've had worse nights."

She smiled, displaying a mouth of swollen gums. "So have I."

"Did you happen to see the man who ran out of this alleyway before me?"

"I've survived this long on the streets by being blind." She spat out a wad of tobacco.

He waited, meeting her gaze.

"It comes and goes. The blindness."

"I understand." Riot went to tip his hat, but found only air. He sighed faintly. He had been partial to that hat.

"Buy me a drink?" she asked.

Riot cocked his head, and offered his arm. "I'd be honored." She tucked his arm close, and nudged him towards a corner saloon.

"May I ask your name?"

"Oh, a real gentleman." She pressed against him. "Most call me Angel. I'm the closest you'll get to heaven. But you can call me Fran MacIntyre."

"A pleasure, Miss MacIntyre. Atticus Riot. Friends call me A.J."

She raised her brows. "I've heard of you, haven't I?"

"Likely so. Although depending on who's doing the telling, it may be bad."

"Mostly bad. For you. You need to be careful 'round these parts."

"I'm a careful sort."

They walked into the Rusty Rose. It was a proper saloon, with a pianist tapping out a playful tune, a long bar, and a buffet. A few working girls sat with patrons, but it was more conversation than business.

As was his habit, Riot surveyed the saloon. A big man with hunched shoulders caught his eye in the corner. Miss MacIntyre had led him true. Riot placed a dollar on the bar. "Lady's choice." He pressed a five dollar bill into her palm. "Take care of yourself, Miss MacIntyre."

"You too, sweetie."

Riot walked to the back of the saloon and stopped at Leonardo's table. The man's shoulders were hunched as he nursed a drink. He didn't react when Riot slid into the chair opposite. "Can I buy you another drink?" Riot asked.

Leonardo glanced up at him, and downed his whiskey. "Why not."

Riot gestured to the bar keep. A bottle and two glasses were set down. Riot poured a draught into each, and raised his glass to Leonardo, who returned the gesture. The bite slid down his throat, washing away the last of Tim's pepper concoction.

"I'm curious," Riot said.

"About what?"

"Do you intend to harm Mr. Nicholas?"

Leonardo shook his head. And then sighed. "I could have if I wanted to."

"I surmised as much." Riot poured another whiskey. "But that doesn't exclude the future. Desperate men do desperate things."

"Do I strike you as desperate, Mr. Riot?"

Riot held his gaze. "No," he said slowly. "You do not. You strike me as careful, patient, and intelligent."

Leonardo chuckled. "If only the ladies thought the same. Nicholas is…a strange boy. I may have sunk low in my life, but I wouldn't harm a boy like that. I'm an honorable man."

"Who doesn't mind a bit of stealing."

Leonardo's hands tightened around his glass. "I needed to make it look like a robbery."

"You were friends with his grandfather."

"I was," Leonardo confirmed. "Are you really a friend of

Nicholas? Because from what I've seen, he don't have friends."

"You spooked him. He hired me to help find his stalker."

Leonardo winced. "I didn't mean…" He trailed off with a sigh. "I only want what's mine."

"And what might that be?"

"How much do you know?"

Riot folded his hands on the table. "Why don't you start at the beginning."

The man across considered his suggestion. "You're that detective I've heard about."

Riot inclined his head.

"Maybe you can help us both."

"We'll see."

Leonardo seemed to accept the vague assurance. He downed another glass, and squared his shoulders. "Nicholas's grandfather and me were partners. His friends called him Teddy. And we were the best of friends. Met him on the boat over way back when. We mined for gold together, we froze together, and starved." He looked at his palms. "Eventually Teddy ended up with a young wife and babe, so we took any job we could find. We worked until our hands bled some days. Times were tough, eh? You are old enough to remember some of it, I think?"

Riot nodded.

"When Teddy and me heard about the blue eggs on the Devil's Teeth, we didn't think twice. We bought a leaky fishing boat, and went to those god-forsaken islands. But the egg company had claim to the southeast island—the lesser of two evils. The north island was left to us—too treacherous for the egg company men. We went twice, and nearly died both times. Lost our load once, and half the next time. The third time was different."

From his position, Riot had a clear view of the entrance. He never sat with his back to a door. Tim hurried into the saloon, tense and ready to spring. When Tim saw Riot, he visibly relaxed and started over, but Riot gave a slight shake of his head. Leonardo was in a talkative mood—there was no need to risk interrupting him. Tim took the hint and sidled up to the bar.

"How so?" Riot asked.

"We did one last haul. The biggest yet. Only instead of risking the Devil's Teeth, we pirated the egg company itself."

Leonardo's eyes were distant. "We boarded one of their boats at sea after they were tired. Even so, they put up a fight. I was shot during the boarding. We didn't harm none of them—not permanently anyhow. We forced the crew into a rowboat, left our leaky boat, and sailed into San Francisco. But I was in a bad way, so I left it to Teddy to sell the eggs and I went off to see to my wound. Only due to us not tossing the crew overboard like proper pirates, our heist was all over the newspapers the next day, along with our descriptions. I was caught, but I never ratted out Teddy to a living soul. I spent five years in prison, Mr. Riot. When I got out, I found his wife and child and learned he had been killed."

"How did he die?"

"On the docks. I figured he was robbed, or someone recognized him and he tried to run."

"Did he sell the eggs?"

Leonardo shook his head. "I didn't think so at the time. His wife wasn't living grand. She was remarried, I think out of desperation. There were more men than women in these parts. Easy enough to find a man, but maybe not a good one."

"Was her new husband unkind?"

Leonardo shrugged. "Hard to tell. She wasn't happy

with me. Blamed me for Teddy's death. Blamed me for leading him astray."

"Did you?" Riot asked.

"I did." Leonardo flexed his fist. "He looked up to me."

Riot didn't reply, only waited as Leonardo lost himself in memories.

The man downed another glass, and sighed. "I asked her, of course. About the money. But she only cursed at me. She didn't even get to sell the rickety fishing boat Teddy had used their savings to buy. At the time, I figured Teddy had to dump the load. Or it was stolen along with the boat. Didn't think about it for years. That was until my sister died a few months ago."

There was the elusive trigger, Riot thought, the catalyst that had put recent events into motion.

"As I was going through her things, I found this letter in her sewing box. Dated three days after our raid." Leonardo placed a well-handled piece of paper on the table. The creases were deep, the paper nearly splitting in the seams. But the hand was still legible.

I've not betrayed you. Only hidden what's yours. Find me on a quieter day. Your friend in arms, Teddy.

"Your sister never showed this to you."

Leonardo gave a rueful smile. "My sister didn't approve of our ways. She was a devout Catholic, and she'd not be a part of ill-gotten gains. She knew what we had done. After she died, I pawned her sewing box for a police badge. Fitting, I thought."

"Why did you think Nicholas knew where the money was?"

Leonardo scratched at his scarred knuckles. "The letter

confirmed that Teddy sold the cargo and hid the money. So I thought maybe Teddy's woman pulled one over on me. When I tracked her down, I learnt that she had died, too. But she had a fine house, and a grandson who'd gone to a fancy university. I wanted my cut."

"I remember eggs were in high demand at the time. A single one cost a dollar. What was the size of your haul?" Riot asked.

"There were at least six thousand eggs. Maybe eight. If you help me find that gold, I'll give you a cut."

"That money belongs to the egg company and the men you sent adrift."

Leonardo slammed his fist down. "Money gotten by theft! The Pacific Egg Company were *thieves*. They had no claim to that island, and they got rich off of those eggs. We didn't hurt anyone. I got a bullet in my gut, and lost five years of my life. What's one load?"

"You were planning to steal the money from Nicholas."

"Only what's mine."

Riot held the man's gaze until he saw the truth in his claim. "I don't think Nicholas knows anything about the gold," he said quietly.

Leonardo sat back. "You're right. I don't think he does, either."

"That was clever of you, if cruel, to stage a robbery in an attempt to find his hiding place."

"It was useless. That boy is peculiar."

"You're right. He is. But Nicholas is also gentle and kind. That's a rare thing."

Leonardo's cheeks flushed with heat. "And I scared him witless." Leonardo broke eye contact.

Riot pushed the bottle closer, and stood. He gathered his stick. "You did."

"I'd like to make it right with Nicholas. He's my best friend's grandson."

"I'll speak with him, but until I say so, don't go near him again. *I* am not a kind and gentle soul."

Leonardo raised his glass. "So I've 'eard, Mr. Riot."

31

A USEFUL THING

WHISPERS WOKE HIM, SOFT AND FLEETING, AND A SCUFF OF feet outside his door. Riot opened his eyes, and winced. He reached to the side, but only found an empty expanse. "Three more months," he whispered.

Riot eased himself up, and limped to a mirror. When his spectacles were in place, he studied the bruises on his lower back and face. At twenty, he would have hopped out of bed and found more trouble, but forty was an entirely different beast.

"*You* knock," a snatch of voice came through his door.

Riot reached for his trousers, and grimaced. By the time he'd slipped on his braces, one of the children standing outside his door finally worked up the courage to knock. "Yes?" he called.

"It's Sarah," a faint voice said. "Can we come in?"

Riot opened the curtains to let in light. "Just a minute, Sarah." When his tie was in place and his waistcoat buttoned, he opened the door. Sarah and Tobias stood outside.

Sarah's face fell. "What happened to you?" she gasped.

Riot gestured vaguely at his eye. "Father and daughter matching black eyes."

"You're halfway there," she said. Her own bruises had spread down her nose and curved under both eyes. It was a wonder her nose wasn't broken.

"I'll have to go and get punched again," Riot said. "Are you willing to punch me, Tobias?"

Sarah's worry turned into a laugh, and she threw her arms around his waist. When he winced, she pulled away. "Do you have more bruises?"

"I'll be fine," Riot assured. He touched the air over her swollen face. "How's the nose?"

"I think it looks worse than it feels. You need ice."

"I likely needed it last night," he agreed.

"Breakfast is ready," Tobias said. "And no, sir. I ain't punching you. Mr. Tim will, I'm sure."

Riot reached for his coat. "You are right about that."

The children followed as he limped down the stairway. "So what happened?" Tobias prompted.

"Did you find the man I drew for you?" Sarah asked. "Is that how you got the shiner?"

"Are the two of you always so alert in the morning?"

"It isn't morning, Mr. A.J."

"It's afternoon," offered Sarah.

"Is it?" Riot glanced out a window. The air was silver with mist. San Francisco had forgotten it was summer again.

"Near to two in the afternoon," Sarah said.

"Have any telegrams arrived for me?"

Tobias slid down the last three steps as he gave a shake of his head. "I would have woken you up for that."

Riot touched the boy's head in gratitude. "You are a wise young man."

"That's stretching it," Sarah muttered.

Lily was putting on her gloves in the entryway. "Good afternoon, Mr. Riot."

"Miss Lily."

She glanced at his face, and grimaced. "There's tea and scones in the kitchen. And Sarah, see that Mr. Riot gets some ice on those bruises."

Lily turned to a mirror and straightened her hat.

"May I borrow Tobias today?" Riot asked.

"Are you taking Sarah, too?"

"I am. It's nothing dangerous."

"I'm not sure you know the difference." Lily gave him a pointed look.

"With a name like mine?"

"Hmmhmm."

Riot opened the door for her, and she stopped on the threshold. "You may take him."

Tobias did a little jig in place as his mother left. "Where we going?" he asked.

"I'm going to the kitchen," Riot said.

"And then?" Sarah asked.

"I thought you might like to know why Nicholas Stratigareas was being stalked."

"*Eggs?*" Three voices asked in unison. Nicholas, Sarah, and Tobias all stared at the man who sat across the table. Riot ran a hand over his gray-streaked beard, feeling far older than he should. The trio in front of him would never know a city where justice was delivered by a swift gun. He and Ravenwood had worked hard for that reality.

"Eggs," Riot confirmed. "We have chickens now, but

there was a time when no one could be bothered to raise them in San Francisco."

"Why on earth would that be difficult?" Sarah asked. "Chickens are easy."

"Everyone was struck with gold fever. They were all mining. Same with laundry—there weren't any launderers, so most sent their shirts on sailing ships to be laundered overseas. Miners couldn't be bothered with trivial tasks."

Tobias and Sarah stared. Nicholas went back to looking at Sarah's drawings. He seemed more fascinated by the sketches than by the possibility of gold.

"It was a different time," Riot explained.

"Sounds lazy," Sarah muttered.

"Obsessed, more like," Riot said.

Tobias's eyes slid over to Mr. Nicholas. Riot cleared his throat before the boy could voice his thoughts. "Mr. Nicholas," Riot said. "Did your grandmother ever talk about your grandfather's trips to the Farallones?"

Nicholas shook his head.

"How did your family come by this house?" Property wasn't cheap in the city. Now, and even more so in years past.

"My grandmother's second husband owned a mercantile, and my father opened a successful restaurant. As far as I know my family worked hard for this home."

"Maybe there's a clue in all those journals and photographs you keep," Sarah suggested.

Nicholas shook his head. "There isn't any mention of gold."

"It may only be a suggestion. Something hidden," Riot said gently.

But Mr. Nicholas wasn't interested in the possibility. He didn't seem to care one jot for it.

"Can we look through your books?" Tobias asked.

Nicholas looked up, startled. "No... no, I've only just put them back in order."

"We'll be careful," Tobias said.

Nicholas looked horrified at the declaration.

"You can look through them yourself if you like," Riot suggested.

"Why would I do that?"

"For the gold!" Tobias said.

Nicholas stared at the boy. "I don't need it."

"Don't you want to find it?" Tobias pressed.

"I have other things to do."

Riot rested a hand on Tobias's shoulder before he could say anything more. "Let me know if you'd like to meet your grandfather's friend, Leonardo."

Nicholas tilted his head. "Should I meet him?"

"That's up to you."

"He ruined my home."

"He did. And he's a rough sort. But family is important to some, and from what I gathered Leonardo doesn't bear your family any ill will. Don't feel like you have to, however."

"He'll leave me alone then?"

"I believe so. I'll check in with you from time to time though."

Nicholas sighed with relief.

"Seems like letting him apologize might put your mind at ease," Sarah said. "Otherwise he'll just be that shadowy face in a window." She glanced at Riot for reassurance, and he gave her a slight nod in return. Sarah was right.

Nicholas looked up suddenly. "Can you draw my roses?"

"Your roses?" Sarah asked.

Nicholas nodded. He carefully closed her sketchbook

and handed it back. Without a word he shot out of his door and into the garden.

"Are all your cases this strange?" Tobias asked.

"I've had a few." Riot slipped on his hat, and the three of them joined Mr. Nicholas by the roses.

"Can you draw them?" Nicholas asked.

Sarah considered the rose bushes. "Will you allow Mr. Riot to look through your journals and photograph albums?"

"Yes," Nicholas said without hesitation.

"I'll do it," Sarah agreed.

Riot tipped his hat to her as he went back inside. Sarah Byrne was a resourceful child.

"That man is odd," Tobias whispered as they walked into the study.

"He's keen on details."

"But not gold?" Tobias asked.

"Or mysteries."

The boy frowned at the shelves of identical journals. "Detective work isn't this boring in *The Bradys*."

"Does your mother know you read those dime novels?" Riot asked.

Tobias shot him a warning look. "I ain't sayin'."

Riot set down his hat, selected the first journal, and settled into an armchair. Tobias selected the next one, and plopped on the floor. "What are we looking for?"

Riot flipped through the old journal. "Treasure."

"What if someone robbed Nicholas's grandfather?"

"A very likely scenario."

After ten minutes, Tobias became bored with deciphering the nearly illegible script, most of which in Greek, and began poking around the study. Riot flipped through a photo album. Old tin-types of Greece and the voyage across seas. Mementos and memories. What was it like being able to trace your family's history? Generations tucked neatly away in a family bible with a thriving tree of names. Riot would never know. He wasn't sure if he wanted to know anything about the blood that ran through his veins.

I leave a son. The words from Ravenwood's last known journal entry came unbidden to his mind. Maybe that was all he needed—he was the adopted son of an eccentric Englishman.

"Mr. A.J.?"

The question snapped Riot out of his musing.

"What are you going to do if we don't find anything here?"

"I'm not sure," he admitted. "As far as Mr. Nicholas is concerned, the case is closed."

"So why are we looking?"

"Curiosity."

"Seems pointless." Tobias picked up the sewing box from the pawn shop, and peeked inside. His face fell when he found it empty. The death of curiosity in the flesh. Tobias plopped down next to Riot on the armrest, and began opening and closing the box with a click as he studied the carvings.

"If I didn't have other pressing matters, I'd attempt to track the boat that Nicholas's grandfather and Leonardo stole. Although harbormasters weren't as diligent forty years ago as they are now. Or I—" He cut off, and stared at the box in Tobias's hands. Something about those markings had caught his eye.

"Or I may retire from detective work altogether and join a society of fools. May I see that?"

"What, this?" Tobias handed the scrimshaw box over.

Riot flipped open his magnifying glass, and studied the box. The carvings were of the sea, but not just any sea. Riot looked up at Tobias, a smile playing at the corner of his lips. "Curiosity is a useful thing, my boy," he said with a glint in his eye.

32

A BROWN STUDY

JIN

Sao Jin stared at the unmoving lump under a blanket. Isobel was like a dead person, and that worried her. In the general run of things, Isobel Amsel vibrated with energy. Jin could *feel* her thinking, even when Isobel sat still.

But Isobel had barely moved for a full day. The hum of her mind was gone. And now, a day later, Isobel *still* lay under her blankets. A plate of food sat nearby. Untouched. At one point a nurse came, but Isobel sent her away with a growling threat. Time ticked on, and a second nurse checked on her. Isobel roused herself long enough to verbally dissect the woman. The nurse had left in tears.

Jin frowned at the lump. She placed a hand on its shoulder, and shook. "Captain Morgan," she said. "Let's go for a walk."

Isobel pulled the blanket tightly over her head.

"Are you sick?" Jin asked.

"Yes," came the muffled reply.

"You are lying. Did the boy die?" Jin asked.

"No."

Jin waited. But Isobel didn't say anything more.

Jin crossed her arms. "I will get the doctor," she threatened.

"I'm tired," Isobel growled. "Go for a walk by yourself."

Jin growled back, and turned on her heel. She slammed the door on her way out, marched across the green, and through an odd game with sticks and arches. She ignored the shouts when she kicked a wooden ball, and walked straight up to one of the private cottages at Bright Waters. She knocked.

No answer.

"Mr. Amsel!" she called.

She knocked again.

"*What is it?*" The door was wrenched open. Lotario Amsel wore trousers, but little else. His arm was out of its bandage. An angry scar marred his otherwise flawless skin. When he saw the girl, he relaxed and smiled. "Oh, Jin. One moment." The door closed, and when it opened again, he was wearing a shirt and vest, the collar undone.

"I have seen shirtless men before," Jin said, scowling up at him.

Lotario waved a hand. "Yes, but I'm extraordinary. Your future husband will never compare if you stare at me overly long."

"I will not marry."

Lotario patted the top of her head. "Wise of you."

If any other man had patted the top of her head, Jin would have kicked him between the legs. But Lotario Amsel reminded her of a cat. And cats were naturally insulting.

"What can I do for you?"

"Captain Morgan is dying."

Lotario blinked at the words. His lips parted, his eyes

widened, and he paled to a color that reminded Jin of milk. "What?" he asked.

"She has not moved for a day and a night."

Lotario was halfway to the door when he stopped. "Is she breathing?"

"Yes."

An audible sigh.

"A nurse came to check on her this morning, but Isobel was..." Jin stumbled over a description. "Disagreeable."

Lotario spun on his heel. If he had been wearing a cape, it would have fluttered. "She's likely in one of her 'brown studies'."

"What is that?"

He waved a flippant hand. "She lies in bed for days. She's irritable, combative, and generally foul-tempered."

"That is exactly it."

"Ah, well. She'll snap out of it," Lotario said cheerfully. "She's dreadful, I know. Shall we go into town? We can peruse the boutiques. My treat."

"Why is she in a 'brown study'? Is she sad?"

"Bel never does anything halfway. Trust me. Just stay away from her right now. If she keeps this up, I'll toss a bucket of cold water on her tomorrow. That generally does the trick. Although she tends to rage for a bit. Best to wait another day. How about a late brunch? In my opinion it's never too late for breakfast."

"No, thank you. I'll try to help her."

Lotario placed a hand on her shoulder. "Jin," he said. "She generally says very hurtful things when she's like this. To drive others away. She *wants* to be alone."

"Words are only words. There is nothing for her to say that I haven't heard already."

Lotario stilled. And he looked at her with the same

penetrating gaze as his twin. "My door is always open if you ever need me."

Jin nodded. She walked straight back to Isobel's room. But this time, she didn't say a word. Jin climbed on the bed, and leaned against Isobel's back. When the woman didn't rage at her, she relaxed. "What happened?"

"Please. Just go," came a muffled reply.

Jin lay down, resting her back against hers.

"You're not leaving," Isobel mumbled after a time.

"No."

Isobel stirred. She sat up, dislodging Jin, and leaned against the wall. She rested her elbows on her knees, and put her head in her hands.

"Does your head hurt?" Jin asked. When Isobel didn't say anything, Jin got up and poured a glass of water. Jin held it out. Isobel moved like an old woman, but she took it, and drank.

"Lotario said I should pour cold water on you," Jin said. "But if you come for a walk with me, I won't."

"Are you threatening me?"

Jin wrinkled her nose. "You smell."

Isobel bit back a comment.

"Or I may run away again."

"You'll run away if I don't bathe?"

"Yes."

"Now there's a threat," Isobel muttered. But Jin could not tell if she was serious or not. So Jin walked to the window, and threw open the shutters. Light poured inside, and Isobel shielded her eyes with a hand.

Jin straddled the sill, waiting.

Eventually, Isobel dragged herself upright, and settled on the windowsill. She looked out into a sun drenched day, toying with the beaded bracelet Jin had given her.

"This is not walking," Jin said.

"One thing at a time."

Birds sang to the sun, and a lazy breeze toyed with leaves. "After... my dream." Heat rose in Jin's cheeks. "You left."

"There wasn't time to explain."

"Where did you go?"

"You helped me solve a case. The twine you found... what you said. Time was important. Titus's life was at risk." Those few words loosened the rest. And Jin listened quietly to the facts.

"Why would John try to kill his brother?" Jin finally asked.

"Jealousy." Isobel gave Jin a pointed look. "Of his father's attention, of his mother's... I'm not sure. But something dark definitely resides in that boy." Isobel rested her head against the wall. "This isn't supposed to be how things end. Nothing was set right. The criminal was caught, and yet... he wasn't. I failed."

Jin reached for Isobel's hand. It felt strange, but she kept hers there all the same. "Titus didn't die in the dark," Jin whispered.

"There is that."

33

JAILBREAK

ISOBEL

Wednesday June 20, 1900

TAP. SECONDS TICKED, AND THEN ANOTHER *TAP.* ISOBEL opened her eyes. Soft breathing broke the quiet. But it was a restful sort. Jin was asleep on her cot. The sound that had awoken her wasn't another nightmare. Isobel glanced towards the shutters. *Tap.* It came again. There were no branches close to the window.

Isobel reached for a revolver, but it wasn't there. She cursed. Grabbing a heavy ashtray instead, she got up and padded to the window. It was too hot for blankets. Too hot for a sheet even. The only reason she wore a nightgown was for Jin's sake. But they had closed the shutter. *Tap.*

It was louder this time.

Isobel opened the shutters. A man stood under her window. He looked up, and nudged the brim of his fedora higher. Starlight touched silver rims around his eyes, and joy filled her heart. Light-headed and without thought, she let her heart pull her over the windowsill. She hung for a second, and dropped to the ground. It felt like she was floating. When she stood, strong arms encircled her, and she leaned back against his body. Lips brushed her neck. Isobel closed her eyes, savoring the dream as Riot's beard tickled her skin. She felt him inhale, savoring her scent.

"I can tell you missed me," she whispered.

"We have less than a minute until the night guard returns," he murmured.

"Can you manage that?"

Riot smiled against her ear. Isobel untangled herself, and took his hand, leading him into the trees. The earth was warm, the night alive with summer, and the forest embraced them. A lantern swung into view, and Riot pressed her against a tree trunk.

"This is familiar," he whispered.

"Not this." She removed his spectacles, and pressed her lips to his. Soft beard, eager lips, and confident hands. Her toes curled into the earth. Weeks of longing went into that kiss, and when they finally pulled apart, the night guard was long gone.

She leaned back, just enough to study him in the moonlight. Isobel touched the skin around his eye. It was puffy and bruised.

"I ran into an old acquaintance," he said.

"You can tell me about it after." Isobel buried her fingers in his beard and drew him closer. "Unfortunately Jin's sleeping in my room."

"This is supposed to be a jailbreak," he murmured against her lips.

"Is this generally how a jailbreak goes?"

"Not in my experience. Your second-story cell had me stumped."

"I prefer a moonlight tryst."

"The night guard will pass by here again."

"To hell with him."

Riot squeezed her bare thigh, but then he released it. The hem of her nightgown slithered down her leg. "I'm serious, Bel. I'm here to break you out. Temporarily. We have a train to catch."

Isobel blinked at him. Her sluggish brain tried to make sense of the words. Riot had a way of muddling her thoughts.

"As much as I'd like to continue… this, I think you'll like what I have in mind."

Isobel arched a brow. "I can *feel* what you have in mind." She pressed her hips against his.

Riot quirked his lips.

"Can't we spare ten minutes?" she asked with a note of desperation.

"Considering how much I've missed you, ten minutes is awfully optimistic."

Isobel laughed, and he silenced her in the most pleasing of ways. As it turned out, she only needed five minutes. After the night guard made his second round, they picked themselves off the ground.

Isobel brushed the leaves from Riot's back as he arranged himself. "I'll get Jin." She stared at the second-story window to her room. It would require running at the wall to catch the protruding beam. Far too much effort after her recent activities.

Isobel looked sideways at him. "Perhaps we should have waited until after I needed to scale a wall."

"I'll give you a leg up."

In short order, Isobel scrambled through her window. She nudged Jin awake, then dressed in shirt and trousers. When Jin dropped to the ground, she caught sight of Riot and pressed her back to the wall.

"Truce?" He offered a hand.

Jin took his hand. "I should not have run away."

"A note would be appreciated next time," he said.

When Isobel returned, Riot took the lead. Only instead of heading towards town, he went to Lotario's cottage. "Why here?" Isobel asked.

"You don't get to ask questions," Riot said as he held the door open.

Isobel arched a suggestive brow. "Sounds more like an abduction to me."

"I'd have thrown you over my shoulder," he whispered.

Isobel gave his beard a playful tug as she walked into the cottage.

Sarah was waiting with Lotario, who was sorting his costume trunk. Sarah beamed, and gave Isobel a hug that stole her breath. "I missed you."

Jin edged against the wall, but Sarah wasn't having it. She greeted Jin with the same enthusiasm, and the smaller girl tolerated the affection without fists or kicks.

"I'm sorry," Sarah said.

Jin sighed. "I am too."

"Good, that's settled," Isobel said. "Now what's going on?"

Lotario looked up from his trunk. "Good Lord," he exclaimed. "You're the only one without a bruise on your face."

"I have some on my neck."

Always one for details, Lotario demanded to inspect

them, and immediately walked over to his dressing table to add fake bruises to his own neck.

Riot gave her a questioning look.

"A murderer," she explained in a low voice. "It wasn't you."

Lotario rolled his eyes. "Stop flirting and come closer. I have to get your coloring right. You've been out of the sun for days."

"I thought you were through swapping places with me," Isobel said.

Lotario batted his lashes at Riot. "He asked nicely. And you're welcome."

"Do you know where we are going, Mr. Amsel?" Jin asked.

"Yes."

"It's a surprise!" Sarah was practically bouncing in place. "Mr. Tim and Tobias are…"

Riot put a finger to his lips, and Sarah shut her mouth with a click.

Isobel studied Sarah for the first time in the light. Wisps of hair stuck out of her braid, and although she was bright and cheerful dark circles ringed her eyes. And fading bruises. There was dirt on her shoes and on the hem of her dress. And Riot had a worn look about him, too. Their tumble under the trees could account for that, but there was something more. When she had climbed on top of him, he had flinched, but she had been too distracted at the time to inspect him for injuries.

Details came to her in a rush. She analyzed, dissected, and came to a conclusion a split second later. "You've been traveling all day," she stated. "Wouldn't you like to rest?"

Riot shook his head. "Our lips are sealed, Bel. If all goes as planned, we'll have you back tomorrow morning."

"Now," Lotario said, pulling out clothes from his costume trunk. "Are you still in a brown study?"

Riot looked at her with concern.

"Not anymore," she said.

"Of course you're not, but do the nurses know that?"

"No," she said. "But Doctor Bright will likely know it's you."

"My dear sister, I think he's known this entire time. You need to put this on."

Isobel arched a brow at her disguise: a worn plaid dress, an old-fashioned bonnet, and a cane.

"And for the finishing touches." He flourished a gray wig. "Sarah and I will do your makeup."

THE TRAIN ROCKED WITH A STEADY CLICK AS ISOBEL watched the sun rise. Jin had fallen asleep on her lap in the first class carriage. She idly smoothed the girl's braid, tracing its intricate weave. Isobel felt the touch of eyes on her. She pulled her gaze away from the countryside to look at the man across from her.

Sarah was asleep, too, her head resting on Riot's arm.

"This isn't how I envisioned a jailbreak," she admitted. Isobel poked at the stiff bonnet surrounding her face. To all outward appearances, she looked like a grandmother traveling with her son, granddaughter, and a servant boy.

"This seemed the safest guise."

Isobel slowly edged out from under Jin. She lowered the girl's head to the cushion, tucked a shawl over her, and squeezed onto the seat beside Riot. "Will you tell me now?"

"Not yet."

"So mysterious."

"I aim to keep you interested."

"Hmm."

Riot could feel her thinking. "You'll never guess it," he said.

"I don't guess, Riot." She felt him chuckle in that peculiar way of his—a silent vibration that never failed to warm her.

"Lotario told me you found the missing boy."

In a low voice, she told him about Samuel Lopez, Sheriff Nash, and the Sheel boys. And in the end she fell silent. Even with Riot at her side, failure left a bitter taste on her tongue.

"I can't let it go, Riot," she said softly. "There must be a way to make the Sheels see sense."

"Would you want to see sense?" he asked. "That boy, their youngest son, would hang by the neck until dead."

Isobel found herself looking at Sao Jin. A furious child with violent tendencies. But then everyone was capable of violence. Even Sarah. Everyone had a trigger. Some were just more sensitive than others. Or perhaps, she mused, defective.

"I don't know, Riot. I can only hope we're never put in that situation."

He reached for her hand.

"It's never like this in the stories," she said. "Every case is wrapped up in a tidy bow, and justice is done. I keep asking myself, as childish as it is, what would Sherlock Holmes do?"

"It's not childish, Bel. At some point, during every case, I ask myself what Ravenwood would do."

"And what would he have done in this instance?" she asked.

Riot was thoughtful for a time, idly tracing her knuckles with his thumb. Soothing circles that lulled her, along with the rock of the train. "There's the rub," he murmured. "If Ravenwood had confronted that boy along with me, the police wouldn't have questioned our story. And neither would they have questioned Holmes and Watson. But I can assure you, when the police marched that boy off in shackles we would have been asking a different question: Should a child, even a murdering one, be hanged? I've seen a boy die at the end of a noose before, and I can't stand to see it again."

His words struck her, as they often did. Isobel squeezed his hand in support. "Doctor Bright thinks he can help John, but I think it depends on the boy's father."

"I'd wager he's the key, but... what do I know of fatherhood?"

Isobel took a deep breath.

"You couldn't have done anything more. We're detectives, not lawmen. We seek the truth."

"Is that all?"

He squeezed her hand. "I think the proof of what we seek is sleeping in this cabin."

Isobel smiled. "Will you tell me now?" she asked suddenly.

"No, ma'am."

Isobel growled. "I can't make bricks without clay, Watson."

"And I'll give you none."

"Cruel man," she murmured. "But you can make it up."

"How so?"

"You can settle an argument I'm having with Lotario."

"That's treacherous ground."

"A viper's nest," she agreed, and went on to explain. "Ari said I was being paranoid because I thought someone was attempting to kill me."

"Clearly you weren't being paranoid."

"In hindsight, yes. I'm usually right," she said without boast. John Sheel *had* been wielding a mirror as she'd climbed the Palisades. "But that led me and Lotario to a conversation about Sherlock Holmes. If Holmes hadn't died at Reichenbach Falls, would he have developed paranoia after his encounter with Moriarty?"

"Did you ask Doctor Bright?"

Isobel pursed her lips. "I value your opinion over a qualified doctor's any day."

"In that case, we're in for a lifetime of trouble."

"I'm serious, Riot."

"I know," he said. "That's what worries me."

Isobel laughed, but quickly stifled her amusement when a car attendant knocked on the door. She slumped and tried to look frail.

"Is there anything you need, sir?" the attendant asked.

"No, thank you. Only our rest." Riot nodded to Sarah on his arm.

The attendant bowed, and ducked his head out.

"Will you settle our argument?" Isobel asked.

"I'm afraid my answer won't settle things. It will only add another to the fire."

She waited.

"Holmes *didn't* die at Reichenbach Falls."

"Yes, he did," she said.

"No, he didn't," Riot said firmly.

"How could he possibly have survived a fall from that height?"

"I'll let you figure that out."

"Riot, do you know Conan Doyle?"

"I do not."

"Then how do you know Holmes is still alive?"

Riot laced his fingers with hers. "Instinct."

"You shouldn't give a woman false hope. It's cruel."

"I'm telling the truth. Holmes is alive and currently in London."

Isobel snatched her hand back. "You're as bad as Lotario."

34

RED ROCK ISLAND

ISOBEL STOOD ON THE EDGE OF A PIER. SALT AIR CARESSED her cheeks, and a piece of her heart seemed to come alive. "A boat?" It was a question full of hope.

"Chartered." Riot gave her an enigmatic smile. "You don't have to wear your disguise once we're aboard," he whispered.

Isobel and Jin stared at the steam trawler. It was as decrepit as its captain. Tim stood on deck waving his cap. Tobias scooted along the gangplank to them. "What took you so long? We got to make the tide." The boy looked for luggage, but there was none.

Riot touched Isobel's arm. "When we're aboard. I promise."

"Tim's going to captain the boat?" she asked uneasily.

"He used to be a—"

"Ferry captain on the Mississippi?"

"Something like that." For the sake of verisimilitude, Riot helped her over the gangplank. "I'm sure you can wrestle for the wheel once we're out of port."

Tim tipped his hat to her, and ordered Tobias to cast off.

Isobel resisted the urge to take over. Instead, she let Riot lead her to the bow. They watched the busy port of Vallejo awaken with the sun. Travelers boarding and docking, others rushing to and from the train depot, all eager to make their exchanges. It was hectic and chaotic. And Isobel tried to take in every detail at once. It was her curse and gift. It gave her a headache more often than not.

Tim sounded a deafening horn, and the steamer chugged out of port into the fog.

"Now then," Riot said. He had their full attention. "Let me tell you about The Devil's Teeth and a young man named Nicholas Stratigareas."

Isobel and Jin leaned forward with every word. But his narrative was a more innocent version. There were details he skimmed over, like the Devil's Acre. His eyes slid to hers: he'd fill her in at another time. In the end, Riot pulled out a scrimshaw box and handed it to her.

"Is this the sewing box where Leonardo found the letter?" she asked.

Riot nodded.

Isobel studied the box in the fog-shrouded bay. After a moment, she gestured for Riot's magnifying glass. She applied the lens to the intricate carvings and immediately recognized the small bumps dotting a jagged, kidney-shaped bay. Fanciful waves had been carved into the shape, but two waves moved against the rest. They made the shape of an **X** next to an insignificant little island that lay midway between Sheep Island and Point San Quentin.

"My God," she whispered.

"What is it?" Jin asked.

Isobel thrust the box and magnifying glass at Jin. "Did you bring shovels?" she asked Riot.

"And pickaxes."

Isobel grabbed the man and kissed him before rushing to the helm. "Are we headed to Red Rock Island?"

Tim stepped aside. "Would you like to take the helm, Captain Morgan?"

Isobel shoved her bonnet and wig into Tim's hands. "I would."

Tim gave her a wink and slapped his cap on her head. "There's a change of clothes down below when you're ready."

"Will you keep a lookout at the bow?"

"Aye, aye, Captain Morgan." Tim saluted, and stomped to the front of the boat.

Salt air filled her lungs, the gulls circled with their calls, and waves lapped beneath her hull. It had been too long. All she needed was a sail. The trawler wasn't her Lady, but it would do. Isobel wiped moisture from her cheeks, smearing her costume makeup.

Under her hands the trawler plowed through fog and over glassy water. Landbound for too many months, she lost herself in the feel of the ocean under her feet. No one disturbed her. They let her be. It seemed a dream. One she had imagined a hundred times over during her time in a prison cell.

Red Rock Island came into view, rising abruptly out of the water. Two hundred feet of stark red rock, clothed in fog. Isobel piloted the trawler around to the north end, to a red sand beach. She ordered the anchor lowered and the rowboat lowered, then went below deck to change her clothes.

She glanced in a small tin mirror, and hastily wiped the tears from her eyes. She dunked a towel in water to scrub off her makeup. Footsteps sounded on the companionway, and then slowed.

Riot came up behind her and wrapped his arms around her waist. "Only three more months," he murmured.

"One hundred days," she corrected. "Thank you for this." It was a threadbare whisper. "This... You..." Words got stuck in her throat.

"I know." He gave her a firm squeeze. "Shall we?"

Her eyes flashed with the hunt. "Yes."

Under the cover of fog, they left Tim aboard and climbed into the rowboat. Riot took up the oars.

"Why are we here?" Jin whispered.

"The box is a map," Isobel explained.

The girl looked puzzled. "To the eggs?"

"Something like that."

Sarah grabbed Jin by the shoulders. "It's buried treasure!" Her voice bounced over the water, and Riot quickly shushed her.

Riot ran the rowboat onto the beach. Tobias hopped off the bow, and helped Riot and Isobel push the boat onto firmer ground.

"What is this place?" Jin whispered, craning her neck to search for a peak. The island was desolate and lonely, and the fog lent it a ghostly aura.

"It's an island," Tobias said.

Jin glared at the boy.

"It used to be a manganese mine," Riot explained.

Isobel hoisted a shovel. "And sailors used to dig up rock for ballast. The old mine is this way." But Tobias was already running towards a steep slope to climb.

"Hold this." Riot handed Jin a lantern.

"Tobias," Isobel hissed. "This way." The boy switched directions.

"I don't think you should tell Miss Lily about bringing him here," Sarah said, frowning at the rugged terrain.

"Probably not," Riot agreed.

Isobel walked towards a cliff.

"We're not going to climb that, are we?" Sarah asked.

"Come and see," Isobel said, as she scrambled over rocks. An archway through the cliff revealed itself. Sarah looked relieved.

They walked under the arch, and around towards the west side of the island. Halfway down the western shore, a path veered off, heading for the jutting rock. A black hole gaped in the side of the island. The entrance to the cave was guarded by a dead seagull, flies buzzing around its corpse.

While Tobias poked at the dead bird, Isobel stopped to study the scrimshaw box. The inside of the lid had a more detailed carving. At first glance, it looked like a botched job, a mess of lines and shapes that made no sense. But Isobel spotted the pattern in the madness. It was the inside of a cave. "Do you see this...?" She showed the lid to the children. "We're looking for this rock formation."

"These look like tiny mountains," Tobias said.

"Or gator teeth," said Sarah. "Except that one." She pointed to an upright carving with a rounded top.

They walked into the mouth of the cave, and Jin bent to light the lantern. The floor sloped upwards, breaking off in different directions. The ceiling was jagged and irregular, and the wash of surf echoed against the rocks, drowning their footsteps.

"I don't think we should be in here," Tobias said.

"You three most definitely should not be in here," Isobel said.

"We should have left you on the boat," Riot added.

"That wouldn't be fair," Sarah said.

As darkness closed around them, Jin stopped. The lantern shook in her outstretched hand. Isobel gripped her shoulder, and bent close to her ear. "You don't have to come. I'll wait outside with you."

The girl gave a jerk of her head.

Isobel waited. But Jin didn't move. She was frozen by memories of whatever dark hell she had survived.

"Hurry up!" Tobias said. He and Sarah stood impatiently at the edge of light.

"Is something the matter?" Riot asked softly.

A ghost-like moan came from the depths of the cave.

Sarah jumped, and Jin nearly dropped the lantern. Isobel plucked it from her hand as Sarah whacked Tobias over the top of the head with a hat. "Stop it!"

Jin trembled in place, unable to go forward or back. Isobel was on the verge of bodily carrying Jin out of the cave when Riot crouched in front of the child.

Riot tipped back his hat, so he might look her in the eyes. "Remember who you're with, Jin," he said softly. "Would Din Gau let anything happen to you?"

Jin's nostrils flared with every panicked breath. But Riot's gaze was steady, and his voice reassuring. Slowly, Jin shook her head. "No, *Bahba*." It was the barest of whispers.

Riot held out his hand, and Jin took it. As Tobias and Sarah continued their bickering, Jin shuffled forward, holding tightly onto Riot's hand.

"Sarah, Tobias, stay focused." Riot's gentle reminder silenced the pair.

The ceiling was high in places, lost to the lantern's light. Isobel had explored this cave as a child, but it was larger than she remembered.

"What if someone dug up the treasure already?" Sarah asked.

"Then we'll have had a pleasant day on the bay," Riot replied.

"Can I go down there?" Tobias asked. "I have matches."

Riot took out a handheld light, and thumbed on the device. "Take this."

Tobias frowned at the flickering light.

"It's trustworthy," Riot defended. "With the occasional slap. We'll meet back here."

Tobias brandished the light. "Come on, Sarah."

"I don't want to go with you."

"I'll go with you." Isobel handed the lantern to Riot.

"I don't think splitting up is wise," Sarah said.

"It's not the kind of cave you can get lost in," Isobel said.

Isobel followed Tobias's spooky moans, until she caught up with him. He put the light under his chin, and grinned.

"You best hope there's no bears in here."

"There ain't no bears on the ocean."

"Are you sure about that?" Isobel asked.

Tobias's face fell, and he handed the device to her. The divergence didn't go far. It ended at a wall of uneven rock.

Isobel pointed the light at a stone protruding from a cairn. It was a grave marker. "Riot!" Her voice bounced off the walls, eventually settling on his ears.

The three joined them in the dead end. Jin looked less pale, and more steady in the light. Riot held the lantern closer to the headstone. A piece of whale bone had been fashioned into a crude cross with the inscription: *Dead I am and salted here; I drawed the cart fourteen year.* It was a miner's grave.

"We're not going to dig him up, are we?" Sarah asked, a note of panic in her voice.

"No." Isobel ran the light over the opposite wall. It illuminated a familiar looking formation of jagged rocks. She aimed the light higher, and was rewarded by a dark crevice. It was nine feet above the cave floor. "There it is." Exactly the kind of place an egger would hide his treasure. High off the ground.

"It appears we won't need the shovel after all," Riot said.

"Slightly disappointing." Isobel stuffed the light into her coat pocket, and climbed up the uneven rock. Once there, she found a suitable foothold, and shined the light into the crevice. "There's a box in here." She reached in, all the way up to her shoulder. Her fingers brushed a leather handle, and a thrill of excitement zipped up her arm. She nearly dropped the light.

Isobel dragged the wooden box to the edge. She estimated it weighed about thirty pounds. Difficult to place alone, but not impossible for a skilled egger who'd climbed The Devil's Teeth with a pouch of eggs. Isobel braced her foot on a rock protrusion, and handed the box down to Riot.

There was no lock. Only a worn hinge that fell off when she opened the lid. Riot raised the lantern. Gold shimmered back. A heaping pile of gold coins with Lady Liberty's head stamped on the front. The children gasped.

Isobel plucked up a twenty dollar piece, and studied it in the light.

Sarah sighed. "Too bad we can't keep it."

"About that…" Riot said. "Mr. Nicholas plans to split this three ways with Leonardo and Ravenwood Agency as payment for our services." Riot handed a gold coin to each child. "For your assistance with the case."

Tobias's mouth fell open. "Think of all the candy I can buy with this."

"We will bury you here," Jin said. "Only it will say, *Dead I am and salted here; I ate candy eight year.*"

Isobel snorted and closed the lid, and Riot hoisted the box. As the children left with the lantern to explore nooks and crannies, Riot glanced at Isobel. "You finally found your buried treasure."

"I did." She smiled. "But I had already found it this past December."

"I do believe it was I who found you."

"You *ambushed* me."

"And you held me at knifepoint," he said.

"Careful, Riot, I may maroon you here."

"As long as you retrieve me for our wedding."

"I'll have to think on that."

If you enjoyed The Devil's Teeth, and would like to see more of Bel and Riot, please consider leaving a review. Reviews help authors keep writing.

Keep up to date with the latest news, releases, and giveaways.
It's quick and easy and spam free.
Sign up to my mailing list
www.sabrinaflynn.com/news

Now available:
Book 6 of Ravenwood Mysteries
Uncharted Waters

HISTORICAL AFTERWORD

Once again, my dear readers, you are likely left wondering what parts are fiction and what parts were torn from history. I wish I could make this stuff up, but I'm afraid even my imagination could not have conceived of an Egg War. Yes, it's true. Eggers, as they were known, raided the Farallon Islands. Rival egg companies fought each other in 1863. There was even a cannon involved. So many eggs were gathered that the egg companies nearly wiped out the local murre population, but thanks to conservationists the population is making a comeback today.

The Morgue (which I'm sure will make an appearance in a future book), Devil's Acre, Spanish Kitty, and the story of Big Louise and Little Josie Dupree were ripped straight from the fantastical history of the Barbary Coast. And in Napa Valley, the Oat Hill Mine Road can still be hiked today, although the mercury mines are off limits due to the hazardous waste our enterprising forefathers left behind.

And Red Rock Island. For decades, I saw that island off the San Rafael Bridge. I even discussed swimming to it with my fellow swimmers, but I never knew that it had such an interesting history. It was mined, and there is still a cave on the island. I found a reference to the miner's headstone buried in newspaper archives, although I'm sure it's long gone. Oh, and I should mention: Red Rock Island is currently for sale. So if any of you have twenty-two million dollars sitting in an account, there you go. I only ask that you let me visit.

ACKNOWLEDGMENTS

I discovered that readers do read the acknowledgements. Now that I know this, the pressure is on. Words don't really do justice to all the people who help me with each novel. Each book goes through an editing gauntlet, and in the course of writing nine books, I've gathered a team (I think they are willing) of indispensable editors and beta readers.

As always, my editor, Merrily Taylor, has supported me through the entire process, including deftly and kindly handling all my frantic emails of self-doubt.

And I'm so lucky Tom Welch agrees to go through every manuscript, line by line, searching for innumerable errors on my part. He's the final polisher, and I feel so privileged to work with such a gifted editor on every book. (Any mistakes are due to my own clumsy fingers.)

Thank you to my beta-readers: Annelie Wendeberg, Alice Wright, Erin Bright, John Bychowski, Lyn Brinkley-Adams, Lorene Herrera, Rich Lovin, and Chaparrel Hilliard. Your insights and feedback are very much appreciated!

And finally to my readers. Thank you so much for continuing to read what I write, and for leaving such wonderful reviews. They mean the world to me.

ABOUT THE AUTHOR

Sabrina Flynn is the author of the **Ravenwood Mysteries** set in Victorian San Francisco. When she's not exploring the seedy alleyways of the Barbary Coast, she dabbles in fantasy and steampunk, and has a habit of throwing herself into wild oceans and gator-infested lakes.

Although she's currently lost in South Carolina, she's lived the majority of her life in perpetual fog and sunshine with a rock troll and two crazy imps. She spent her youth trailing after insanity, jumping off bridges, climbing towers, and riding down waterfalls in barrels. After spending fifteen years wrestling giant hounds and battling pint-sized tigers, she now travels everywhere via watery portals leading to anywhere.

You can connect with her at any of the social media platforms below or at www.sabrinaflynn.com

GLOSSARY

Bai! - a Cantonese expression for when something bad happens (close to the English expression, 'shit')

Bahba - Dad

Banker - a horse racing bet where the bettor believes their selection is certain to win

Bong 幫 - help

Boo how doy - Hatchet Man - a hired tong soldier or assassin

Capper - a person who is on the lookout for possible clients for attorneys

Chi Gum Shing 紫禁城 - Forbidden Palace

Chinese Six Companies - benevolent organizations formed to help the Chinese travel to and from China, to take care of the sick and the starving, and to return corpses to China for burial.

Chun Hung - a poster that puts a price on someone's head

Dang dang - Wait!

Digging into your Levis - searching for cash

Din Gau 癲狗 - Rabid Dog

Dressed for death - dressed in one's best

Faan tung 飯桶 - rice bucket or worthless

Fahn Quai - White Devil

Fan Kwei - Foreign Devil

Graft - practices, especially bribery, used to secure illicit gains in politics or business; corruption.

Hei Lok Lau - House of Joy - traditional name for brothels at that time

Hei san la nei, chap chung! 起身呀你個雜種！- Wake up, you bastard!

Highbinders - general term for criminals

Kedging - to warp or pull (a ship) along by hauling on the cable of an anchor that has been carried out a ways from the ship and dropped.

King chak - the police

Lo Mo - foster mother

Mien tzu - a severe loss of face

Mui Tsai - little Chinese girls who were sold into domestic households. They were often burdened with heavy labor and endured severe physical punishments.

Nei tai - you, look

Ngor bon nei - I help you

No sabe - Spanish for 'doesn't know' or 'I don't understand'. I came across a historical reference to a Chinese man using this phrase in a newspaper article. I don't know if it was common, but it is a simple, easy to say phrase that English speakers understood.

Pak Siu Lui - White Little Bud

Sau pan po - 'Long-life Boards' - coffin Shop

Si Fu - the Master

Siu wai daan 小壞蛋 - Little Rotten Eggs - an insult that implies one was hatched rather than born, and therefore has no mother. The inclusion of 'little' in the insult softens it slightly.

Slungshot - a maritime tool consisting of a weight or "shot" affixed to the end of a long cord, often by being wound into the center of a knot called a "monkey's fist." It is used to cast a line from one location to another, often a mooring line. This was also a popular makeshift (and deadly) weapon in the Barbary Coast.

Sock Nika Tow - Chop Your Head Off - a very bad insult

Wai Daan 壤蛋 - Rotten Egg

Wai Yan 壤男人 - Bad Men

Wu Lei Ching 狐狸精 - Fox Spirit

Wun Dan - Cracked Egg

Wun... ah Mei - Find Mei

Yiu! 妖! - a *slightly* less offensive version of the English 'F-word'.